JERI SM

"... is one of r
—P. C. Cast, *New Y*
of the Hou

LUST FOR LIFE

"A perfect conclusion to my favorite modern vampire series. Jeri Smith-Ready is the perfect DJ for this universe, spinning a high-stakes story with heart, humor, and more than a little bite !"

—Seanan McGuire, *New York Times* bestselling author of the October Daye series

BRING ON THE NIGHT

"Packed with complications, offbeat humor, and believable characters, and of course the playlist is spot on! Great stuff!"

—*Romantic Times* (4½ stars)

"Jeri's writing is majestic, spellbinding storytelling that keeps you on the edge of your seat. . . . Along with a spine-tingling twist in the WVMP world that will have readers feeling as though they've just come off the Tilt-A-Whirl, this book is an engaging, fast-paced read that you won't want to put down."

—*The Official Fiction* (5 stars)

BAD TO THE BONE
Nominated for the Pearl Award

"Offbeat and hugely entertaining."

—*Romantic Times*

"Believable, captivating characters abound. . . . By turns funny, sexy, and gripping."

—*Library Journal*

"This truly clever take on vampires is fresh and original. . . ."

—*Romantic Times*

"Jeri Smith-Ready has created a set of strikingly original, fascinating characters, rich with as much style and rhythm as the music her vampires love. Lyrical and uncompromising, *Wicked Game* is a winner I'll be reading again."

—Rachel Caine, bestselling author of *Thin Air*

"Clever, funny, creative, and way too much fun. . . . A sure-fire winner."

—*The Green Man Review*

"A wicked delight. . . . Urban fantasy that makes an irresistible playlist and an irresistible read."

—C. E. Murphy, bestselling author of *Urban Shaman*

"Sharp and smart and definitely not flavor of the month, *Wicked Game* is wicked good."

—Laura Anne Gilman, bestselling author of *Flesh and Fire*

"Will make your corpuscles coagulate with corpulent incredulity. It's for young bloods and old jugulars alike."

—Weasel, WTGB 94.7 The Globe, Washington, DC

"An imaginative tale that adds new dimension and limitations on the otherwise long-lived lives of vampires. . . ."

—*Darque Reviews*

"Excellent dialogue, skillfully crafted characters, and unique plot. . . ."

—*Romance Reviews Today*

ALSO AVAILABLE FROM
JERI SMITH-READY

WVMP Radio novels

Wicked Game

Bad to the Bone

Bring On the Night

"Let It Bleed" (self-published novella)

Lust for Life

Aspect of Crow novels

Eyes of Crow

Voice of Crow

The Reawakened

Shade novels (teen fiction)

Shade

Shift

Shine

Stand-alone novel

Requiem for the Devil

LUST *for* LIFE

JERI SMITH-READY

POCKET BOOKS

New York   London   Toronto   Sydney   New Delhi

Pocket Books
A Division of Simon & Schuster, Inc.
1230 Avenue of the Americas
New York, NY 10020

This book is a work of fiction. Names, characters, places, and incidents either are products of the author's imagination or are used fictitiously. Any resemblance to actual events or locales or persons, living or dead, is entirely coincidental.

First Pocket Books paperback edition December 2012

POCKET and colophon are registered trademarks of Simon & Schuster, Inc.

For information about special discounts for bulk purchases, please contact Simon & Schuster Special Sales at 1-866-506-1949 or business@simonandschuster.com.

The Simon & Schuster Speakers Bureau can bring authors to your live event. For more information or to book an event contact the Simon & Schuster Speakers Bureau at 1-866-248-3049 or visit our website at www.simonspeakers.com.

Manufactured in the United States of America

10 9 8 7 6 5 4 3 2 1

ISBN 978-1-4391-6350-4
ISBN 978-1-4391-6351-1 (ebook)

To Adrian,
at last

For small creatures such as we, the vastness is bearable only through love.

—Carl Sagan

Author's Note

For the complete WVMP RADIO story, check out Book 3.5, "Let It Bleed," a novella available for free download through Summer 2013 at www.jerismithready.com/books/let-it-bleed (and for sale at all major e-book retailers thereafter). Instead of being an offshoot side story like most novellas, "Let It Bleed" is an essential piece of the WVMP Radio puzzle, bridging the events of *Bring On the Night* and *Lust for Life*, as well as providing a rockin' good time. Enjoy!

Playlist

"All Day and All of the Night," The Kinks
"Season of the Witch," Donovan
"Shake Your Moneymaker," Elmore James
"Fire and Rain," James Taylor
"Tubthumping," Chumbawamba
"Flavour of Night," Robyn Hitchcock
"Monsters," Matchbook Romance
"Death Letter," Son House
"Unbelievable," EMF
"It's Only Over When . . . ," Bad Religion
"Wish I Was in Heaven Sitting Down," R. L. Burnside
"Forty Miles of Bad Road," Duane Eddy
"Crystalised," The xx
"Radar Love," Golden Earring
"Get Together," The Youngbloods
"Atlantic," Keane
"Rehumanize Yourself," The Police
"Runaway," The National
"No Surrender," Bruce Springsteen & the E Street Band
"Ciara," Luka Bloom
"Break on Through," The Doors
"I Will Follow You Into the Dark," Death Cab for Cutie
"One Day Like This," Elbow
"Asleep," The Smiths
"After the Gold Rush," Neil Young & Crazy Horse
"Telstar," The Tornados
"Good Lovin'," The Grateful Dead
"Where Did You Sleep Last Night," Nirvana
"One Love," Bob Marley

LUST *for* LIFE

1

Somebody to Love

Halloween is a great day to be dead.

Or, technically speaking, undead. A vampire like me can be just a bit more herself in public, fly the freak flag a few feet higher. At WVMP, the Lifeblood of Rock 'n' Roll, we hide our secret in broad daylight all year (not literally broad daylight, unless we want to spontaneously combust). But come October, we revel in it.

The station's Halloween parties at the Smoking Pig are legendary, and tonight's is no different. The bar is packed to near-fire-code-violating density, our listeners dressed as their favorite musical icons from decades past.

This year I gave in and dressed as Courtney Love, lead singer of Hole and widow of my fiancé Shane's idol, Kurt Cobain of Nirvana. My messy blond hair, white baby-doll dress, and torn stockings enhance the riot grrl 'tude. So does being undead.

Our latest '60s DJ—Vincent, who is, alas, not a vampire—cranks up the energy with the Kinks' "All Day and All of the Night." The crowd cheers and bounces, heads bobbing.

I spy my best friend Lori leaning against the far end of the bar, near the restrooms. I clomp over in my one-size-too-big combat boots. "It's one of your favorite songs. Come dance!"

She passes a hand over her forehead. "You go ahead. I'm tired." Her face is almost as pale as her white-blond hair, but maybe it's just her Madonna circa Blond Ambition costume.

I examine her glass, which holds only ice. "Too many sea breezes?"

"No, I'm sticking to ginger ale. My stomach's been funny lately."

When I was human, I would've backed away fast to avoid a dreaded intestinal virus. But that's not so much an issue for vampires, so I gently loop my arm over her shoulders. "If you're sick, then go home."

"I will, after Shane gets here. How much longer?"

I don't bother glancing at my watch. "Half an hour. I've forbidden myself to stare at the door for another thirteen minutes." I look at the front entrance. "That was a glance, not a stare."

She gives me a wan smile as she subtly adjusts her "bullet" bra up a few inches. "Are you nervous?"

"If by 'nervous' you mean 'ready to drag him into the nearest alley and rip off his clothes,' then yes." I let go of her and do a goofy little shuffle dance, very un-Courtney-like. "I am so stoked. And in six nights, day-light savings time'll be over!" Winter means to me now what summer meant when I was human: freedom.

Lori goes to take another sip, then realizes her glass is empty. "You're not worried Shane'll be different after boot camp? They're teaching him how to kill."

"The Control's first precept is 'cooperation before coercion.'" I recite it like I'm back in basic training myself. "They teach us how to avoid killing."

"But, Ciara"—Lori draws out the two syllables of my name, KEER-ah, in that lecture-y tone that somehow soothes me—"you didn't train as an Enforcement agent like Shane. That division is hard-core. David's told me stories of his days in uniform."

Lori's right—I do wonder if Shane has been changed by his training with the International Agency for the Control and Management of Undead Corporeal Entities. I wonder if they've turned my laid-back, grunge-DJ vampire into a hardened warrior, carved out his gentle soul and replaced it with the heart of a killer. I wonder if they've cut his hair.

I take a sip of my beer and change the subject. "Seen any of our advertisers tonight?"

"Mel from Creaky Antiques is dressed as Chuck Berry, and Bernita from Waxing Nostalgic is pulling off a pretty sweet 1980s Grace Slick."

"Good to see our clients getting into the holiday spirit. What about Ray from the Pontiac dealership?"

"Franklin's got him now." She points past me, near the bar's side door, where our sales and marketing director is chatting up one of our most fickle advertisers. Neither is in costume, but Franklin might as well be, with his animated, garrulous, downright swishy public persona.

It's all an act, especially these days. His boyfriend, Aaron, died of the same mutant chicken pox that would've killed me permanently had I not been turned. Since then, Franklin's real-life demeanor has been even grimmer than usual.

The slithering strains of "Season of the Witch" creep out of the speakers, and the partygoers wrap around each other in pairs, slinking together in the darkness.

Our punk/Goth DJ Regina spies us and starts to head over. Lori dashes for the bathroom, covering her mouth. I'll assume those events are a coincidence.

Regina strides toward me, the chains on her black leather boots and jacket clinking, because she wants them to. She has the stealth of most vampires, but she likes to make an entrance.

I step forward to meet her at the corner of the bar. "Vincent's playing your song."

"Ha ha." She taps her black-lacquered fingernails on the bar's polished brass railing, so softly it's barely audible under the blaring music. Still, Stuart the bartender turns instantly.

"Another Bass ale?" he asks Regina, who just smiles.

I pull my list of clients from the pocket of my denim jacket and take a surreptitious glance around, trying to figure out who I've yet to schmooze. "Vincent's great with the crowd. Best we've had since"—I clear my throat to force out the name stuck there—"since Jim."

"Vincent's totally brill." Regina leans back against the bar, crossing her arms over her chest. "Shame we're going to lose him."

"Not another one!"

"He put in his two days' notice tonight."

"Two *days*? What did you guys do to him?"

"Nothing, swear. We even let him play cards with us."

"You didn't."

"Just wanted him to feel like one of the gang."

Playing poker against creatures who can sense the

slightest rise in body temperature or heart rate is the surest path to poverty. "How much did you take from him?"

"Total last week? About six grand."

"Regina . . ."

"David needs to hire one of us to replace Jim. That's the way it's always been."

"The job description does not include the word 'undead.' Besides, Jeremy's a DJ and he's human."

She scoffs. "Despite his best efforts."

Ever since he discovered vampires were real, our emotastic '00s DJ has tried to become one. Nothing's dampened his enthusiasm—not even watching me bleed and suffocate on the cold dive into death, then scream and shudder on the twisting climb into un-life. Jeremy likes pain.

I spy him on the far side of the bar and offer a wave. Jeremy waves back with an actual smile, making his lip ring glint in the overhead light. The cute (and surprisingly straight-edge-looking) girl with him probably has something to do with his unusually sunny mood.

I elbow Regina. "Isn't that Lea from Legal Grounds?"

She glances away from the stage over to Jeremy. "I guess."

"He told me months ago he had a crush on a girl who worked at the coffee bar. I figured it was Emma-Rae, the only person in our zip code with more tattoos than he has."

"Opposites attract, right? Look at me and Noah. Or you and Shane."

"You think Shane and I are opposites?"

"That boy is a marathon brooder. But nothing bothers you."

"Would I need six months of therapy after that zombie battle if nothing bothered me?"

"Most people would need six years of therapy after what you've been through."

She has a point. In a four-week span last spring, I became a vampire to avoid death by mutant chicken pox; staked my Control commander to save the entire town of Sherwood, Maryland, from zombies; impaled myself on a fallen tree (don't ask); and had my throat nearly torn out by one of my coworkers.

I'm either resilient, shallow, or totally lying to myself, but whatever the reason, I feel glad to be "alive." Especially now that the nights are getting longer.

"We interviewed a new candidate for the sixties job," Regina says. "Adrian's the real deal. Metaphysically, musically. He's even got the hair." Her lip curls a little. Punks aren't fond of hippies, even though their music shares a call for revolution.

"I don't care if he's a mummy with a mullet, as long as he keeps the ratings up." I chatter on, making alliterations with monsters and hairstyles, while another part of my brain has zoomed in on the name Adrian.

First, the silliness test: The Vampire Adrian. Not bad. Many names are too tame or diminutive to work with the vampire title. Someone named Bob, for instance, better switch to Robert after he's been turned, or he'll be laughed at. By me, at least.

Second, the barrage of Adrian anagrams, which I can't stop: A NADIR, AD IRAN, AND AIR. I'm particularly proud of RADIAN—extra points for keeping it to one word.

Vampires tend to develop obsessive-compulsive behaviors, a nasty side effect of our "temporal adhesion," which is a fancy way of saying we get stuck in time in the era we were turned. Most vampires still dress and speak as we did when we were alive—we're basically walking, stalking time capsules.

So the OCD quirks help us feel in control as the world changes around us. Usually the weirdness takes years to manifest, but I started obsessing over wordplay and correct grammar on my first night.

The phone rings behind the bar. I flinch as the sound cuts through the background noise to scrape my spine. Stuart keeps the ringer turned all the way up so he can hear it—he doesn't know it hurts our sensitive vampire ears, since, like most people, he doesn't know vampires exist.

He answers after one ring. I turn back to Regina.

"What do you mean, this Adrian guy is the 'real deal'?"

"I mean, he's a bleedin' flower child. If Jim is Altamont, Adrian is the Summer of Love."

I cringe inside at the name of my stalker and the violent incident she equates him with. Jim loved the sixties for its recklessness, not its idealism. He was one of that decade's darkest children.

I spy Lori heading for the front exit with David, her husband and WVMP general manager. She gives me a wave and a weak smile. Poor girl.

I wave back, then turn to Regina. "So I guess we won't be hearing a lot of Doors or Pink Floyd from Adrian."

"He's more folk-rock." She examines the pointy end of one of her long black spikes of hair. "He's still mad at Bob Dylan for going electric."

She might be kidding, but I laugh, anyway, mostly from relief, and the fervent hope that WVMP has finally left the DJ-Jim era behind. If the programming lineup can move on, so can I.

Suddenly my laughter fades. Not because I've seen or heard or smelled something that stopped my breath. It's a sense beyond senses, which in my more rational moments I don't even believe in, because I don't believe in much of anything.

But now, as I turn toward the front door, where I know Shane will appear twenty minutes early, I believe.

"What's wrong?" asks Regina, in a tone that suggests she doesn't care, though I know she does.

I hand her my half-full bottle of beer. "Nothing's wrong now."

Even in combat boots, my feet seem to float as I cross the room. The crowd parts a little, leaving me a path. Then it parts a lot, revealing Shane framed by the wide wooden doorway.

I stop to drink him in as he searches for me. With his lithe form dressed from neck to toe in the black Control Enforcement uniform, he stands like a statue: a monument to badassery. Thick-soled, calf-high boots add even more height to his six-foot-five-inch frame.

My sigh mixes desire with relief, at seeing him "alive" and well, and at the fact that they didn't make him cut his hair. The light-brown, nape-length strands still frame his face, making the uniform look borrowed—or, better yet, stolen.

When his pale blue eyes find mine, eight weeks of loneliness melt like snow on a sun-drenched road.

We take a long step toward each other, but the crowd

suddenly surges between us, pushed by a force at the other side of the bar.

Stuart is shoving his way toward the stage, his tan-weathered face twisted with urgency. He speaks to Vince, who shuts off the music mid-song. The crowd goes silent and tense.

Stuart takes the mic. "Ladies and gentlemen, I'm gonna have to ask you to leave the bar calmly but quickly. Please walk to the nearest exit—do not stop for your coats—and once you're out, get as far from the building as you can." He pauses, jaw shifting as he mulls his next words. "Don't panic, but a bomb threat's been called in."

The fear scent of two hundred and fifty people hits me like a shot of pepper spray. I squeeze my eyes shut and stagger back. Everyone is screaming, even the guys. Terror pitches their voices into an eardrum-piercing octave.

I slap my hands over my ears and struggle to open my eyes.

"Ciara!"

Shane's voice breaks through the siren in my head. A watery glimpse shows him pushing through the crowd toward me, fighting the flow of fear and frenzy.

I lurch forward, wanting to swipe aside the people between us like bowling pins. A woman dressed as Cher stomps on the ridge of my foot with a spiked heel.

Shane, closer now, calls my name again. I put out my hand, but a crazed, um, person dressed as Boy George shoves me aside with the world's pointiest elbow.

I'm trapped by my superhuman strength, afraid to push these people for fear of shattering ribs and limbs. But instinct reminds me what'll happen if I'm touched by fire or sun.

I won't scald, blister, or scar. I'll disappear. After about ten shrieky, melty seconds, that is. If I burn like flash paper in front of all these people, the world will know vampires exist.

"Ciara!" Shane pulls me tight to his side. "Don't let go."

I let him lead me, my eyes shut against the sting of human fear. Someone to my left has literally pissed herself.

Near the door, the panic and pressure grow as people sense that survival is close but not quite within their grasp. I focus on keeping myself and everyone around me upright. *Please let the door open out instead of in.*

My foot hits something soft. I look down to see a hand, then behind me to see a body, stretched and inert. Its pale blue shirt is torn and scuffed.

"Franklin!" I pull away from Shane and fight the crowd to stop in my tracks. It's like trying to tread water in a rushing river.

"Franklin, get up!" I tug at his wrist, then travel hand over hand up his arm like I'm climbing a rope, making my way to his shoulder.

More feet stomp over his chest. I want to rip them off and leave these people bloody stumps for legs.

Instead, I hunch over Franklin as I lift his upper body, shielding him with my less-breakable torso. His head lolls back on his neck.

If I pick him up as easily as I can, I'll be busted as supernatural, but I don't care. There's no time to ask for help just so I can pretend to be a weak human girl. I slip an arm beneath his knees and the other under his shoulders. Fighting the crowd's own field of gravity, I stand up straight.

Shane is there, looming in front of me. "Give him."

"No time. Just hold me up and push us forward."

The mass of flesh is thinning as the last wave of people squeezes out the door.

A step from the threshold, it happens: a sudden shift in air pressure, lasting a millisecond, which to a vampire can seem like an eternity.

A roar, a thrust of air, and the world begins to melt.

2

I Walk the Line

"Ciara, wake up." Shane's voice is muffled, like he's speaking through a wool scarf.

A cool mist touches my cheek, and I hear the faint rush of water. I swipe it from my face, then realize I have hands with which to wipe. Hands with fully functional fingers, not melted stubs.

I open my eyes to see the edge of a roof and, in the corner of my vision, a traffic light. A siren screams, piercing the cotton wall of my ringing ears.

"There you are, thank God." Shane's face appears above me. The front of his uniform is shredded, revealing hints of unbroken flesh beneath.

I touch his chest through one of the holes. "You're okay?"

"Yeah, we got thrown pretty hard, but we were lucky—the fire missed us. I carried you around the corner before the paramedics could see you."

"Franklin? Is he—"

"He'll be fine." Shane helps me sit and lean against him. "They took him to the hospital for some bruises and burns, maybe a cracked rib, plus the concussion that knocked him out. You saved his life."

"Too bad he's not in charge of payroll." Ah, good, my quip powers are undamaged. "Did everyone else get out safe? And by 'everyone else,' I mean primarily our friends."

"The other DJs were first out the door. You know how quick vampires are, and how good at self-preservation. Regina grabbed Jeremy and his girlfriend. Some of the humans near the back where you were got burned pretty bad, but I haven't, well, smelled any dead."

I look at his outfit, or what's left of it. "I thought we weren't supposed to wear our uniforms in public."

"It's Halloween. I figured people would think it was a costume. Besides, I couldn't wait to see you, not even long enough to change." He leans in to kiss me.

My phone rings, making me sigh with frustration. I pull it from my jacket pocket, marveling that it survived the impact against the concrete.

"Ciara, thank God you're okay!" Lori shouts. "Wait, this is Ciara, right? Not some bystander who grabbed her phone from the pile of clothes she left behind?"

"Very subtle, Lori."

"Sorry. David and I just got home. We heard it on the police scanner. For once I'm glad he's started playing that thing every night before bed."

"That's weirdly vigilant of him." I wonder what prompted his sudden protectiveness.

"You sure you're okay?"

"Yeah. I'll see you tomorrow night at the office. Wedding powwow, remember?"

"Of course I remember! This time, don't forget to bring the binder."

"Riiiight. I won't."

"I'm so glad you're all right. When I heard there was fire . . ." Lori makes a weird gulping noise. "I gotta go. Sick again. Sorry."

Blinking at the strobe of ambulance lights, I survey the chaos. Half a block away, flames lick the sky above the bar. Through the smoke I see police redirecting traffic, which obeys with only a few honks of protest.

Stuart is stalking past the front of the Smoking Pig, face streaked with ash and sweat. He's ranting at someone on his cell phone, maybe his insurance agent.

He hangs up and strides down the street toward us. "You guys okay?" We've barely nodded when he erupts. "What is wrong with you people? This is the second time the Pig's been firebombed during a WVMP gig. How can one radio station make so many enemies?"

"Wait, Stuart." Shane lays a hand on the bartender's shoulder. "The bomber could've been after anyone at that party."

"They weren't." Stuart shrugs him off—no easy feat. "Whoever called the police to warn us said the bomber was out for revenge against WVMP."

"What'd we do n— I mean, we haven't done anything." Not in the last several months. "Did they say who they were?"

"It was anonymous." He catches himself and glances to both sides. "And I think I wasn't supposed to tell anyone it was a threat against the station. So don't spread it around until you hear the police announce it, okay?"

I begin a mental list of enemies we've made. It's a long one, but my mind latches onto the most recent addition: our former sixties DJ Jim, who was taken into

Control custody after attacking and almost killing me and my sixteen-year-old cousin. Maybe he escaped, or has an ally on the outside.

Stuart, Shane, and I watch the husk of wood and metal that was once the Smoking Pig collapse into rubble. It feels like somebody died.

"If I ever rebuild this place again, I swear I'm changing the name." Stuart gives a heavy sigh. "There's the fire chief. I better go hear the bad news." He shuffles off, a broken man.

"You think it could be the Fortress again?" I ask Shane. "They did firebomb the Smoking Pig three Halloweens ago." The religious cult that sprang from a schism in the Control seemed so pious on the surface, but they were secretly slaughtering vampires to "purify" themselves with undead blood.

"It's not their MO." Shane rubs my back soothingly. "They threw a Molotov cocktail through the window after all the customers had gone home. That attack was a warning, but this"—he gestures to the wreckage—"this was terrorism. Whoever did this doesn't care about the lives of vampires or humans."

Hmm. Jim was psychotic, but his targets were very specific. I can't see him endangering innocent civilians in his rage.

But who called in the warning? Was it the bomber's accomplice, a fellow terrorist with a conscience?

Shane breaks my sleuthy reverie. "Are you supposed to be Courtney Love?"

I examine what's left of my dress. "I think the bombing enhanced my costume."

"It's perfect." He lays an admiring glance on my torn

stockings and combat boots, one of which was stripped of its laces. "You wore this for me?"

I answer with a smile much too unironic for the woman I'm impersonating.

"I love you." Shane draws me close. "I missed you." He kisses me with starving lips. One hand threads through my hair, his fingers lighting up the nerves all over my body.

When we finally take a breath, he murmurs, "I'm not letting you out of my sight until we know who's behind this attack. I know you like your independence, but—"

"Shh." I press my face to his neck, inhaling the mix of skin and smoke. Later I'll be annoyed at his overprotectiveness and worry that the Control has turned him into a robot soldier. But for now I just want to be with him. Preferably naked.

And after living without him for eight weeks—after almost going up in a whoosh of flame and fabric—independence is the last thing on my mind.

I lie in bed with Shane's arms around me for the first time in two months. His sleep is light, since it's only five a.m. My limbs are languid from lovemaking, but I don't want to sleep. I want to imprint the feel of him upon every cell of my body and brain, dwell in this moment of gratitude.

But his return, combined with my near death, takes me back to the night Jim attacked me, especially the moments after my maker Monroe staked him with a handful of pencils to save my life.

Jim lay thrashing on the floor in agony. Like all vampires, he wouldn't die until the stakes were pulled out and his body sucked itself through the wound. But we couldn't finish the job—Jim had told me that he'd drunk my sixteen-year-old cousin Cass to the point of death. We needed him to bring her back as a vampire.

Or so we thought. He lied about that, like so many other things. When Shane showed up a moment later, he knew Cass was nowhere near dead. He could've ended it all.

But he didn't. Halted by my misguided pleading to spare Jim's life, Shane hesitated. That one moment of suspension was long enough for the Control agents to restrain Jim and take him away, still "alive" with a half dozen pencils through his heart.

Jim remains in Control custody to this night (I called to confirm, eliminating him from our list of bombing suspects). No doubt they're now studying him, a half-dead vampire, to see how much we can take without dying, studying our tolerance for pain. The thought of our former friend trapped in a Control lab hurts worse than the thought of him dead.

I stroke the curve of Shane's upper arm, feeling the contours of his triceps even at rest. His lashes flutter, then his pale blue eyes open, long enough to take in the room with one sweeping glance. He closes them again and pulls me closer to his chest. His hand splays over the inside of my left shoulder blade, as if to protect my heart against an assault from behind.

Has the Control turned my easygoing grunge boy into a hypervigilant soldier? Or did Jim do that the moment he set his sights on me?

And if it means I can survive, do I even mind?

3

Sunshine, Lollipops, and Rainbows

I'm a big fan of organization. I have to be, living with a vampire whose OCD-ness manifests itself in sorting. But the *Brideosaurus rex* binder is a bridge too far.

"T minus six weeks!" Sitting beside me at her desk, Lori slaps open the lace-edged three-ring binder, then licks her finger and turns to our current to-do list. "Second fitting for your gown is scheduled for next Tuesday." She glances at my figure. "At least we don't have to worry about you changing weight before the wedding."

Lori went through all of this less than a year ago. I was her maid of honor but was fortunate enough to be away at Control orientation—Indoc, it's officially called—for most of the final month. So I missed her bridal gown's progressively more tearful second, third, and fourth fittings (Lori's weight fluctuates when she's stressed).

When it came to the actual wedding, though . . . okay, I missed that, too, thanks to Jim killing my cousins a few minutes before we were supposed to walk down the aisle. He called a Code Black, which meant the rest of us vampires had to come help him "clean up" the evidence.

The forsaken joys of Lori's wedding—and the troubles our friendship endured when I was first turned—are my prime motivation for letting her micromanage my own ceremony and reception. That and the fact that she's an excellent (and free) wedding planner.

She pulls out another list. "These are the standard songs people usually dance to at receptions. I crossed out the father-daughter one but added an in-law dance so Shane can dance with your mom and she won't feel left out. When he dances with *his* mom, you can dance with Monroe. Since your dad is . . ."

"In federal prison. Right." Monroe agreed to walk me down the aisle. I'm not crazy about the whole idea of being "given away" like a prize cow, but it seemed like a good maker-progeny bonding opportunity. Maybe it'll keep me from crying over my rat-bastard father. I don't usually miss him, but the bridal magazine father-daughter photos are getting to me.

A knock comes at the station's front door, which is locked from the inside to keep vampires safe. Even indirect sunlight will roast us, so we stay indoors until civil twilight, roughly half an hour after sunset and before sunrise.

"It's Franklin," says someone who sounds a lot like Franklin.

Since it's nighttime, I open it wide. "You look like hell."

"Coming from you, that's a compliment." He winces as he climbs the last two stairs, leaning on the iron rail with the hand not holding a cup of takeout coffee. "By the way, fuck you for saving my life."

Coming from him, *that's* a compliment. "You're welcome. I expect a weekly donation of your best blood.

Slightly chilled with a shot of vodka and a dash of Tabasco sauce. If it's convenient."

He raises his middle finger as he shuffles away to his office. Lori flutters about him, concerned.

"Franklin, you should've taken the whole day off. You need time to recover."

He eases himself into his desk chair with an audible grunt, sounding much older than his thirty-nine years. "Phoning a few advertisers isn't exactly bricklaying."

She stops on the threshold to his office, where his gruffness creates a psychological barrier few dare to cross. "Couldn't you call them from home in bed?"

He looks past her at me. "I have other business."

I turn away before he can see my smile. He was checking up on me.

"Did the FBI talk to you guys yet?" he asks us.

"Shane and I were interviewed last night. Of course, they brought up the Fortress bombing from three years ago. This one was totally different, but I wouldn't mind a free investigation to see if the Fortress still exists." After we fought them, most of their members ended up in jail, in comas, or in the ground.

"The FBI and Homeland Security were here this morning." Lori rubs her arms. "Makes me so nervous when cops come to the station. One of these days they're going to search the DJs' apartment."

"Not without a warrant," I remind her. "The media wants to turn it into another War on Halloween story. Talk about a manufactured controversy."

"I hereby declare war on every holiday except Labor Day." He winces as he reaches for his Rolodex. "Who's in David's office?"

"David and Shane are interviewing Adrian," Lori tells him. "The new vampire DJ."

"Do we have to hire someone to replace Jim? Can't we just pretend the sixties never happened?"

"As a history major, I say no." Lori gestures to the heavy-duty cardboard cutout of Eric Clapton near the front door. "Sixties music is the lifeblood, no pun intended, of any classic rock station."

"We're not a classic rock station," he says. "You can tell because we have more than a hundred records in our rotation."

I smile, partly at his snark and partly over Lori's use of the word "lifeblood." Funny, I never used to like puns.

"At least this one's a vampire," Lori says.

"Like that's a good thing." Franklin adds in my direction, "No offense."

I wave off his insult. "It is a good thing. I'm tired of playing the 'gimmick' for the human DJ fill-ins. I'm tired of pretending that we're pretending to be vampires. It's like every day's a Code White." That's when we meticulously scrub all evidence of vampire existence from a room or building. Like a Code Black without the dead humans.

Franklin nods. "It's like keeping your house buyer-ready all the time. Feels like it's not even your place anymore."

"When did you try to sell your house?"

"This summer. I needed a change. The memories were getting to me."

Of Aaron. It's been six months, and the hurt is still fresh on Franklin's face. As much as it ever was—he's pretty stoic. He and Aaron were together longer than Shane and I, and if anything ever happened to Shane . . .

"I de-listed the house two weeks ago," Franklin says. "Market's complete shit right now. Anyway, what do we know about the new guy, not that I care?"

Lori recites Adrian's personnel file. "He was turned in 1965. He's originally from Phoenix, but his last gig was in Albuquerque. He worked at an independent station there for ten years before he had to move on."

"Because of the whole not-aging thing?" I ask her, curious if his departure had a more scandalous reason.

"Pretty much. His focus is more on folk rock, like early Dylan, Mamas and the Papas, Peter, Paul and Mary. Super granola type."

Franklin's lip curls. "A real hippie? Actual peace, love, and understanding? Not the fake shit like Jim?"

"It'll be good for our image." I rub my throat. "Besides, having almost been killed by a psychopathic psychedelic, I'll take a crunchy folk rocker any day."

"We already have Noah." He pours the rest of his takeout coffee into his favorite mug, the one that says FUCK OFF. "Rasta Man brings enough peace and love for one workplace."

"It'll be nice for Noah to have a kindred spirit." I hear David's door open. "Ooh, there he is now." I wave Franklin to join me. He mimes shooting himself in the head.

"Ciara, Lori, Franklin." David comes out of his office. "Come meet our new DJ."

A tall vampire glides past my boss and stops next to Lori's desk. He looks like he just stepped out of the Woodstock movie—after a long shower. His thick, wavy, golden-brown hair falls almost to his waist. White daisies are woven among the strands, stems intertwined with small loose braids. The tassels on the sleeve of his white jacket sway as he reaches to shake my hand.

"Hi." I meet his mahogany eyes, then out of habit look down. I'm not as easily mesmerized as I was when I was human, but older gorgeous vampires still turn my brain to goop. "Welcome to WVMP."

My gaze falls on his bare feet, sticking out from under the frayed cuffs of his blue jeans. Vampires are fairly insensitive to cold weather, but still, for November, that's hard-core.

Lori lets out a soft giggle, falling under the new vamp's spell. "Yeah, welcome to . . . here."

"Thank you," he says in a voice like velvet. "I'm looking forward—"

Something crashes behind me. I spin to see Franklin standing over what's left of his mug. Creamer-laden coffee has splattered against the front of my desk.

Franklin's not mourning the mug. He's staring at Adrian, slack-jawed. Slack, period, like he overdosed on muscle relaxants.

I look back at the hippie vamp, who seems just as captivated. I've never seen anyone look at Franklin that way, not even his late boyfriend.

"Hi," they say in unison. Then they laugh the same laugh, the same length and pitch. Weird.

David clears his throat. "Um . . . Adrian, this is Franklin, our sales and marketing director. Franklin, this is—"

"Adrian." Franklin puts his hand out, fingers stretching like he's fallen off a cliff and reaching for that saving grip.

Adrian takes Franklin's hand between both of his own. "Pleased to meet you."

"Yes," Franklin breathes, and it sounds like he's agreeing to a lot more than this being a pleasurable meeting.

I look at David and Lori, whose foreheads are as scrunched-up as mine feels.

Adrian speaks again, his voice resonating against the walls. "Thanks, I'd love some coffee."

"Good." Franklin drops his hand and stares some more, then realizes Adrian just made a joke. "Oh! You mean this." He surveys the damage around his feet. "Shit."

Since Franklin doesn't seem capable, I collect the four largest pieces of the mug. FUCK and OFF are in separate pieces. I shove them together and try to make an anagram.

Huh. There's no anagram for FUCK OFF.

"So!" Lori says brightly. "David tells me you've been working in Albuquerque. What's it like there?"

"It's beautiful." He's still looking at Franklin.

Vampire stares always have at least a spark of predatory threat. It's what lots of humans get off on: that danger mixed with seduction. They think they can tame us (they can't).

But Adrian's stare contains only pure, helpless fascination. With Franklin, of all things.

David babbles, since no one else will. "Adrian was turned when he was twenty-seven, like the rest of our DJs, but of course that wasn't a consideration in hiring him, heh." The public loves the fact that our DJs have a connection to the so-called Club of 27, the group of legendary musicians who died at that age. "He's looking forward to moving in downstairs, but I told him we needed to get Jim's stuff out first. We've been putting that off for too long." David inhales like he's going to add another sentence, then seems to lose interest in his own half of the conversation. I offer him a polite "Okay."

I've seen some pretty amazing things. I've watched people die and come back to life. I've seen the Great Beyond and felt the comfort of a higher being that loves all creatures, alive, dead, and undead. I've seen a zombie cheerleading pyramid.

None of it has freaked me out as much as the sight of someone falling in love with Franklin. Except maybe the sight of my vampire-hating, hippie-ripping coworker falling in love with Adrian.

I shoo them toward the stairs. "I just made some fresh coffee in the lounge. You two should get some while it's hot."

Lori snickers. Replaying my own words, I try not to echo her.

Shane comes out of David's office as Adrian and Franklin disappear into the lounge together. He holds up his phone and beams like a little boy who just caught his first fish.

"Hey, I just twittered about the new DJ."

"Great!" I move to his side and give him a quick kiss, avoiding Lori's eyes so we won't laugh at the fact that it took Shane three full minutes to compose a tweet. Considering most vampires his age see cell phones primarily as devices to call people with, and not as handheld computers/entertainment sources/life managers, Shane's pretty advanced.

David looks between Lori and us, then back at her. "Ready to tell them now?"

"Yes!" She twists her hands together. "We have big news. It's good and bad."

"Give us the bad news first," Shane says.

"It's the same news, with good and bad aspects." Lori spreads her fingers over her tiny belly. "I'm pregnant."

My life flashes before my eyes, but her smile short-circuits my panic. "I'm so happy for you!" I exclaim as I hug her.

She hesitates, then hugs me back. "You are?"

"Of course." I let go of her and look at David, who's getting a hearty handshake from Shane. "You wanted this, right? I mean, you guys just got married six months ago, but he's not getting any younger."

"Hey, I'm only thirty-five," he says.

"And when your kid graduates from college, you'll be almost sixty." I whisper the last word.

"We were trying, but I can't believe it happened so fast." Lori grabs my arm. "And no one else can know until we get past the three-month mark in case . . ."

"In case what?"

She gives me a blank look. "In case I lose it. Between eight and sixteen percent of pregnancies miscarry in the first trimester."

"I had no idea." As an only child and out of touch with most family members, I'm ignorant of all things baby.

She turns to Shane. "Do I smell different? Will the older vampires be able to tell?"

He leans close to her shoulder and takes a deep whiff. "Maybe. Their noses are more sensitive than mine. But they're so wrapped up in their little worlds, they won't care."

"Good." She turns back to me. "Anyway, the bad part."

My mood dims. I've dreaded this since Lori and David got engaged—that divide between those with kids and those without. Eventually she'll make fellow child-bearing friends, and she'll have more in common with them than with me. But at least we'll always have that donor-vampire bond.

"I can't be your donor anymore."

My eyelid twitches. "Oh." I hurry to add, "I understand. You need to keep up your strength while you're pregnant."

"And then I'll be nursing."

"Not to mention sleep deprived." I force my tone to stay light. "Don't worry, I know it's just temporary. We'll get back on track once your kid's eating solid food."

Lori hesitates. "Unless I'm pregnant again."

Now I get why Lori is so nervous. She's breaking up with me.

"So how far along are you?" Shane asks, easing the tension—on the outside, at least. This is a standard question I should've thought of.

"Seven weeks, they say."

Desperate to sound clueful (the opposite of clueless?), I add, "Twenty-nine more weeks to go!"

Lori fidgets with her gold heart pendant. "Actually, more like thirty-three. Pregnancy lasts forty weeks."

So much for having a clue. I dread the barrage of pregnancy facts for the next eight months, and then a barrage of baby facts for the next, um, however long babies are considered babies, and then a barrage of toddler facts for—okay, I give up. I don't even technically know what a toddler is.

David takes a deep breath. "This is going to sound crazy, and feel free to say no, but . . . we'd like you two to be the godparents."

The room falls silent.

My brain fixates on the "god" part of the word while my mouth searches for a tactful response.

"Wha?" I finally utter.

Shane slips his hands into his back jeans pockets, a sign of discomfort. "Are you sure? I mean, we're, you know, unholy."

"Don't worry," Lori assures us. "It's just a ceremonial thing to make our parents happy. David's family is Episcopalian and mine is Lutheran. They were scandalized when we had a Unitarian wedding, so we figured baptizing their grandkid would soothe them."

"Baptizing. With holy water." I cradle my right arm, remembering the agony as it plunged into a basin of the substance. It took only moments to cure myself with my mind, but nothing will erase the memory of melted flesh.

"You guys won't have to stand near the baptismal font," David says. "You'll be off to the side."

"This is an amazing honor." Shane shakes David's hand again. "Thank you for asking us."

"Does this mean you're saying no?"

"It means we need to think about it."

I want to hug Shane so bad right now. Instead I just send him a grateful smile.

"What's to think about?" Lori rubs her abdomen, which is still perfectly flat.

"I think Shane would be a great godfather." I swallow hard. "But how can I be a godmother when I don't even believe in God? Not a Bible God, anyway."

"You're a good person," she says, "and that's all that matters."

"I'm pretty sure your churches would disagree."

"It's a big responsibility," Shane says. "We're supposed to be the kid's religious role models."

Lori sighs. "Come on, don't take it so seriously. It's a symbolic thing, a sign of our friendship."

"A symbolic thing?" Shane asks. Uh-oh, he's getting his Catholic on. "Like Holy Communion is just a symbolic thing?"

"Hey!" I grab my coat from my chair, before the office turns into Little Belfast. "I know where we could finish this discussion—or, better yet, have an entirely new one. Our favorite Smoking Pig substitute: O'Leary's Pub!"

"I can't drink," Lori says forlornly.

"And I can't eat, so we're even." I pick up the bridal binder and wave it hypnotically. "We can talk about favors, or hotel goody bags for out-of-town guests."

Her mouth tugs into a smile. "Do you promise to sit still for my entire lesson on seating charts?"

I knew she couldn't resist the lure of wedding planning. It's like a drug to her.

The four of us head off for the pub, me riding with Lori and David with Shane. Maybe on the way the guys will finish the theological argument—or, more likely, start a new one about football.

But tonight Lori and I steer clear of prickly topics like birth and death and the ways our friendship is evolving. If I meet her halfway—or further—on things like my wedding that make her happy, maybe we'll be okay.

4

The Boxer

Just as I suspected, they're making Shane a killer.

I sit on the bleachers of the Control headquarters gymnasium with Captain Elijah Fox, who's overseeing Shane's combat training. My own muscles, despite their vampire strength, are still a bit shaky from the session Elijah and I just finished. It's worth the pain and humiliation, though, to help me feel safe and strong.

In front of us, Shane is practicing swordsmanship with Agent Tony Rosso, a small, wiry vampire Enforcement agent I recognize from Indoc. Agent Rosso can chop the legs off a spider on a wall at twenty paces, using eight separate knives. I'd hire him as a bodyguard if I could afford it—and if Shane wouldn't be insulted.

Rosso's long, dark hair sails around his head as he demonstrates the debilitation blow on a practice dummy. A vampire can recover from any weapon-delivered wound except decapitation or a wooden stake through the heart. So whenever possible, bilateral fibular dismemberment (chopping off the legs) is the best way to defend against a vampire we want to take into custody. The limbs will grow back eventually—months or years for a younger vampire, weeks or even days for an ancient one—but in the meantime, they can't chase us or run away.

When it's his turn, Shane doesn't hesitate. In one fluid motion, he steps forward, crouches, and swings the katana sword down and across. The legs of the practice dummy thump on the floor, neatly severed. I feel like applauding, even as my stomach curdles at the sound and sight.

Beside me, Elijah sits forward, elbows on his knees, watching Shane's every move. He scribbles notes in a shorthand I can't decipher, then taps the end of the pen against his broad, dark chin, deep in thought.

"How's Shane's doing?" I ask him.

"Boy's got potential, if he can stop thinking with his fists. I keep reminding him he's got other body parts he can hurt with. And he hunkers down too much when we go hand to hand. He'll get more force behind his blows once he learns to let it rip. But his defense is solid. He blocks like a brick wall."

I lean forward, mirroring Elijah's pose and resting my chin on my folded fists. Violence has never been Shane's way—at least, not in the time I've known him. But the night I became a vampire—and Jim revved up his fixation with me—Shane resolved to keep me protected by any means necessary.

"You think he's cut out for Enforcement?" I ask Elijah.

He jots another note. "I think Agent McAllister is cut out for whatever he sets his mind to."

"But if you were making the personnel assignments, and Shane's preference didn't mean jack, which division would you put him in?"

Elijah doesn't answer right away. Instead he watches as Shane loads a holy-water pistol. Hands covered with latex gloves, he tips the bottle into the funnel leading into the chamber of the long black plastic pistol. Then he crosses himself, which is not official procedure.

"Immanence Corps," Elijah says finally. "I'd put him in IC."

"So he could be my partner?"

"So he could channel the divine in him."

I've never heard Elijah talk like this. "Divine what?"

Captain Fox moves his hand in a circle. "Essence, nature, whatever. He's got it. We all do, but some people are more connected to it."

The term "immanence" has many meanings, but in the Control it refers to the divine presence on earth. It also means "inherent." Since the Control considers magic a form of divinity, the IC is populated with those supposedly born with paranormal abilities.

I say "supposedly" because I'm a diehard skeptic, and that's where my power lies. My blood as a human—and my mind as a vampire—can reverse the effects of holy water, which is supposed to leave permanent scars. This magic runs in my family, but no one's blood was as powerful as mine. Too bad I had to die and deprive vampiredom of their best ever skin-care regimen.

"Lanham stuck me in IC," I point out to Elijah, "and I'm not connected to the divine at all. I think that was his point."

"What do you mean?"

"I think the Control wanted to see if I could neutralize my comrades and their alleged paranormal abilities."

"Huh. As long as they're not using you to mess with your fellow vampire agents, in the fine tradition of the Immanence Corps."

I grimace at his reference to Project Blood Leash, the movement spearheaded by my former IC commander ("former," because I killed him). Last April, Colonel Petrea and his daughter Tina raised most of the corpses lying in Sherwood Cemetery. He manipulated the zombies' actions through blood magic, hoping to use that same kind of control on his fellow vampires. An unintended side effect was the spread of a mutant chickenpox virus that killed me and Franklin's boyfriend, Aaron.

"IC wouldn't dare mess with vampires while the Project Blood Leash investigation is going on. They'll be sanctioned as it is. But even if they try to use me that way, it won't work. I'm not that powerful. It's not like I can de-vamp someone."

Shane and Agent Rosso take aim at the person-shaped targets, the water in their pistols colored blue and red, respectively, so they can see where they hit.

"Hmm." Elijah rubs his chin. "If someone had that power, to unmake a vampire, wonder how many of us would volunteer?"

Agent Rosso's voice rings out. "Fire!"

They aim for the heads. Shane starts out too low but adjusts his angle until the target's face is soaked in blue water. A real vampire's eyes would be gone.

"Wouldn't it be safer to practice with regular water?" I ask Elijah. "That's what we did in my basic training."

"Enforcement agents have to learn to handle holy

water and get used to the splash back, because it does happen, no matter how you protect yourself." He pushes up his left sleeve, displaying the lighter underside of his forearm, where half a dozen black scars lie scattered like seeds.

"Isn't that the arm you lost in the zombie attack?"

"Yep." He rubs the dark brown skin. "When it grew back, all my old scars were there. Funny, huh?"

Agent Rosso lowers his weapon and turns to us. His look of warning shuts us up.

We stay quiet while Shane and Rosso finish their target practice, then Elijah steps down for a round of hand-to-hand training. Shane pummels the shields Rosso holds up. His legs and arms blur as he executes the maneuvers I remember from orientation, and many more complex ones. I wouldn't want to meet Shane in a dark alley. If I were anyone other than myself, of course.

When they're finished, Shane and Agent Rosso walk over—or rather, Rosso walks, Shane staggers. He towels off his face and gulps water, looking human in the best way possible.

"Hey." He leans over and gives me a quick kiss.

I look past him at Elijah and Rosso. "Can you guys come work him out like this at home? I love it when he sweats."

Shane grimaces and pinches the front of his damp T-shirt. "I'm off to take a shower. Be back in five."

I watch him stride toward the locker room with Rosso, his gait much steadier than a moment ago. Then I hop off the bleacher and help Elijah collect the equipment.

"So how does your arm feel?" I ask Elijah while we drag the mat off the center of the floor. "Now that it's back."

"Itches like a motherfucker, deep inside where I can't scratch, so I guess it's still healing." He drops the mat on the stack beside the wall, then reaches back and undoes the Velcro straps on his stakeproof vest. "But at least I'm back on the job."

We collect the holy-water pistols and punching pad thingies and carry them to the equipment closet, where I nudge the light switch with my shoulder.

Elijah puts the punching pads on a shelf. "But you know what? If I hadn't been injured, I probably would've been on strike anyway."

"Because of Petrea and Project Blood Leash?"

"You know it." He gives me a look of regret. "It's hard for recruits to understand, especially when you're left all up in the air about when you're gonna serve your tour of duty."

"Why would I be dying to join an organization that wants to control my every move—literally?" I hang Elijah's stakeproof vest on a wall hook. "I just want to start so I can get it over with. Sorry, I know this is your calling, but I'm only here because I have to be. Same with Shane."

"Maybe you'll change your mind once you're in."

"You mean once I'm brainwashed by the military machine? I don't think so."

"Beats working at a desk job."

"I like desk jobs—climate-controlled environment, frequent snack breaks, office gossip with my best friend. Oh, and if I screw up? No one dies."

He shakes his head and says with a chuckle, "Sounds boring."

"You looked hot working out in that gym," I tell Shane as we enter the Control headquarters command building. "It's a macho side of you I don't get to see much."

"You know what they say." He swings his gym bag in an exaggerated fashion. "Some men choose machismo, and some have machismo thrust upon them."

I'm about to make a comment about having machismo thrust upon *me* when I hear footsteps around the corner. We slow as we approach the main command hallway. It's a human female, judging by the sound of her heels clicking on the spotless, polished floor.

I instinctively drop Shane's hand, to adhere to the no-PDA-in-uniform rule, before realizing we're not in uniform.

The woman approaching is quieter than most humans, so I bet she lives with vampires. When I was a human living with Shane, it was hard to get used to his stillness, but ultimately I found it soothing and became hyperaware of my own noises. As a vampire myself, I've found the hardest part of passing as a human is learning how not to go completely motionless around them, like a predator among prey.

Which we are, of course. The Control knows this, and yet, thanks to people like Colonel Lanham, it treats us with respect instead of fear. Except when it doesn't.

We turn the corner to see a face from my worst nightmares.

"Special Agent Codreanu-Petrea." Shane nods to the

fiftyish flame-haired woman, then takes my hand again, knowing I need his touch.

I swallow, glad we're not supposed to salute indoors. My hand would be shaking all the way up and down. I clear my throat to address her, but she steps in to save me.

"Agent McAllister. Agent Griffin." She gives us a warm smile. "Please, call me Anca. My last name is a mouthful."

It's more than a mouthful—it's a horror. Codreanu was the name of the founder of the Iron Guard, a fascist group that terrorized Romania during the thirties and forties. Their anti-Semitism was so vicious, even the Nazis asked them to ease up. (I know, because they were the subject of my last college paper.)

And Petrea? That's the surname of the man I killed.

"How is your training coming along?" Anca asks Shane in a faint Romanian accent.

"Very well, thank you." Shane blinks twice—a gesture I've noticed has replaced his old smirk. He's about to say something ironic. "It's more to my liking than I would've thought."

"Excellent. We need good vampires like you in Enforcement."

"Good vampires, as opposed to good humans?" I ask her. "Or good vampires, as opposed to bad vampires?" I'm not being pedantic . . . okay, I am being pedantic, but this isn't about my compulsion. I want to know how she feels about vampires now that her undead husband is dead forever.

Her smile tweaks into a crooked curve. "We need good people."

That didn't answer my question, but she's a superior officer (agent, whatever), so I can't go all *Law & Order* on her.

She shifts her leather file folder to her left hand and reaches out to touch my arm. "And, Ciara, how are you handling your new life?"

Suddenly thirsty and extraconscious of the heat of her skin relative to mine, I resist the urge to step away. "Fine, thanks. It's not that new. I've been a vampire over six months now."

She gives me a bemused smile. "If there's anything I can do, please let me know. Even just a chat, woman to woman. I'm not a vampire, but I lived with one for thirty years. I've fought beside them. I teach Advanced Human-Vampire Relations at orientation. So I know what you're going through." A business card appears between her fingers. "Call me? I feel responsible for what you are, and I am so very sorry."

"It wasn't your fault."

"My daughter stole my necromancy texts to raise those *cadaveris accurrens*." That's the Control term for zombies. It means "running carcasses."

"I know, but—"

"Tina did it because she thought Stefan and I were disappointed in her lack of magic." Her voice is nearly as mesmerizing as a vampire's. "If we'd been more supportive parents, she wouldn't have had to prove herself in such a shameful way. And you wouldn't have died."

The rage still simmers inside me. Tina got a reduced sentence in a Control correctional facility in exchange for ratting out her dead-undead father. But

I want to see her in a civilian prison for the deaths she caused.

I hold it all in and just say, "Thanks. I'll call you."

I don't realize until after we say good-bye and turn down the hall that I actually mean it. Special Agent Codreanu-Petrea could be useful in more ways than one.

5

No More Words

Lieutenant Colonel Winston Lanham usually sports a head shaved so close, you can check your lipstick in the reflection—not that I would recommend it. But every so often he lets it grow out to a quarter-inch buzz cut, as if to prove he still has a full head of hair.

Right now he has about three weeks of light brown growth the length of indoor-outdoor carpeting.

As we enter his office, he turns from his vast, wall-size bookshelf. "Griffin. McAllister. You're early."

I check my watch. "We're five minutes late, sir."

"For you, that's early." He points to a pair of chairs on the other side of his wide oak desk.

Even in the act of sitting, Lanham shows more precision in movement than any other human I've met. He could end us without breaking a sweat—I know from experience.

I try to keep my eyes away from the nameplate on his desk, LT. COL. WINSTON LANHAM, to stop myself from making anagrams of his name.

Too late. SHAMAN LINT NOW.

"I trust your training is going well?" It's a question only because Lanham lifts his voice slightly at the end of the sentence. There is but one correct answer.

"Yes, sir," we both say.

"I'm looking forward to activating both of you soon in your respective divisions. Naturally, you'll want to start your service as close as possible to each other."

"Thank you, sir." I add, "And we'll have off the week of December twenty-first for our wedding, right?"

He raises an eyebrow. "You plan a long honeymoon?"

"Sadly, no." Sunlight makes travel risky for vampires, which is why we chose the shortest day of the year to get married. We plan to spend a few nights in a nearby vampire-friendly B and B. "But my mom's getting out of prison just before the wedding. I'd like to have some time with her." Assuming she doesn't permanently pass out when she discovers her daughter's a vampire.

Lanham's eyes soften for a moment, as if I just made him sad. If my already keen observation skills weren't further enhanced by my vampirism, I'd think I was mistaken. He's never shown anything resembling personal concern for me. He saved my life earlier this year, but probably because I am useful to him.

"I understand." He makes a note on his legal pad with a glistening bronze-colored fountain pen.

I look at his nameplate again as my anxiety ratchets up a notch. *INHALANTS MOWN*.

Shane speaks up. "Sir, we ran into Special Agent Codreanu-Petrea in the hall."

"Oh?" Lanham adjusts his dark blue tie. The cracks in his composure, however tiny, are making me nervous. "How would you describe the nature of your interaction?"

"She was nice," I tell him. "Too nice. Either she still doesn't know I killed her husband, or she's buttering me up as part of a vengeance plot."

"The details of Lieutenant Colonel Petrea's death are classified. Anyone not present on the scene only knows that he was killed by a fellow agent in self-defense. And anyone who *was* present on the scene—"

"—is either dead or one of us. Except the agent who was Petrea's sidekick. The only one Elijah didn't shoot to death. If the agent was loyal to that family, why wouldn't he tell Ms. My-Grandfather-Was-a-Fascist?"

Lanham frowns. "First, we don't know for certain that Anca is related to Cornelieu Codreanu. Second, we're preventing the agent in question from speaking to anyone we haven't authorized. As one of the key conspirators of Project Blood Leash, he's in a Control penitentiary, awaiting trial."

"Sir, if I may ask, how is that investigation going?" Shane's respectful demeanor contains an edge of anger. "The vampire agents are getting restless. They want results, or more of them will walk."

"The investigation is proceeding as fast as I can push it. But I'm only one man—one man who has been known to bend over backward to accommodate vampires." He pauses to glare at us until we nod in acknowledgment for all he's done. "As for Anca, she's been extremely cooperative in this investigation. She's eager to clear her family's name of the wrongdoings perpetrated by her daughter and her late husband."

Hmm, that's the second time Lanham has referred

to Agent Codreanu-Petrea by her first name. I wonder if they're friends, or if he's just saving time and syllables.

Lanham pulls my personnel folder in front of him on the desk, signaling subject change. "Now, for the reason I called you both here to meet me."

I eye my folder, which looks four times as thick as the last time I saw it, then glance at his nameplate. AH SNOW-MAN LINT. "You said it was urgent."

"Yes. Several months ago I alluded to preliminary conclusions our research division had drawn about the blood you donated when you were a human. Your 'anti-holy blood,' as you call it." He opens a long envelope and pulls out a sheet with charts and figures on it. "The results were inconclusive at first, so we ran several series of tests. It was unfortunate that your death prevented us from collecting more blood."

Right. *That* was unfortunate about my death. "Sorry I inconvenienced you."

I expect Lanham to reprimand me for interrupting him, but instead he nods. "I apologize. That was ill put. Your death was a personal tragedy for everyone who . . . who has an interest in you." He swallows and shifts the folder an inch to the left.

Whoa. This is the first time I've seen Lanham show a speck of human feeling about my death. I'm not sure which bothers me more: the fact that he might care about me, or the fact that I sort of care whether he cares about me.

I steal a glance at Shane, who's gripping the arms of the chair like the sides of a lifeboat.

Lanham clears his throat. Moment over.

"I know it has always pleased you to think of your

heathen self as anti-holy. When a vampire drinks your human blood, their holy-water burns heal instantly. You were able to heal your own holy-water burn—and that of your maker—with the power of your mind alone. But your power, such as it is, is not specifically anti-holy. Holiness is just one form of magic."

"Magic, sir? Can you define?" He can't mean like a dude onstage sawing a lady in half or making the Statue of Liberty disappear. Those are mere illusions.

"Any sort of supernatural occurrence or being. A vampire, for instance, exists because of blood magic. To look at it another way, all forms of magic are a manifestation of the divine, whether or not they reside in overt religious forms. This is why simply being a vampire is enough to qualify you for the Immanence Corps."

"Okay." I have no idea where he's going with this. My breath quickens and I take one last peek at his nameplate.

SHALT MAN WIN? NO.

"Sorry, sir, I just have to . . ." I reach out and turn his nameplate so I can't see the letters. "There. Thank you."

Colonel Lanham eyes the nameplate, two vertical lines appearing between his brows. Then he closes my file and folds his hands atop it. "We have reason to believe that your blood—and, in fact, your entire being— is not anti-holy. More broadly, it's anti-magic. Anti-supernatural."

"Is it genetic?" Shane asks. "Some of her family has anti-holy blood, too."

"We're not certain. There's an inherited component but also a more, shall we say, philosophical one."

"My skepticism." I love the idea that this ability is

partly under my control—as much as beliefs or lack thereof are under anyone's control.

"Exactly," Lanham says. "Your anti-magic abilities are part of your essence, you might say."

"Cool."

"Not entirely cool." Lanham shifts a pen from the left side of my personnel folder to the right side, for no apparent reason.

"What's wrong?"

"I'd like to ask you a few questions about your experience as a vampire, and you need to be completely honest. It's the only way we'll be able to help you."

My hands fumble for the ends of the chair's armrests. "Help me what?"

"Survive."

Shane takes a short, shallow breath. Every muscle frozen, I can't turn my head to look at him. It feels like my tongue has descended into my throat.

"Huh?" is all I can manage.

Lanham holds my gaze as if to hold me up. "How long did it take for your fangs to manifest?"

"A day or two." For most vampires, it's a matter of minutes.

"Have you experienced a decreased sensitivity to pain?"

I latch onto this. "Yes! I heal fast now. A zombie broke both my legs and I was back on my feet in less than a minute."

"That wasn't my question. I asked about the pain, Griffin. The pain."

"A headache, for instance?"

"A vampire bite, for instance." He lowers his voice,

as if that will change anything. "I apologize for the personal nature of these questions."

"I don't—" Finally I turn to Shane, with my whole body instead of just my head.

The look in his eyes sinks my soul. It's not disbelief or bewilderment. It's *oh-God-I-knew-it*.

My mind races. I want to get this over with and hear the truth.

"I hate being bitten." I stare at the blank side of his nameplate. "It feels like being stabbed."

"I see. Have you also—"

"I've had a word obsession since the day I was turned. I make anagrams from everything. I can't pass a drugstore without buying a word puzzle book." I give him a pleading look. "Can you help me?"

Lanham gives a nod that somehow isn't a nod. A nod that says, *I hear you, but no.*

"We're not sure how to remedy your unique situation. But rest assured the Control is doing all we can to keep you around as long as possible."

My brain cells feel like they're playing leapfrog. "Keep me . . . around? Like in the Control? I just started my contract and you're already talking about extending or renewing it?" Please let that be what he's talking about.

"I mean, in this world. The blood magic that makes you a vampire is having trouble taking proper hold in your body and soul. Your essence puts up too much resistance."

I spring out of my chair. "But I believe I'm a vampire! I'm not skeptical about that."

He shakes his head. "This power isn't completely under your control, any more than breathing or blinking are. Based on what you've told me, I conjecture that you will fade faster than most vampires—than *any* vampire." He swallows again. "I'm sorry, Ciara."

I sit down hard, barely registering the fact that he called me by my first name.

"This is bullshit," Shane says. "If her essence resists magic, why did she become a vampire in the first place? Why didn't she just die?" His voice shudders over the last word.

"I almost did." I choke back the panic. "You thought I wasn't coming back, remember? I went all the way into the white. The other vampires said that when they died, they only saw a white light from a distance."

His face shadows. "Or not at all."

Shane thinks he was on his way to hell when he turned, because he saw only darkness before Regina brought him back from his suicide-by-vampire attempt. So we've both had anomalous vampings: mine of complete light, his of complete dark. This does not calm me.

He turns back to Lanham. "There's got to be something we can do to make her stronger."

"Agent McAllister, I believe she will strengthen physically just like any vampire." He speaks to me again. "It's your mind that concerns us. We believe it will age more quickly. Your compulsions will intensify and your temporal adhesion will be more rigid. You'll lose vitality."

Vitality. My mind seizes on that word. It comes from the Latin *vita*, meaning life.

As in, I don't have much.

"So I have the vampire version of a terminal illness? Is that what you're saying?"

"Essentially, yes."

The world feels like it's floating. "I just died. I don't want to die again."

"You won't." Shane puts his hand over mine. "We're going to stop this."

I want to cry and beat my fists against the floor, against the walls, against my own body. I want to go full tantrum, denial and anger.

I'll do that later, safe in Shane's arms. For now, I need to fight.

I reach forward, take Lanham's legal pad and fancy-pants fountain pen. "What do I have to do?"

On the drive home, Shane and I fill the fear space between us with chatter and task lists.

"The easiest part is music." I gesture to the stereo. "I already listen to the satellite alternative station, but I could switch to the indie station. They discover new bands sooner."

"I guess it couldn't hurt," Shane says, "except my ears."

"Hey, a lot of it's good and you know it." I check the list. "I'll get a new hairstyle every year, even if the old one looks better on me."

"Don't forget fashion."

"Right. I'll buy the new seasonal lines from all the cutting-edge designers, even if I hate the clothes and can't afford them."

"And technology. Get a new cell phone before you're eligible for an upgrade."

"Ooh, good one. Same with my laptop and software. And I'll start Contemporary Awareness training next week. That'll be so boring. They'll probably teach us how to tweet."

"Then you'll get an A." He taps his fingers on the steering wheel. "You need more direct donor blood, less bank blood."

That was on Lanham's list, too. "Is this one of those good-nutrition-is-the-foundation-of-good-health talks?"

"I know it still bothers you to drink from a human."

"It makes me feel pathetic. I keep seeing myself from the outside, on my knees like a dog, lapping up scraps." Using my toe, I smooth a wrinkle in the floor mat. "Now I can't even drink from Lori, since she's pregnant."

"What about the donors you've been sharing with Monroe and Regina?"

"Those are the worst. I don't know them, they're just walking veins. I feel like an intruder—like they want to be with the 'experienced' vampire and they're only feeding me to be polite."

"There's still Jeremy. You're due to drink from him this weekend, right?" When I nod, Shane adds, "It's time for you to bite someone. Might as well be him."

I stare out the side window at the highway lights whizzing past, keeping my eyes away from the green signs with their irresistible white letters. "I guess. If I bite too hard and it hurts, he won't care."

"No, he'll enjoy it."

"Ugh." I look down at my list. There's only one item left. "Lanham wants me to resist my compulsion."

"I can help you. I'll put tape over all the labels in our

kitchen. I'll be more careful about using correct grammar." He hesitates. "I'll recycle your stash of puzzle books."

I thought I'd hidden them. But there was that time—okay, several times—I shoved a puzzle book under the sofa cushion when Shane came home early.

"Okay." My voice is as tiny as my resolve. "Maybe I could just cut back? Not stop cold turkey?" My palms are sweating at the mere thought—and it takes a lot to make a vampire sweat.

Shane sighs. "What if you just finish the ones you have and don't buy more?"

My fingers curl around the door handle. I have only two puzzles left in my current book. The rest are all completed.

I think of a guy on *Mission: Organization* (Shane's favorite Home & Garden Network show) who broke down in tears at the suggestion he throw away stacks of old magazines. Am I that sick?

"I don't know if I can do that. I can't just stop thinking about words." My throat closes up. I try to breathe and swallow at the same time, and next thing I know I'm hiccuping.

A vampire. With hiccups.

"Hey." Shane clicks on his blinker and pulls onto the shoulder, the tires rumbling over the grooves designed to wake drowsy drivers. He puts the car in park, slaps on the hazard lights, then draws me into his arms.

"We're going to fight this, Ciara. I don't care what we have to do. We'll keep you whole and bright for a long time."

I cling to his shoulders, my lungs tightening from the

pressure inside and out. He's not in denial like he was when I was a dying human. He's stronger now. And with his strength, I can tell inevitability to fuck off.

He strokes my hair and starts to sing. Tears flow down my cheeks as I recognize the song he wrote for our engagement, back when I was alive and we thought our future together would be short and sweet. Before we were given a form of forever.

In his song, he vowed to love me when I'm an old human, weak in body and mind. And now, in his embrace, I know he'll love me when I'm an old vampire, strong of body but not of mind.

Still I weep, at the injustice of false second chances.

6

Trouble Me

Funny thing about dying, either slow or fast: the world doesn't stop while you mourn yourself. Bills must be paid.

Just after midnight Friday morning, I sit alone at my desk in the radio station's main office, making myself useful. Ever since I "changed my work shift"—i.e., became a vampire—my job has absorbed all the duties that don't require being awake at the same time as the rest of the world. Lori's taken over many of my sales clients, and in turn I now do most of the accounting.

There was a day when I'd sooner dig ditches than keep books, but being a vampire makes it easier to focus on mundane tasks. Perhaps it's the predator's patience, or the obsessive-compulsiveness.

The door at the bottom of the stairs opens. A head of golden-brown hair appears.

"Hey, Ciara."

"Adrian. How'd your first show go last night? Sorry I missed it. I was . . ." *Absorbing my accelerated mortality.* "Out of town."

"I only screwed up the lead-ins to commercials four or five times." He tilts his head back and forth. "Possibly six or seven."

"The equipment must be different at every station."

"It's similar enough to lull you into a false sense of competence." His smile fades when he sees Franklin's office empty. "I was on my way out downstairs and saw the light on under the door."

"It's just me here. Sorry. So be honest—how does WVMP measure up compared to other stations?"

"It's, um, rugged."

"Yeah, when you look up 'low-budget' in the dictionary, there's a picture of WVMP too broke to afford their picture in the dictionary."

Adrian laughs, which makes me glow a little inside.

"It's worth it, though," he says, "to be around other vampires. Being oneself is a beautiful freedom."

I jut my thumb at Franklin's office. "Plus, we have a hot sales-and-marketing director."

Adrian actually blushes, which I'm not sure I've ever seen a vampire do. "I like Franklin. He's different."

I lean over to see his feet. Yep, still bare. "You're one to talk."

"But Franklin's different in a different way than I'm different."

I wiggle my toes in delight at his repetition of the word, and an anagram of "different" flits across my mind (*FIFE TREND*!). Then I remember I'm not supposed to care about words. Clinging to them to feel sane is tantamount to giving up.

"Are you guys actually going on a date," I ask him, "or are you skipping straight to happily ever after?"

"I thought maybe some musical dinner theater."

"Franklin hates musicals. He does like dinner, though, so if you leave before everyone starts singing, you might come out ahead."

Adrian chuckles. "He might be more open to new experiences than you think." He turns Lori's desk chair around and straddles it, a move that reminds me of Jim (but without the sinister threat of imminent assault). "Franklin told me you saved his life in that bomb blast. I think it changed him."

"How would you know? You met him after the bombing."

"I can tell when someone's struggling with a new reality, especially life and death." Adrian picks at the threads on the chair's top edge. "Before I was a vampire, I was studying to be a doctor. In med school I dealt with a lot of terminally ill patients."

"Oh." I turn away, shuffling papers to cover my reaction. "That must've been hard."

"Hard, yes, but sacred. The closer they got to death, the more they believed they were going somewhere afterward." He sighs. "That's one trade-off to immortality. Vampires don't have that certainty that there's anything beyond. We get that one glimpse of white light as we change from alive to undead, and that's it. No vampire's ever come back from a second death."

"I did."

"You're kidding." Adrian folds his arms on the top of the chair and rests his chin on them. "Tell me."

Something about this guy makes me want to speak, with none of the inner resistance I feel during therapy sessions. I set down the papers and turn to him. "I was in a battle, and someone unloaded a round of holy water right here." I open my mouth and point my finger up toward my palate to demonstrate. "Boom—burned straight into my head, completely annihilating my brain."

"Whoa."

"Exactly. For a few seconds, I wasn't anyone or anywhere. I was just . . . suspended in a place—no, 'place' is the wrong word. It was more like a state of being. Like there's solid, liquid, gas, and—that."

"Fascinating."

"Whatever and wherever I was, I wasn't alone. There was a presence, but not a singular presence like people think of God. It wasn't one being. It was like everyone and everything was in one place and time. Does that sound too far out?"

Adrian gestures to his clothing. "Do I look like I know the meaning of 'too far out'?"

I laugh for the first time today. "Anyway, if my experience is any indicator, vampires do have something to look forward to when they die for good." My heart sinks as I remember the new reality. "Then again, I'm not like most vampires."

"How so?"

I shrug, not ready to reveal my weakness to everyone yet. "I don't know. I'm not afraid of dying as much as I'm afraid of fading. Drifting through the world with no comprehension, becoming a monster."

He nods sadly. "I heard Jim faded early. That's why he was taken away."

That is ultimately the truth, so I don't deny it. "It was bad."

"His listeners still miss him. I got thirty-one calls during my show asking when he'll be back."

"We've told listeners he's gone for good," I say with a sigh. "Maybe you'll be the one to finally satisfy their hippie vampire DJ needs."

"I could never take Jim's place. He's a legend."

I try to remember Jim at his best: jamming at a gig to the Doors, weaving a spell as magical as Morrison himself. But all my memory shows is his half-melted face surging toward me while I struggled beneath him. Instead of music I hear my own screams as he plunged his fangs into my throat.

Was Jim crazy only because he was fading, or was there something wrong with him to begin with? Will *I* turn into a monster who has to be carted off to a Control nursing home? Will Shane be allowed to visit me?

"You think they'll ever let Jim out?" Adrian asks.

I hope not. "Fading's a one-way trip, right? The Control can only slow the process or keep old vampires from hurting people."

"Hmm, maybe." Adrian glances at the mantel clock on the never-used fireplace behind me, then stands and puts Lori's chair back under her desk. "I gotta scram now. But, Ciara, I still think there's hope for Jim, and for all the old vampires." He fingers the tassels of his jacket sleeve. "I'm probably just naïve. One of the side effects of living in a time when we believed anything was possible."

"I almost envy you." I pull out my keys. "Here, I can let you out the front. It's quicker."

Once outside, Adrian turns to me, his hair shimmering gold in the porch light. "It was good talking to you, Ciara."

"It was."

As I close the door and lock it, I realize I wasn't just being polite. It *was* good for me to talk to Adrian. He's the first person I've met who didn't know me as a human.

The lightness he leaves me with doesn't last, though. Within minutes, the dread of what I learned from Lanham last night forces its way into my mind, laying a heavy gray blanket over every thought.

I'm going to fade.

Suddenly I know who I need to talk to.

In the downstairs lounge, I make a new pot of stronger-than-dirt coffee, then pour two cups.

In the adjacent hallway outside the studio, I find Shane and Monroe in quiet conversation. They look at me, faces tight with tension.

"You told him?" I ask Shane.

"Was I not supposed to?"

"I was just coming down here to do that." I hand the extra coffee mug to Monroe, who takes it with a kindly nod.

Shane leans forward and kisses my temple. "I've gotta get back in. Song's ending."

My maker and I walk in silence down to the heavy steel door that leads to the DJs' apartment. It's almost too heavy for a human to budge, and even I have to pull with both hands. Monroe opens it with one dark finger curled around the handle.

The apartment has six small dormitory-type rooms that lead off from a common area, which includes a small kitchen to the left and a big living room to the right. Most of the decor is vintage seventies, though the kitchen appliances hail from the late nineties, when this bunker-style apartment was built beneath the ancient shack upstairs. Beyond the kitchen is a small hallway containing the bathroom and laundry area.

The apartment isn't glamorous, but it is safe—from fire, the sun, probably even a nuclear detonation. Best of all, there's always music playing.

I sit at the small dining table across from Monroe and wait for him to speak first, which is usually a losing bet.

"I'm sorry, child." He takes a sip of coffee. "It ain't easy getting old at any age."

Monroe still has the face of a twenty-seven-year-old man, though he comports himself like the ancient vampire he is. An aspiring Delta-blues guitarist back in the thirties, he went to a Mississippi crossroads at midnight to meet the devil, in the hopes he'd become a prodigy. Instead he found the vampire who would give him a different kind of immortality.

"What do you do to stay sane?" I ask him. "You're almost a hundred now, and you're not crazy like Jim was."

"I probably am, just in a different sorta way."

"In a way that doesn't kill people and make a million maniacal progeny."

The station's phone rings. I glance at the extension on the nearby side table. It's the studio line, probably someone making a request. I let Shane answer it.

"One thing I do," Monroe says, "is I keep to myself."

"I've noticed that."

"It's hard when you got friends. They take it personal,

like you don't like them anymore. But you gotta take care of yourself first. No one else will."

"Shane will."

"For now. But he's fifteen years older than you. What if he fades first? What if he dies?"

It's hard to breathe when I picture that. "I can't think about it when I'm trying to survive myself."

"That's what I'm saying. Let him worry about him and you worry about you. Then you worry about each other."

That makes a strange kind of sense, and reminds me of the way I used to think years ago when I was a con artist. I put myself first, but I wasn't a total bitch. I cared about people. I had Lori.

"So you're saying if I want to stay sane, I need to be alone?"

"Not be alone. Be by yourself." Monroe sets down his coffee cup and slides it slowly across the table, just past the halfway mark. It comes to a halt two inches from mine, his fingers still resting on the handle. "You ain't never gonna be alone."

I slide my own mug to close the gap, leaving my hand on the smooth ceramic surface after the soft clink.

The phone rings again. Shane is still on the line with his caller. I sigh and go to answer it, irritated at the interruption to a rare moment of genuine connection with my maker.

"WVMP, the Lifeblood of Rock 'n' Roll." I keep my voice chirpy. "How can I help you?"

For a moment, nothing. Then a woman's sob.

"Hello?" I try not to sound annoyed. People request songs in all moods, but especially heartbroken.

"Is Shane there?" she asks.

"I'm sorry, he's on another line. May I take a message or—"

"What about Jim? Where is that son of a bitch?"

Beside me, Monroe tenses visibly.

"Jim no longer works here," I tell the caller.

A shocked gasp. "Where'd he go?"

"I'm not sure which station he moved on to. But he's not coming back to WVMP."

"Then I need to talk to Shane."

The voice sounds vaguely familiar. "Can I have your name?"

"It's Deirdre."

My heart flutters. "Shane's, um, friend who used to live off Greene Street?"

"I'm still here. What's left of me, anyway, after Jim was through."

Deirdre was once one of Shane's donors, but he traded her to Jim after we started dating. The vampire's bite is such an intimate experience, Shane wanted to show his commitment to me as a boyfriend by not putting his mouth on other women.

But after Jim went into Control custody, we contacted his donors to let them know he wouldn't be visiting them anymore. According to Jim's records, he hadn't seen Deirdre in months because she'd supposedly moved away.

The studio line goes dim. "Deirdre, Shane's free now. Hang on."

I put her on hold and race down the hall to the studio. The ON THE AIR sign is dim, and a Robyn Hitchcock tune is playing over the speakers. I peer through the studio window to see Shane flipping through a stack of CDs.

He motions me inside. "What's up? Who's on the phone?"

"Deirdre."

Shane's fingers freeze, their tips barely curled under the flipped-open CD. "My Deirdre? I mean—Jim's Deirdre?"

"Yes, your Deirdre." I clear my throat to erase the jealousy. "Something's wrong."

He slowly picks up the phone. "Deirdre, what's wrong?" He listens for a moment, then holds out his palm, as if she's standing in front of him. "Slow down. What do you need?"

Through the receiver I hear the word "blood."

"I'm sorry," Shane says, "you can't be my donor anymore. Maybe Regina or—oh. Oh God. Oh, no." He leaps out of the chair, smacking it against the table holding the DJs' equipment. Good thing he was playing a CD and not a vinyl record or it would've skipped.

"What's wrong?" I ask him.

His head jerks up so he can see the clock. "I'm off at three a.m.," he says into the phone. "We'll come help you."

7

Sour Girl

The nature of Deirdre's emergency sounds time-con-suming, so before heading to her place, Shane and I stop home to feed our vampire dog, Dexter, and take him for a walk. I offered to come home on my own to take care of Dexter, but ever since the Halloween bombing, Shane won't let me out of his sight unless absolutely necessary.

Deirdre lives in the same cute town house as always. But no flowers line the walkway now, and the roof is missing several shingles.

A rolled-up note on blue paper protrudes through the curved handle of the screen door. I pull it out—just to bring it to her, I tell myself, not to snoop. In big print, the words FINAL NOTICE catch my eye.

"It's open!" she says when Shane knocks.

Deirdre greets us in the dark kitchen just inside the door, a bottle of red wine—the cheap stuff, nothing like what she used to have—in one hand, a pair of wineglasses in the other.

"I started without you." She sets the bottle on the counter with a hollow clonk. "Oh, you brought her again. Just like old times." Her laughter is weak, like the rest of her. Deirdre slumps against the counter, pawing through a forest of empty wine bottles and plastic shopping bags.

I head to the microwave and start heating one of the servings of blood we brought from the station. I refrigerate the other four servings in their brown paper shopping bag.

"Here they are." Deirdre finds what she's looking for: a pack of cigarettes and a lighter. "So—hey!"

She protests as Shane's hand zips out, faster than a snake, tearing the lighter away from her.

"You're too young to use fire," he says.

"Jim used to let me light my own." When Shane holds out his hand, she reluctantly gives him the cigarette. He lights it for her and hands it back, grimacing at the taste.

Smoking itself isn't dangerous for vampires of any age: we can't get cancer or other diseases. But the act of lighting up, combined with carelessness or a stray breeze, can instantly turn us youngsters into a pile of nothing. We should all wear T-shirts that say WARNING: FLAMMABLE.

"When did Jim turn you?" Shane asks.

She blows out the smoke and rubs her nose. "Last December. Just in time for Christmas, the prick."

I try to point out the bright side. "At least it was a dark time of year. Not much daylight in—"

"I lost my kid!" Deirdre flails her hand at the stairs behind her. "I had to give him to my ex-husband. That asshole has full custody now, and my poor baby thinks I don't . . . that I don't love him." She starts to cry. "When

I do see my son, I can barely hug him for two seconds, and then I have to push him away so I don't bite. He smells so good," she finishes in a whisper.

Shane lowers his head. "I'm sorry. I can't imagine how hard that is."

"No, you can't." She gulps a couple of breaths to stop crying. "What good is living forever when you lose everything worth living for?"

The microwave beeps. Quietly I fetch the last clean wineglass and pour Deirdre a drink of blood. My foot brushes a stuffed blue dog her kid must have left behind.

"Come on." He puts a gentle hand on the back of her shoulder. "Let's sit and talk."

Deirdre leans into him as we walk downstairs into the living room. A large window looms over us. No way would its torn shade block all the sunlight.

"That's where I sleep." She points her cigarette at the storage room under the stairs. "Only safe place in the house."

I peek inside. Despite the utility-type remnants, like a toolbox and vinyl shelves, it looks like a decent fallout shelter bedroom. A thick towel hangs over the knob—probably to stuff into the crack beneath the door to block every photon of sunlight.

"It was an accident." Deirdre sinks onto the couch and taps her cigarette into the ashtray. "I don't know if that makes it worse or better."

"Jim drank you too deep?" Shane sits beside her, but not close enough to touch.

"Jim always drank me too deep. He wasn't careful like you." She shrugs. "At first I loved that about him.

I always had a thing for bad boys. Like my ex." Deirdre gives Shane a look of longing. "You were the exception to my rule. My one white knight."

I clear my throat. "Did Jim take care of you after he made you a vampire?"

"For a few weeks he was great, then he got bored, I guess. I almost starved to death a couple times."

The longest I've been without blood was twelve hours, and it was hell. The physical symptoms—thirst, weakness, bone-creaking chills—aren't even the worst. It's the way our minds change. Suddenly it seems okay to kill.

And all that soul-shriveling misery can be swept away with one slurp of a blood-filled sippy cup.

"I'm so sorry," Shane tells Deirdre again. "If I hadn't—" He cuts himself off before he can say what we're all thinking: if he hadn't traded Deirdre to Jim, she'd still be alive.

It was her choice to stay with Jim, of course. But vampires are as addictive as any drug, and no one as abusive as Jim would ever be easy to leave, even if one wanted to.

To my relief, Deirdre shakes her head. "It's not your fault, Shane. You trading me to Jim was the right thing for all of us—at the time, at least. You had no idea he'd go crazy." She takes a long gulp of blood, closing her eyes with relief, then a drag on her cigarette. "Where's he been, anyway?"

"In Control custody."

"Oh my God!" She coughs on her smoke. "Why?"

"*Why*?" My voice twists. "Because he was a psychopath. He should've been locked up a lot sooner."

Shane's tone stays gentle. "He attacked Ciara, among other things."

"He almost killed my sixteen-year-old cousin," I tell her. "And he tore my throat to shreds."

Deirdre hunches in on herself, crossing her arms and closing her legs. "I'm not surprised. Nothing was ever totally against my will, but sometimes it came really close to the line."

I nod. Jeremy told me back in April that Jim had come up with some new donor game that made him really uncomfortable. *He's developing a taste for fear*, he said.

"So now what?" Deirdre makes a weak attempt at a grand two-handed gesture. "What's to become of my glamorous immortal life?"

"You're one of us." I hear the words after they've left my mouth.

Shane looks surprised.

"She is," I tell him, "as much as I am. Jim made her, and he was one of us, just like Monroe." I turn back to Deirdre. "We'll make sure you get enough to drink. Did Jim teach you how to bite?"

Her gaze thunks to the floor. "Not safely."

Oh God. She's hurt a human. No wonder she's hiding out here.

"I can't train you, Deirdre," Shane says. "It would be, you know—"

"Too sexy?" she says with a sneer. "Jim says there are no rules and no barriers when it comes to vampires. Everyone does everyone and everything."

"Remember when we said Jim is a psychopath?" I snapped.

"Ciara and I are engaged." Shane points to my left hand. "So I won't be doing anything without her."

"I don't mind if she comes along, remember?" She reaches for Shane. "You can teach both of us together."

He stands up, out of arm's length. "No."

That seductive longing in her eyes is ten times as strong as it was when she was a human. I can see it now as clearly as if it were yesterday: Deirdre spread-eagled on her bed, begging Shane to fuck her, withholding the blood he needed until he agreed (which he wouldn't). We weren't even dating then, but it was awkward with me sitting across the room. Really awkward.

"I don't know the other vampire DJs." Deirdre seems to shrink into herself again. "Jim never introduced us. Maybe he was ashamed of me."

"I'm sure it was nothing personal," I tell her. "You were the twenty-fourth vampire he made. If he brought all of his offspring to every party, it'd be really crowded."

She stares at me. "Twenty-four?"

"He was going to turn my cousin. He said she would've been his twenty-fifth."

"He was going to turn a child into a vampire? Who does he think he is, Lestat?"

"He was doing it to coerce me, but yeah, he probably would've changed her, no matter what I did." Deirdre's anger encourages me. Maybe it'll be a rope to help her climb out of her sorrow.

"So the Control busted in and saved the day?" she asks.

"Monroe staked him with a handful of pencils."

"Staked? But you said he was in custody." Deirdre puts a hand to her own chest. "Besides, Jim told me I'd be in agony if he died." Her face turns stormy. "Or did he just say that to keep me from killing him?"

"He's not dead." Shane rubs his forehead with the side of his hand. "The Control agents got there before we could pull out the stake—pencils, whatever. They took him."

Her jaw drops. "They wouldn't put him out of his misery?"

"They said they could give him something for the pain," I tell her.

"That's crazy." She turns to Shane. "Were you there when this happened? Why didn't you pull out the stakes?"

"I was ordered not to."

"Since when do you take orders from anyone?"

"Since we joined the Control. It wasn't voluntary." Shane lifts his gaze to mine. "But I'm not sorry."

"I *thought* you looked different." Deirdre stands and faces him straight on, examining him from head to toe. "More confident, less . . . slackerish."

Shane's eyebrows twitch, like she's insulted him but he doesn't want to show it. "It's temporary."

"It better be." She sighs and turns to the dark fireplace. "I'd like to keep living here, if it's okay."

"Good," he says, "because there's no room at the station, and you're not living at our apartment."

"I get that." She heads for the stairs—to show us out, I guess. "You and I have a past. It'd be awkward." Deirdre emphasizes the last word of each sentence as if to mock them.

Shane rolls his eyes at me, then follows her. "I'll talk to the other vampires about taking you on as an apprentice."

I head up after them. "Noah'd be a good match, don't you think, Shane?"

"Ooh, Noah!" Her step takes on a bounce. "I saw him at a show once. He's cute."

Noah's Rasta pacifism is just what Deirdre needs to balance her own wild tendencies. She was reckless to begin with, and with Jim's blood in her now, she could be a powder keg without the steadying influence of a straight-edged mentor like Noah.

In the kitchen, Deirdre tries to hug Shane. He accepts it, but with stiff arms.

I point to the fridge. "There's a day's worth of blood in there, so drink half of each container every three hours." I turn the knob on the front door and swing it open. "We'll bring more tomorrow and—"

Everything freezes.

Standing on the porch, mouth agape, fist raised to knock on the door, is Jim.

8

Paint It Black

Our eyes meet, and for one tick of the wall clock, I know that I am dead. Dead for good.

Something blurs between us. I leap back. Jim surges forward. As he rushes past me, I see his eyes go wide with—could it be fear? Not predatory fervor or a victorious gloat?

Shane smashes him against the wall next to the coatrack. Jim's hands bounce against the coats, then rise, reaching for Shane's throat.

A second blur and he stops. A third blur and he sinks to the floor as Shane steps back, right hand up in a defensive posture and left hand—

Oh.

In Shane's left hand, a wooden stake drips blood.

"No . . . time," Jim gasps, rolling over on his back, grasping for anything. A white faux fur coat falls across his lap. Within a few seconds, it's soaked in a flood of scarlet.

Deirdre pulls in a squeaky breath, then another, making pre-scream noises. I shove the front door shut a second before she looses a caterwaul of grief and horror. The sound crawls up my spine and wants to burst out the top of my head.

Jim writhes under his fountain of blood, mouth opening and closing. He reaches toward me, pleading, just as he did the night Monroe staked him to save my life. I shake off my shock and prepare for another attack. If Shane's blow missed, Jim will heal and be on us in a flash.

Shane stands over him, ready to strike again. His face is the cold stone of a professional assassin. Except this was no hit job. This was a split-second, kill-or-be-killed-along-with-your-fiancée situation.

Jim's body goes limp.

"No!" Deirdre lurches forward, hands outstretched. Shane stops her.

"It's not safe," he says. "Get behind me. Both of you."

But when he lets go of her, she drops to her knees next to Jim.

"Let her say good-bye," I tell Shane.

"But if he's not—"

"It's her choice."

Deirdre keens and wails against Jim's chest, one hand in his dark-brown curls. His white linen shirt, drenched in blood, rides up to expose his pale belly. I look down to see red drops splashed on my jeans, the kitchen wall, and the stuffed blue dog in the corner.

As long as Jim's bleeding, he's still "alive." The moment he starts to die—*if* he starts to die—it'll run backward into the wound, along with the rest of him.

I don't know what to do or what to feel. It's like I'm in a movie, and the director just shouted "Action!" but I don't know my lines. I don't even know which character I'm playing. I wish someone would yell "Cut!"

"What do I do?" I ask Shane.

"Just wait." His voice drops to a whisper. "I'm sorry."

I'm not sure who he's talking to: me, Deirdre, or Jim. Or all three of us.

The bleeding just stopped. I think.

I hold my breath.

For a long moment, the blood on Jim's chest and the floor beneath him becomes a still pond.

Then the pool begins to shrink. My breath sucks back into my lungs, mimicking the action of the blood. It's begun.

Shane slowly gets to his knees, crosses himself, and closes his eyes.

"What's happening?" Deirdre whispers.

She's never seen a vampire die. Did it have to be her own maker? "Deirdre, come with me." I look at Shane. "I'll take care of her."

He nods, never taking his eyes from Jim. Once, years ago, they were friends.

Jim's flesh begins to crawl, sliding toward the hole in his chest.

"NOOOOOO!" Deirdre's scream of horror is cut off when her own breath stops. She falls back, flailing. I catch her before her head can hit the wall.

With some difficulty, I pick her up, carry her into the dining room, and lay her gently on the floor, away from breakable objects.

The moment I put her down, she starts writhing, clawing the air and the carpet beneath her. With one hand I clutch her wrist, and with the other I pull out my phone and call Jeremy. To survive this, she needs fresh blood.

When he answers, I say in a preternaturally calm voice, "We need you to save a vampire."

"What? Who? I'm on the air."

I look at the clock. It's almost 5:30 already. Morning twilight is in forty-five minutes. I have no desire to spend the day in the house where Shane killed Jim. "We'll bring her to you."

"'Her'?" His voice pitches up in panic. "Is Regina—"

"Not Regina. Just get ready." I hang up. "We have to take her to the station so Jeremy can save her." Shane responds with only a nod.

I look down at Jim's body, which is starting to fold in on itself. Then I turn and watch his mirror image in Deirdre. She scrapes at her dress, exposing the skin that's bruising from the inside. A blue and black circle widens across her ribs. Her eyes roll up, showing nothing but white in her agony.

Jim's back arches. Deirdre's back arches.

Jim's back breaks in half with an earsplitting crack. Deirdre falls to the carpet, mercifully unconscious. I check her pulse, erratic but strong, and focus on the rhythm of her breath instead of the sucking, snapping sounds from the kitchen.

In the corner of my eye, the stuffed dog seems to shudder as a small red cloud rises from its fur. The blood drifts up, against gravity, over the dog's outstretched paw. It hovers, then flies across the room into the wound, which is now an unrecognizable vortex of flesh.

The last few drops enter the hole, and I wait for the soft pop that came with the three staking deaths

I've witnessed—including Colonel Petrea's, the one I inflicted.

The wound explodes like a firecracker. I cover my ears and hold back a scream, half expecting Jim to reappear, inside out, rejected by the realm of the truly dead.

But he stays gone.

I lower my hands, and for several moments all sound is muffled, like after a concert where I've sat too close to the speakers.

Shane rubs his ears, then bends over and collects Jim's clothes: a pair of black leather pants, white button-down poet shirt, and pointed-toe black boots. Every drop of blood is gone.

Something rattles on the floor as Shane lifts the shirt.

"Whoa." I go over and gather the stack of pencils, the ends of which are shaved off and smoothed out. "That's how he survived. The Control kept these in his heart."

"His body probably healed around the wounds. He might not have felt it. Or maybe they did give him something for the pain." Shane refocuses. "Right now, we have to save Deirdre."

As we pass the radio station studio, Shane carrying Deirdre in his arms, Jeremy is standing there in the open doorway.

"Holy shit," he says. "What happened to her?"

"Maker died," I tell him. "She needs blood. Meet us in the DJs' apartment."

"Be there in three minutes. I have to set up the last song and record an outro so it sounds like I'm signing off."

We enter the apartment and shut the heavy steel

door behind us. Everyone is gathered in the common room, looking somber. I called ahead and told them what happened, and not to tell Jeremy until after he'd fed Deirdre.

"Put her on the bed," says our fifties DJ Spencer.

The couch has been folded out, just like when my own life hung in the balance—and then toppled over into death and reanimation. I have the urge to set this couch on fire.

Instead, I set the pile of Jim's clothing on one of the dining room chairs, hidden under the table where Jeremy won't see it. Two of the sawed-off pencils tumble onto the floor, in a noise that shatters the silence. Regina watches them fall but makes no move to pick them up.

Shane carefully lays Deirdre on the thin mattress. Spencer sits beside her and feels the pulse at her wrist.

"How old is she?" he asks me, lines of concern framing his dark eyes.

"Jim turned her last December. So less than a year old."

I look across the sofa at my maker. Monroe's watching me, probably thinking what I'm thinking: if he died right now, this is what I'd go through, if not worse.

"Will she live?" Noah asks Spencer, anxiously twisting the end of one chest-length dreadlock.

"She's fading fast." Spencer brushes the hair off Deirdre's forehead and lifts one of her eyelids. "It'd be best if she could wake up to drink, but I reckon one of us can feed her the first few drops until she does."

Shane and I exchange a look. I give him a reluctant nod.

"I'll do it," he tells Spencer. "I'm the only one she knows."

The silence stretches out. We all focus on the wall clock, waiting for Jeremy to arrive, rather than talking about the biggest thing to happen to the station since, well, ever. They've lost one of their own.

Someone knocks on the door to the hallway. Regina opens it for Jeremy.

"Let me wash up." He hurries into the kitchen, yanking off his gray hoodie.

Shane calls over, "Jer, we're gonna need to do the neck. It's faster, and she needs blood, *stat*."

Jeremy's eyes light up with anticipation. "Sweet," he whispers, pulling his T-shirt over his head. The action ruffles his bleached-blond hair and pulls off his glasses, which clatter on the kitchen floor.

I pick them up and look through them at the recessed ceiling light. Huh, they're real.

I set them on the counter next to the sink as Jeremy cranks up the hot water. "I always thought these were a fashion statement."

He snorts. "I'm shallow, but not that shallow."

I pull a pair of clean dish towels from a drawer and hand him one. Then I notice a bandage on his right arm. "What happened to you?"

"New tattoo." He wets the towel and pours antibacterial soap onto it. "Just got it today."

"What's the occasion?"

Jeremy gives me a bashful smile as he washes the sides of his neck with the soapy towel. "You are."

This pleases me more than it should. Donors usually get enthralled by the vampires who feed from them, but Jeremy and I have always butted heads, trading snipes at every chance.

"Let me rinse." I push him gently to bend over the sink, then I wet the towel and squeeze it over the back of his neck to wash away the soap. Jeremy takes the dry towel, smelling fresh and clean and very, very chompable.

But it won't be me chomping him this weekend as planned. After feeding Deirdre, he won't be able to donate again for two weeks. Lori's taken herself out of the rotation because of her pregnancy. Shane said I need to drink from more humans to stave off the fading. What am I going to do?

I pull my mind back to the present. Save Deirdre. Nothing's more important now, right?

As Jeremy and I head toward the bed, I realize that this is what it means to be a vampire. Our survival is tenuous, and a constant obsession.

Shane sits a few feet away from Deirdre on the fold-out couch. A stack of clean towels has been placed near her head, and two are folded next to her, where Jeremy will lie.

Jeremy reclines between Deirdre and Shane. Though this is for survival and not for fun, his heartbeat quickens in anticipation. Even Jeremy's sweat smells different the moment before he's bitten.

He turns his head toward Deirdre so he can see her face and give Shane access to his neck. "Who was her maker?"

Shane freezes as he leans over. The other DJs go completely still, then Noah shuffles his feet nervously.

Jeremy's going to freak when he hears that Jim's dead. He might not even be willing to donate or help us after he knows Shane killed him.

I don't want to lie to him. "We'll tell you later."

"But—"

"Shh." Shane's left hand covers Jeremy's mouth as it lifts and turns his chin. "Hold as still as you can."

Jeremy flinches, and for a moment that prey freak-out look comes into his eyes. But then he closes them and exhales, making himself relax.

"Thank you." Shane's lips, then tongue, stroke the skin of Jeremy's neck, searching for the vein.

Shane slides in his fangs. Jeremy's body stiffens for two seconds, then seems to sink deeper into the mattress. They moan in unison, Shane at the taste and Jeremy at the sensation. I envy Jeremy his pleasure. Why can't I feel something when I'm bitten besides fiery pain?

On Deirdre's other side, I slide my hands under her shoulder and lift her to sit halfway up. Now comes the part I've been dreading.

Shane takes his mouth from Jeremy's neck, full of his blood, leans over, and kisses Deirdre, feeding her the way a bird feeds its nestlings. His tongue moves in her mouth, forcing in the life-giving substance.

But she just lies limp in my arms. Shane breaks away and strokes her throat. "Come on, swallow." Her mouth hangs open. "Deirdre, wake up. If I've killed you, too . . ." he whispers with agony.

Jeremy's eyes open. "What do you mean, 'killed her, too'?"

"It was self-defense," I tell him. "Her maker tried to kill us."

"I don't understand." He puts his hand to his neck, catching the thick blood as it oozes out.

Deirdre surges out of my grip. "Shane . . ." She

kisses him, making soft, urgent noises in the back of her throat.

Shane pulls away. "No. Here." He turns Jeremy over on his right side. "Drink."

She pouts. "I'd rather take it from you."

"This'll be faster. It'll save you. By the way, his name is Jeremy."

"I don't care." Deirdre falls on our friend, teeth snapping together.

Shane's hand whips out and catches the back of her neck. "Easy. No sucking, no chewing." He withdraws the stake from his back pocket. "I'll be watching."

She snorts. "I guess I should feel lucky you're giving me a warning. Jim didn't get that courtesy."

Jeremy starts. "Jim? What?"

Shane lets Deirdre go. "Drink now."

"Wait! You guys!" Jeremy's cries are silenced as Deirdre starts to drink. But tears form in his eyes, and when they overflow, I can smell their salt, mixing with the scent of his blood.

I watch Shane watching Deirdre feed on Jeremy. As a Control Enforcement agent, his training demands he protect humans from vampires. I want to reach for him, hold him, let him tell me and show me how much the last hour has shattered him. If it has.

Jeremy's hand thumps on the mattress as Deirdre drinks from him, long and deep.

Reality is starting to catch up to me. Shane killed Jim. If it weren't for the pile of Jim's clothes on the chair, topped with a stack of sawed-off pencils, I'd think it was a dream.

Deirdre finally pulls back, then gazes down at Jeremy, who looks at her through heavy-lidded eyes.

"You saved my life," she tells him.

His shoulder twitches in a tired shrug. "Glad to. I like vampires."

She lays her head on her thin pillow, facing him. "What was your name again?"

"Jeremy. Is Jim really dead?"

Her only response is to draw him close in an embrace. They weep together for the guy who brought them so much pain.

After a few moments Spencer slips a hand between them. "Gotta clean the boy up now."

As Spencer bandages Jeremy's neck, Shane steps away and watches the sobbing Deirdre with heartbreak in his eyes. But when he looks at me, the heartbreak turns to pride. He's not sorry he saved my life. I'm not, either.

Deirdre begins to wail. Clearly her strength has returned, at least to her lungs.

"How could you?" She launches herself off the bed and totters toward Shane. "You didn't even give him a warning. It was like you planned it."

"I did plan it." He grasps her shoulders. "I ran this scenario in my head a million times. I killed him in my imagination, until it became second nature."

"Why?"

"Because he's twice as fast as I am, and ten times as strong. Surprising him was our only chance for survival."

"Speaking of planning," I say, "funny coincidence that Jim showed up while we were there."

Deirdre gapes at me. "Are you saying I set you up? I hadn't seen him since February."

"Then why did he come to you?"

Spencer clears his throat. "Maybe it was the only safe spot in Sherwood."

"It's not like he could come here," Regina adds.

"Why come to Sherwood at all?" Noah asks. "Why not run away? This is the first town the Control would look for him in."

Deirdre turns back to Shane and clutches his T-shirt. "I swear to God I didn't know Jim was coming."

"We'll see about that." I go to her purse and pull out her cell phone.

"What are you doing? Stay out of my stuff!"

Shane holds on to her as I scroll through the incoming and outgoing calls. The lists are sadly short. "Is Ben your ex-husband?"

"Troy's my ex-husband. Ben's my son. I know eight's a little young to have a cell phone, but I gave it to him so I could call without his dad around. Sometimes in the middle of the night."

The phone shows no call to or from any unknown numbers. Just a bunch to Ben, a few to Troy, and two to a pizza place. I wonder if Deirdre bites the delivery boys.

I slip her phone back into her purse, disappointed. She could've deleted a call from Jim from her list. If I could prove she had contact with him, maybe we could get more information out of her.

"What is most puzzling," Noah says, "is how Jim escaped from Control custody."

"Either he went all Hannibal Lecter and killed a guard," I point out, "or someone released him, either on purpose or by mistake."

"Could he have mesmerized some sap into letting him go?" Spencer asks. "A human guard?"

"His eyes were super-powerful." I tap my chest. "Speaking as a human who had to look into them on a daily basis."

"He had beautiful eyes," Jeremy says.

We all fall silent as the weight of loss bears down on us. Jim is gone forever. He'll never again recite trivia or overplay his poker hand or tell us something is groovy.

Shane turns away and walks swiftly, silently, to his room. The door closes with a soft click.

I shift my weight from foot to foot, uncertain whether I should follow. Maybe Shane wants to be alone to think or mourn. Then again, he might want comfort. What would I want? Hard to say, since I've never killed one of my longtime friends.

I decide to err on the side of too much.

I knock softly on Shane's door, then open it slowly, expecting to find him pacing or maybe sitting on the edge of the twin bed in quiet sorrow, staring at the floor or the wall.

Instead, I find him backed into the far corner of the bed, knees pulled to his chest. He's chewing his thumbnail, eyes scanning nothing. He looks like a ten-year-old boy worried he'll get caught for shooting out a window with a BB gun.

When he sees me, his lips part but make no sound, like they're waiting for the words to enter from the outside.

I have none to offer, so I climb onto the bed and take him in my arms.

Shane sobs without tears, heaving great, shuddering breaths that quake my body. He holds on to me so tight that for a moment I feel like I'll squish up like a stress ball. But I'm made of strong stuff now, and I can take it.

He pulls away finally and rests against the wall, tilting his head up to stare at the ceiling. "We need to call Lanham."

"He better find out how the hell this happened. If someone knew Jim escaped, they should've warned us."

"Yeah, that, too."

"There's something else you want to talk to him about?"

He lowers his chin to look straight at me. "Asking for a transfer."

"Out of Enforcement? I can understand why you'd want to do that after your first kill, but you've worked so hard, and if you start over in a different division, you'll have to do a whole new training." I can't believe I'm arguing for him to stay an Enforcement agent. "Besides, Lanham will never let you do it. He'll only color outside the lines when it's his idea."

Shane's face remains impassive. "I don't mean change divisions. I mean change locations. If you'll come with me."

My spine turns cold. "You want to leave?"

"I can't stay here at the station. I know what I did was justified." He swallows, and I wonder if that was the truth. "The other DJs will say they know it, too, but I can see it in their eyes. They think I'm a murderer. I was the one to end him, to plunge that stake into his—" Shane shifts his lower jaw from side to side, and I wonder if the tears are finally on their way. "They can't mourn him with me here."

"I'd have to get a transfer, too. You think the Control would do that?"

"Married agents usually stay together. Like Agent Sellers and Captain Wayne-Sellers from Indoc?"

"But they're both in the same division with jobs at headquarters." I point to my lonely engagement band. "Besides, we're not married yet."

"Then let's change that. We'll move the wedding up."

"Shane, no. I'm not rushing our wedding. We won't give Jim the honor of turning our lives upside down." I put my hand on his knee. "Think about it before you decide what you want. It would mean leaving the station, leaving Sherwood, probably leaving Dexter."

He gives me a sharp look. "Dexter?"

"If the Control deploys us somewhere, it could be some field situation where we wouldn't have a permanent home. That's no life for a dog. Plus, he's a vampire, which makes him extra freaky about routine."

"Okay." He runs a hand over his head, back to front. "We stay for Dexter."

I offer him an out. "If you still feel this way at the end of our contracts, and you want to stay in the Control, then we'll ask to be deployed somewhere stable away from here. Somewhere we can keep Dexter."

"That makes sense."

"In the meantime, we need to go deal with the DJs."

"I know." He gives a long sigh. "I've lived in Sherwood for more than ten years. It's probably time for a change."

"You're a vampire. Change is bad."

"Usually." He shifts to sit on the edge of the mattress. "Maybe not this time."

9

Stand by Me

The DJs are still gathered in the common room when we enter. Noah and Regina sit together on one end of the foldout couch. Spencer is in the kitchen, pouring Jeremy a tall glass of blue Gatorade. Deirdre is slumped over the table, her cheek pressed against the marbled linoleum surface, an open bottle of rum in her hand. Monroe sits in one of the overstuffed brown armchairs with his gleaming red acoustic guitar, softly picking an old blues tune that I recognize but can't name. I'm glad Adrian hasn't moved in yet—at least he's spared this tableau of misery.

Shane comes with me to the center of the room by the coffee table. He starts to cross his arms, then drops them and simply stands straight, eyes forward. Like a soldier. "If you guys have something to say to me, say it now."

Deirdre lets out a growl. "I have a lot to—"

"Not you. You're done."

Spencer spreads his hands. "What do you want us to say?"

"I think he wants a round of applause." Regina throws up her arms. "Or maybe we should do the wave."

Spencer looks confused by the latter term. Then he turns back to Shane. "You gonna defend what you did? Killin' one of our own with no warning? Deirdre told us you didn't say a word to Jim. You just staked him like an animal."

Shane stares straight ahead, as if he's making an official report, not discussing the death of a friend. "Jim has demonstrated his superior strength on numerous occasions. In the time it took me to say a word to him, he could've torn off my head. More likely Ciara's head, since she was closer."

I resist the urge to rub my neck. "It's true. You guys remember Thanksgiving three years ago. He threatened to kill Shane in front of all of us." I glare at Spencer. "You've seen the way Jim acted around me when he thought we were alone."

"I seen it." Monroe sets down his guitar with a low hum, then stands and comes toward me. "I was the one found them, remember? In his room, covered in her blood. The way he was at it, he woulda chewed straight through her neck if I—" He stops, his hand halfway to me. It starts trembling, which I've never seen it do before. Monroe lowers his hand, then stares at it like it's not even attached to him. "This is all my fault. I shoulda ended it that night."

"I stopped you. We thought my cousin Cass would die if he died. We thought we needed Jim to bring her back."

"We were wrong."

"Then look at it this way: if we'd killed Jim that night, then Deirdre would've died, alone in her house. As young as she is, she'd never have survived her maker's death."

Deirdre shows no reaction to this, just keeps scraping the black-and-white label off the rum bottle with her jagged thumbnail.

Noah speaks up at last. "I never support killing, you know that. Yet I cannot help but admit I am relieved that Jim is no longer a threat."

"What if he wasn't a threat?" Jeremy's voice is faint from loss of blood. "What if that nursing home rehabilitated him? Isn't that what they're there for?"

"You think maybe he didn't escape?" Regina twists her studded leather bracelet so hard it squeaks. "Maybe they let him go on purpose because he'd gotten better?"

"He wasn't better!" I tell them, nearly yelling. "After Halloween I checked to make sure Jim hadn't escaped and set the bomb at the Smoking Pig. Lanham said nothing had changed. Jim was still a prisoner under guard."

"Maybe Lanham lied." Regina gasps. "Oh, no, wait, Colonel Stick-up-His-Ass has never lied to you. Except all the times he's lied to you."

She has a point. Lanham has saved me so many times, literally and professionally, it's easy to forget his motives could be mixed at best.

Spencer examines the bits of pencils scattered on the chair. They're smooth at both ends, like unsharpened golf pencils. "Looks like these were shaved off flush with his skin."

He holds one of the pencils up to the kitchen ceiling light. "His body mighta healed around the wound and sealed it off. Which woulda made 'em harder to get out."

"And if only one or two actually pierced his heart," Noah points out, "it could still pump. He could still live." He rubs a spot on his chest an inch down and to the right of his heart, probably remembering the time he took a crossbow arrow there. "Also, it would leave room for the final killing blow."

No one but me looks at Monroe or Shane, the ones who delivered Jim's wounds.

"So he was walking around with those things still inside him." Regina shudders. "I wonder if he could feel them."

"I bet the Control wondered, too." The DJs won't like my next conjecture. "They might've wanted to study him. How often do they get a half-staked vampire in their midst?"

"They could make one anytime," Regina says with a snarl.

"Technically they could, but politically? No way. Not with the uproar over Project Blood Leash. Right now the Control is tiptoeing around the undead so we don't all quit. Another anti-vampire injustice would destroy the agency."

Deirdre scoffs. "How is keeping Jim alive with stakes in his heart *not* an anti-vampire injustice?"

"Every society treats their criminals worse than they treat regular people." Noah sits on the corner of the couch. "They don't have the same rights, so they are used and discarded."

"If Jim was useful to the Control as some sort of lab specimen, they would've had him under maximum security." Shane examines his left hand, stretching and flexing his fingers. "But they obviously didn't."

"Then they did let him go on purpose." Jeremy sips his Gatorade. "Maybe the Control sent him as an assassin."

"But why would they?" Noah asks. "He was a danger to humans and other vampires. Releasing him would go against everything they say they stand for."

"They stand for 'whatever it takes,'" Regina growls. "If the Control wanted you and Shane dead, the best way to do it would be to let Jim go. They wouldn't whack you directly."

"But we're valuable to them." I glance at Shane. "Right?"

"You *were* valuable," Regina says. "With no more anti-holy blood, you're just another vampire."

"She was a vampire when she saved my life." Monroe points to the left side of his head, where a holy-water blast took his skin, skull, and brain, all of which grew back. "She had the power with just her thoughts and her words. This girl's more than just another vampire."

"True," Regina admits, then says to me, "You do have a lot of enemies. It's one reason why I like you."

"We may never know how Jim escaped," Shane says, "but we should assume it wasn't an accident, and watch our backs."

"I bet Jim could tell you how he escaped," Deirdre snarls. "Oh, wait, he can't because he's dead." She takes another chug of cheap rum.

The phone on the end table rings. It's an inside line, from David's office. He often comes in at seven a.m. to set up the syndicated morning news programs.

I go to answer it, then hesitate. "Does David know what happened?"

"We told him." Spencer is lining up the pencil segments on the table in order of size. Deirdre reaches out to the pile of Jim's clothes. Spencer pushes it closer to her.

I answer the phone. "Hey, David."

"You okay?"

"Better than I could be, I guess. What's up?"

"Colonel Lanham's here to see you."

"Already? Who called him?"

"No one. Apparently Jim had some kind of tracking device in him. All the high-value prisoners wear them."

I eye the line of pencils. "Spencer, did you hear that? Is it in one of those?"

He squats down level with the table, then selects the smallest pencil and hands it to me. Sure enough, next to the graphite inside lies a silvery gray fiber.

David continues. "The sensor also detects the temperature difference between a vampire's body and the surrounding air. That way they know when and where an escaped prisoner dies."

Makes sense. No point wasting resources trying to find a vampire who's already gone *poof*.

"Lanham wants you and Shane to debrief him," David says. "Bring Deirdre, too."

Shane and I help Deirdre stagger upstairs to the office. She insists on bringing the rum. Whatever keeps her quiet.

Lanham is waiting in David's office, his height and presence making the room look even smaller than usual. "Griffin. McAllister. I understand there was an incident and that James Esposito Jr. is now dead."

Deirdre lets out a wail and slumps to the floor next to Lori's desk.

I speak over her noise. "He's dead because he got away from you guys. How the hell did he escape?"

"We're looking into it. There's been a report of an incident outside the facility where he was staying. Perhaps it was a diversionary tactic."

"Your security must suck if you have to jab prisoners with tracking devices." When he glares at me, I add, "Sir."

His jaw shifts. "I can't reveal details about our correctional facilities' methods. But remember, ever since the vampire agents' work slowdown, we've been understaffed agency-wide."

A convenient excuse. Or the truth. Or both.

Lanham looks down at Deirdre, who's clutching the legs of Lori's chair and whimpering now instead of wailing. "This must be Ms. Falk."

"Jim's most recent progeny," I tell him. "She called us for help because Jim abandoned her and she was starving. While we were there, he showed up. I guess he was looking for sanctuary before the sunrise."

Lanham gives me a sharp look. "You 'guess'? He didn't state his purpose?"

I shut my mouth. Shane can tell him, and he does:

"Sir, I acted immediately, in the belief I was defending my life and those of Agent Griffin and Ms. Falk." Shane swallows, almost imperceptibly. "I struck without warning."

"I see." Colonel Lanham fingers the rim of his black cap. "Which part of your training led you to believe this was the right tactic?"

Shane stands even straighter. "The part where we're taught how to fight those older and stronger than ourselves, sir. We're to use any weapon at our disposal. Including surprise."

Deirdre practically spits. "There's a difference between surprise and cold-blooded murder."

Lanham holds up a hand. "Before anyone says another word, I need to interview the three of you separately, lest one account color the others." Lanham looks at Deirdre and gestures to Franklin's empty office. "Ma'am?"

She lifts a bewildered gaze from the floor to his face.

A tear hangs from each set of eyelashes. Lanham squats in front of her and extends his hand to help her up, like she's a child, and not a vampire who could tear out his throat with one leap.

"Would you join me for a few minutes, please?"

I've never heard his voice so gentle. But his other hand, hidden from her, hovers near the stake holstered at his ankle. I know from experience, Lanham is the world's fastest-drawing bureaucrat.

Deirdre stares up into his eyes. Maybe she trusts him, or maybe she can smell the wood of the stake. But she grasps his hand and lets him lead her to Franklin's office. They shut the door softly.

A car rumbles into the parking lot outside. Lori's, judging by the engine sound.

"I called Lori and told her what happened," David says. "I figured she'd want to know right away, and that you could use her support." He gives me a grim smile, and I want to hug them both.

Less than a minute later Lori jerks open the door at the bottom of the stairs. She must have sprinted from the car.

"Ciara, oh my God, are you okay?"

She tackle-hugs me, once again forgetting how dangerous it can be to do that to a vampire. But I just embrace her, holding my breath so I can't smell her blood, close to her skin from running.

"I'm okay. It's good to see you. It's good to see anyone normal."

Lori examines me, picking over my shirt and hair, as if the trauma has left stains or lint. "Did Jim hurt you?"

"He didn't even touch me, thanks to Shane."

She beams at him. "Our hero! A knight in flannel armor."

"I don't feel much like a hero right now."

Lori puts a hand over her mouth. "I'm so sorry. He was your friend."

Shane looks at his feet. "Not for a long time."

An uncomfortable moment passes. There'll be a lot of these to come, I'm guessing.

Finally Lori says, "David told me that Jeremy saved Jim's progeny. Denise?"

"Deirdre. He didn't even hesitate." I guess there's more than one kind of hero today.

She moves toward her desk and peers at the *Cats of Greece* calendar hanging above it. "Weren't you supposed to bite Jeremy this weekend? Wasn't Sunday the big day?"

I find it funny that she remembers that. Then again, I have been talking about it a lot, out of nervousness and anticipation.

"Shit," Shane says. "Now you can't even drink from him for at least two weeks." He puts his hands to his head. "Worst possible timing."

David and Lori each say a variation of "Huh?"

Shane gives me a gentle but pointed look. "Do you want me to tell them?"

"No, I'll do it." I suddenly need to sit down. On my way to my chair I search for words that will convey the seriousness of my situation without throwing Lori into hysterics.

I speak to the floor. "The same quality about me that let me heal holy-water burns also . . . doesn't want me to be a vampire. So I'm a crappy vampire. It's maybe why I hate to be bitten and why I can't bring myself to bite a human. And why I—why I'm already acting old, with the obsessive-compulsive business. I'm fading."

The room is silent except for the murmur of Colonel Lanham and Deirdre's conversation behind Franklin's door.

I finally look up at Lori, expecting to see tears running down her face, or at least filling her blue eyes. I expect whimpering.

Instead she gives Shane a sharp look. "Unacceptable. What can I do to help her?"

His smile is warm and wry. "Keep her up-to-date on all the latest everything. TV shows, music, fashions. Take her to every new movie. Teach her all the—" He gestures to my phone sitting on my desk. "—the technology things."

"Got it. What else?"

"Be understanding."

"Got it. What are you doing?"

"Racking my brain to find her a new donor. You're pregnant and now Jeremy's out of commission for two weeks. I've gotta find someone for her to drink—and preferably bite—as soon as possible. She needs the best nutrition she can get."

Lori's lower lip trembles. Great, now she feels guilty for not being my donor anymore.

"Just a second." She turns on her heel and drags David into his office. Before shutting the door, she reaches out to the volume control and cranks up the music in the upstairs speakers.

"Ow." I rub my ear as his office door slams shut. "It had to be Regina's show, didn't it?" Bad Religion grinds their chords from the ceiling into my brain.

"Hang on." Shane walks stealthily toward David's office. He presses his ear to the door. It swings open.

"Geez, a little privacy?" Lori snaps at him, then strides over to me. "Ciara, we've agreed. You can bite David if Shane supervises."

My mouth falls open. "Bite . . . David?" I can't even look at him. The first time I saw him after I turned, we practically jumped into each other's arms. The attraction wore off once I got into a regular feeding schedule and David got used to me being, well, magnetic. But we have a history.

The love of his life—before Lori—was a woman named Elizabeth who broke his heart and their engagement when she became a vampire, but fed on him (and only him) until she died permanently. At which point he got me and her mixed up inside his heart, because we looked sort of alike and he was lonely. At the time, I was insecure about my future with Shane, so we almost—

"I can't do that," I tell them.

"Ciara," David says. "It'll be all right, I promise."

"The important thing is to make sure you're okay," Lori adds.

Shane's face displays a hundred and two emotions.

"What do you think?" I ask him.

He comes and sits on the edge of my desk, taking my hand. "I think we should do whatever it takes to keep you well."

I look at Lori. "Do you want to be there when I—"

"No." She takes a step back. "I love you guys. I trust you guys. But I do not want to see it."

I lower my head, feeling relieved and grateful but also very sad. I can't believe it's come to this.

10

Kashmir

Obsessive-compulsive disorder has at least a hundred different manifestations in both humans and vampires. Shane sorts. Regina counts. Spencer cleans. Noah watches where and how he walks, aligning his feet with the pattern of the carpet or grains of hardwood. Monroe and I share an obsession with words, rearranging the letters on signs or parsing definitions (he's learned to do it all in his head, while I often blurt out a grammatical correction in a rude and embarrassing way).

Jim? He was a hoarder.

I always knew this in the abstract, because he was such a trivia buff. But apparently he collected more than facts. On my only other visit to his room, I was too busy trying to escape to notice how much stuff he had. Besides, he kept most of it below.

Regina, Spencer, Noah, and I gather around the four-by-eight-foot trapdoor in Jim's floor. It lies open, revealing part of a tomblike cavity.

"How far does it go?" I ask Spencer.

"Bigger than this room. Pity is it's not nearly so tall."

"Can't we just leave all that shit there?" Regina's hands are twitching, and I can tell she's dying to jump down and count the boxes and their contents. "Nail the door shut and put the rug back over? Pretend it doesn't exist?"

"Adrian should have a clean place to live," Noah says. "Free of Jim's bad energy."

The skeptic in me hates to admit it, but there's some seriously unhealthy vibes in this room. Then again, I almost died here, so I could be biased.

Spencer holds out a box of latex gloves in one hand and a box of garbage bags in another. "Let's get started."

One by one we drop into the crap-oleum (like a mausoleum for crap, is where I'm coming from, linguistically). I put on the gloves—not because I can get an infection or even a cut that'll last more than a few seconds, but because something down here might be icky. Like I told Lori, I'm a terrible vampire.

"Ciara, do you need this to see?" Noah holds up a fluorescent lantern, the kind used for camping.

I peer around at the darkness and marvel as the shapes and shadows come into sharp focus. "No, my eyes are adjusting. But thanks." Next to Shane, Noah's by far the most considerate vampire DJ. He's too polite to say it out loud, but he seems to sense my uneven development. One day soon (or one hour soon) I need to tell them all that I'm fading fast.

The closest box has a distinct metallic smell, like stale blood. Ugh, did he keep leftovers down here?

No one else is touching it, so, not wanting to be a wimp, I pull up the flaps to see stacks of dark-blue cardboard folders marked "Lincoln Cents" in faint gold letters. I open the top one.

Turns out that coppery smell actually was copper, not blood. Jim collected pennies.

"Wow." I run my finger over the rows of coins, some shiny and gleaming, some as dull as wood. The scent is making my fangs want to pop.

I pull out an older folder, from 1941 to 1974. Most of these are dark with age, Abe Lincoln's face barely distinguishable. But a single penny winks at me in flawless silver. "How come this one from 1943 is different?"

Without sound, Spencer appears at my shoulder in an instant. I'm used to that by now.

"During the war, they needed copper for shell casings, so the pennies were all made out of steel that year." He brushes his thumb near the coin, wiping away invisible dirt. "Jim's daddy bought that for him on his eighth birthday in 1951. That's why it's in mint condition. All the rest he collected himself."

So he was a collector even as a human. My heart twists at the thought of an eight-year-old Jim, maybe wearing a birthday hat, unwrapping this silver penny. Beaming at this relic from the year of his birth, when evil came in obvious forms, like Nazis and kamikazes.

My American History professor told us that countries keep the basic personality of the time in which they were born. The United States, formed during the Enlightenment, has held fast to that era's focus on individual freedom. Despite the efforts of religious zealots and reactionaries, it still puts reason above blind obedience to authorities like churches and kings and even presidents.

It's the same with vampires. Though we all have individual personalities and characters, we're still the children of our times. Jim was made in 1970, a period of great anger, when the sparkling hopes of the sixties were beginning to wither and transform into cynicism and rage. Dr. King and RFK were dead and, for a while, so were their dreams.

A heavy wooden thunk comes from behind me. "Bo-nus!" Regina shouts.

Spencer goes to her, peeling off his gloves and taking a new pair from the box (for the third time). "What all'd you find?"

"Jim's progeny trunk. Look at these files."

Noah and I join her and Spencer at the trunk, made of heavy mahogany and lined with orange velvet. Clearly purchased in the seventies.

"He had twenty-four progeny," I tell them.

"Thanks for the info, Encyclopedia Brown," Regina mutters. "Don't you think we know that?"

It kills me not to know who Encyclopedia Brown is. I'd look it up on my phone's Web browser, but no way I'd get cell reception this far underground.

"Looks like it's in reverse chronological order." Regina hands me a thick accordion folder. "There's your friend Deirdre, Jim's latest and lamest."

I run my thumb along the green card-stock covering. It'd be helpful to know more about Deirdre to see if we can trust her, but it feels like a violation of privacy. "I'll give it to Shane. He probably already knows most of it, since she was his donor."

"Whatever." Regina pulls out progressively thicker file folders from the piles in the trunk and lays them on the floor, where Spencer straightens their contents without reading them.

I open the next box, which is nearly overflowing with

trinkets and pieces of paper, each tagged with a name and date.

I pull out a ticket stub from the Winterland Arena in San Francisco on June 17, 1975. "Wow, Grateful Dead during their heyday." A tag attached to it says, "With Carl and Bonnie."

"Oooh, look at this one." Regina grabs another ticket stub. "The Place des Nations in Montreal. I used to love that venue." It's rare to hear Regina speak fondly of her native country. "But—gag—Jefferson Starship. One incarnation away from 'We Built This City,' possibly the worst song ever."

I lift the tag attached to it and read Jim's chicken-scratch handwriting. "He went to the show with some-one named . . . Gary?"

"Oh God!" She yanks her hands away like the ticket is coated with holy water, leaving me holding it by the tag. "Cashmere."

Spencer and Noah gasp in unison and take a step back from me and the ticket.

"Cashmere? Like—" I rub my thumb and forefinger over the sleeve of my sweater, even though it's one hundred percent cotton.

"With a *K*!" Regina hisses.

"Oh, Kashmir." I emphasize the second syllable, wondering what a Jefferson Starship show has to do with the contentious Himalayan region between India and Pakistan.

Regina creeps closer to me. "Kashmir is the name Gary took after Jim turned him."

I roll "The Vampire Gary" over my mental tongue. "I can see why he changed it. But why Kashmir?"

Noah explains. "After the song by Led Zeppelin."

Oh, right. I keep forgetting that's the title. I think of it as the "dan-nan-nan, DAN-nan-nan" song with the "ooooh, yeah, yeahs" at the end.

"That song used to make me laugh." Regina twists the ends of her spiked black hair. "It reminded me of *Fast Times at Ridgemont High*. But then I met Kashmir." Even in the nearly nonexistent light down here, I can see her pale. "He was batshit."

"Crazier than Jim?"

"Yes," Noah says. "He was far gone when we met him"—he looks at Regina—"ten years ago?"

"Eleven years, two months." She sends me a glare of warning. "Kashmir is Jim to the Jimth degree."

I swallow a whimper at the thought. A sped-up slide show flips through my mind of Jim at his worst, and the way his eyes would simultaneously light up with joy and go dead with treachery.

I turn back to the box of memorabilia. "It'd be cool if some vampires could be neutered like dogs so they can't make new ones." The others stare at me. "That would be wrong, of course," I add.

"That would be fascist," Regina says. "But I agree about Jim. His own makers wouldn't let him create a new vampire. They knew there was something wrong with him. Jim didn't make Kashmir until after he left his makers' coven in England and came back to America."

"When was that?"

"Seventy-five—same year as the Zeppelin song." She riffles through the box of memorabilia. "This whole half of the box is Kashmir stuff."

Noah takes another step back and crosses his arms. "We should burn it."

"No!" I grab the box flap, as if that will protect it. "We should learn everything we can about these vampires in case they ever turn up."

Regina paces, thumbing the silver hoop in her lip. "Blondie's right, Noah. We need to go through it all, bad mojo or not."

He turns away, arms still crossed. "Then send me a memo with pertinent details. Leave out the murder sprees." He crosses the dark cellar floor, ducking to avoid a spiderweb.

I turn back to Regina. "Murder sprees?"

"Jim and Kashmir made a lot of vampires together. First here, then eventually he went back to England to make more vampires, rub it in his makers' faces that he had his own coven. As you can imagine, some of his progeny weren't very stable."

"Did the Control ever go after them?"

"They investigated but couldn't prove anything. As crazy as Jim was, he was always careful. He'd take his progeny out into the forest around Yosemite. They'd attack hikers and make it look like a mountain lion attack. Or just make the bodies disappear. If someone's buried long enough, it's hard to tell exactly how they died."

"What about forensics labs?"

"This was the seventies. The era of *Barney Miller,* not *CSI.*"

"You know about *CSI?*"

"We have to read commercials for it during our shows." She narrows her eyes at me. "Despite what the Control claims, we *are* capable of learning new things. We just choose not to change the way we live. You'll understand when you're older." She shrugs and turns back to the rows of containers. "Okay, people! Four down, thirty-three boxes to go."

Spencer looks at his watch. "I'm on the air in a half hour, and we're gonna need reinforcements for this little project here. I'll go call Shane and Jeremy."

I kneel next to Kashmir's box and sift through the memorabilia until I find a photo of him and Jim, taken at a dark place punctuated by neon lights.

They have the same sable hair, but Kashmir's is straight where Jim's is curly. Almost a foot taller than his maker, Kashmir's body is long and lean as a cheetah's. His clothes accentuate his height, a blue silk shirt open to the navel, tucked into white bell-bottoms that flare over boots that match the shirt.

In the picture, he's wearing wide, magenta-colored sunglasses, slid down his nose to show his amber eyes. The light reflects in them slightly off center, making his pupils look shifty, like he's peering past the camera and into the brain of the observer. Or maybe that's just me.

His stance is half a step ahead of Jim's, but his arm reaches back to his maker's shoulder, maintaining the connection even as he poses.

Jim's not posed at all. He just looks happy.

Over my shoulder I watch Regina and Noah work together, coordinating the dispersal of the boxes' contents. Despite their differences, they're in sync with each other, from years of working together—and months of sleeping together. He's got fewer years on her than Shane has on me, so they could grow old together, too, assuming Regina doesn't screw things up.

The radio station keeps our vampires in touch with both their "Life Times"—as the Control calls our original eras—and with current events (by reading news reports on the air), so it could be decades before Noah and Regina fade. I wonder if they know how lucky they are.

I sigh and turn back to the box of Kashmir. It's full of crime and destruction and decadence, but also music and friendship and love. It's full of life.

You'll understand when you're older, Regina told me, not realizing I already am.

11

Secondhand News

On Saturday night, Shane and I join the other DJs for a poker game, and I try to figure out how to tell them all I'm dying.

How will they react? With pity? Scorn? Fear? I was the one who campaigned hardest for Jim to be put away when he started fading. Will they want me to put *myself* away to protect the station? Would they be right? How long before I jeopardize the secrecy that keeps us safe?

Spencer insists on total silence during play, so we can speak only between hands. I use that as an excuse not to drop my bombshell.

At midnight Shane leaves the table to start his show, planting a soft kiss on my cheek and murmuring, "Call me if you need me."

In a few minutes Regina enters from the studio just as the door to the outside passageway opens. Adrian staggers through, sets two suitcases on the floor, then leans on the doorjamb.

"Hey," he says with a weak smile.

"What the hell's your problem?" Regina asks, taking Shane's vacated seat at the table.

Spencer slides back his chair. "What she means is you look like forty miles of bad road. What happened to you? Need blood?"

"There's plenty in the fridge." I set down my cards. "I'll get it for you."

"No, I'll get it. Right now, I just need to rest." Adrian slouches over to the sofa and lets himself sink into the cushions with a whump.

The lamp next to Adrian shows his face alarmingly pale, his eye sockets hollow. Even his hair looks dull and limp. Nothing like the bright flower child I saw two nights ago.

"I'm getting you blood," I tell him, "so just stay there."

When I return, warm cup in hand, the other DJs have resumed the poker hand without me.

I sit beside Adrian and nudge him with the cup. "Wakey-wakey, eggs and bakey. Okay, just blood, actually."

"Huh? Oh, you didn't have to do that." He takes my offering and uncaps the straw.

"You might not've survived the trip down the hall."

Adrian gives me a mere shadow of his heartwarming smile. "I've survived worse." But as he sips, his eyes go distant, like he just heard his own lie.

"So what happened? Franklin turn you down for a date?"

He blinks a few times, hard and fast, golden eyelashes fluttering like hummingbird wings, and just like that, life has returned to his face. "No! He said yes. We're seeing *Hair* Friday night. And it won't even be our first date."

"Considering how Franklin feels about *Hair*—both the musical and the subject—that's probably best. So what's your first date? Don't tell me *Jesus Christ Superstar*."

"No," he says, chuckling. "It was tonight, sort of. He helped me get through a tough time, the thing that caused my current state of being."

The only time that was tough enough to make me look like that, I'd taken a tree branch through my stomach. "Did you get hurt?"

Adrian shakes his head. "It's personal—too personal even to tell you or Franklin. That's what's cool about him. He didn't even ask what had happened."

"That's because he doesn't care."

"Exactly. No matter what I've done or what I've become, he accepts me."

"No, I mean he really doesn't care. About anyone." My lips twitch at one corner so Adrian knows I'm kidding. Mostly.

"Franklin cares about you, Ciara."

I stretch and sigh. "Well, I am very important."

"The cards are being dealt," Regina says in a sledgehammer voice.

Without a word, I go over and pick up Adrian's suitcases. They're surprisingly light. He follows me into the hallway and past the studio, where Shane gives us a quick wave through the window.

In the DJs' apartment, Monroe is sitting on the couch, tuning his guitar.

"Hello there," he says, standing to greet Adrian with a bright smile. "Welcome to our homestead. Be sure and let me know if you need anything. Anything a'tall."

Wow, that was one of the longest speeches I've ever heard from my maker.

"Thank you." Adrian shakes Monroe's hand, then looks embarrassed at the sight of me carrying his stuff.

"Adrian's not feeling well, so I'm his butler. For one night only, and no, that offer doesn't apply to other vampires."

Monroe bestows a rare smile on me as well. Wow again. Adrian has a funny, sunny effect on people who aren't Regina.

I stop outside Adrian's new room. "This is your place. Jim had his own special decor, which you're welcome to change if you want. We moved his stuff out yesterday."

He jerks his head to look at me. "What stuff?"

"Old records of donors and progeny, receipts from concerts. Don't worry, we're keeping all the historical pieces in off-site storage." Until we can sell them on eBay to finance next year's holiday party. Or maybe that's just *my* plan.

"What about his personal records? You said donors and progeny."

"We have that, too, but we won't give it away to anyone." Except the Control, if necessary.

"As long as you didn't throw it out. Jim is a legend among vampires *and* DJs."

"So you've told me." I give him a set of keys on a peace symbol chain. "The small one is for this door, and the other one is for the outside back entrance. As you already know, the upstairs front door unlocks from the inside, for vampire safety. Only the humans have keys."

"Why?"

"Because vampires can be absentminded. David worries we'll accidentally open the front door and burst into flames or set a fellow vamp on fire."

"But you have a key and you're not human."

"I was when I started working here. David doesn't have the heart to ask for my key."

"Good. It's not like you have to worry about fading anytime soon." Adrian opens his door with the small key. "Holy moly."

As he steps in, I hit the light switch inside. The lava lamp and the wave machine turn on, casting lurid glows over the layered Oriental rugs and the velvet curtains draped over the sprawling bed. The drapes seem to wave in the flowing light.

"It's . . . it's . . ." Adrian searches for the word.

"It's something." I set down his suitcases and stand at the threshold, with no desire to enter again.

He sits on the edge of the bed and caresses the lush coverlet. "This place is . . . not me in the least."

I sigh with relief. Maybe if Adrian changes the decor, I'll feel more at home here. Or less at home, whichever is better.

"You can get different sheets from our laundry room. For everything else, Sherwood has a million antique stores. There's even an antique mall. Which is a mall with antiques, not a really old mall. Although there is also a really old mall." Huh, I never thought about that before.

"Thanks, Ciara. Wherever Jim is, I hope he doesn't find out I changed his room."

Behind me, Monroe's guitar goes silent. I guess I'm the one to break the news to Adrian about his idol.

"He won't find out. He's dead now."

Adrian's shoulders slump. "I figured it was a matter of time, stuck in that Control hellhole. When did it happen?"

"Two nights ago."

"Did he attack one of his guards?"

"No, he—" I wipe both hands down my face, realizing I can't avoid what happened, not even with one person. "He escaped from the nursing home and showed up at Deirdre's house. She's one of his progeny who lives here in town. Anyway, the last time we saw Jim, before he went into Control custody, was when he was attacking me." I step forward. "Right in this room, as a matter of fact."

Adrian's mouth has slowly opened during my speech, but on the word "attacking" it dropped all the way slack.

"Attacked you how?"

"He almost ripped my throat out." I look away from Adrian's shell-shocked face. Among vampires, biting without permission is tantamount to rape. "When he showed up at Deirdre's, Shane killed him. To protect all of us, but especially me."

Adrian slowly shakes his head. "I can't believe this."

"Believe it." Monroe enters, his footsteps silent on the layers of rugs. "I was the one staked him right here. And I'd do it all again, 'cept this time I'd pull 'em right back out again. Let him die with some dignity, 'steada wasting away in one of them Control places."

"I stopped you. Long story," I tell Adrian, deciding to spare him the account of Jim almost draining my teenage cousin dry. "Can we get you anything else? The kitchen's pretty basic. Instructions for the microwave are taped on the front, in occasionally insulting language, depending on who made the latest sign."

"No," Adrian whispers, looking as pale and drained as when he entered the station lounge tonight. "I just need some time alone with my thoughts."

On our way out, as I shut the door softly behind me, I share a glance with Monroe, wondering if he's thinking the same thing I am:

Alone with our thoughts is the most dangerous place a vampire can be.

12

Question

Sunday night. Bite night.

Waiting for David, I pace through my living room, but productively, to hide my nervousness, as if Shane wouldn't guess.

Now seems as good a time as any to work on Dexter's "Heel!" command. With his strength and predatory drive, it takes more than muscle to keep this monster in line. It takes discipline, praise, and blood-soaked liver treats.

Unlike human vampires, Dexter still enjoys eating solid food, if it has a trace of dog blood on it. Dogs have blood banks just like humans, and just like humans' blood, their blood expires, or turns out not to be usable for transfusions. Which is fortunate, because the neighborhood schnauzers and poodles aren't exactly lining up to be chomped by our undead Great Dane–black Labrador retriever mix.

Drinking a beer near the stove, Shane watches Dexter and me circle from the living room to the kitchen and back.

"He's doing great now," Shane says. "He listens to you."

"When I have food." I turn abruptly to the left, cutting off Dexter's path. He nimbly keeps pace, not missing a beat. "Good boy."

"You ever wonder if the Control could make him mortal again?"

"He's undead like us. That's a one-way street, right?"

"But he's not naturally supernatural. He was vamped in a lab. So maybe the lab could un-vamp him."

I come to a halt next to a framed painting of a field aglow with fireflies, one of our few pieces of art. "I've never thought about it."

"Even when you were human, you never wished you could take him for a walk in the sunshine? Let him play with his own kind? Let him just be a dog?"

"If we let him be a dog, he'll die." I hold up the fingers of my left hand to signal Dexter to sit. He obeys. "The ones his size are old when they're six. Besides, Dexter is who he is—not only in how he was born but how he was made." I lower my hand and my boy lies down, still looking up expectantly.

It's not part of the training session, but I sit and wrap my arms around his thick neck. He thwacks his tail against the floor, hard as a puppy, and rubs the side of his head against my hair, petting me without hands.

Shane comes over. "I guess it's the same trade-off we all make. A longer life, but one lived in darkness and isolation."

"Dexter's not isolated. He has us. He has Lori and David and all the DJs. As long as dogs are part of a pack, they're happy." I look at Shane over Dexter's broad black shoulders. "Trust me, I know this stuff."

I'm no Dog Whisperer, but I used to volunteer with animal rescue. I'd socialize and train dogs at the shelter so they'd be more adoptable. Unfortunately, once I had a dog of my own, not to mention a full-time job and part-time college, I couldn't fit in volunteer work. The vampires were a big enough charity case.

Shane sits beside me and scratches behind Dexter's ears in the way that only he knows how to do. Dexter's eyes roll up and he starts to kick his back leg, in the throes of doggie ecstasy.

I ponder Shane's words about us living in darkness and isolation. "Would you be human again if you could?"

"I try not to think about it, especially now that you've turned, too. I don't want to dwell on all the things that've been stolen from you. Sunlight. Food. Freedom."

"What food do you miss most? For me it's mac 'n' cheese. Or doughnuts, I can't decide." Surprisingly, we've never had this conversation. Maybe it's Dexter's presence between us, or maybe it's the fact that David will be here in a few minutes, so we can't talk too long or get too maudlin.

Shane thinks for several moments, sipping his beer (which thankfully, being a liquid, still tastes like beer to us). I envision his mind sorting all the possibilities alphabetically, then letting go of that list to rearrange them in order of preference. Whereas I'm fine with two top choices, being inherently dichotomous, he probably wants to declare one single food the victor, as if by setting his target more precisely, it becomes more attainable.

"Pancakes."

"That's a good one." Unfortunately, I know from experience that even though pancake batter is technically liquid, it tastes like milk of magnesia. Coffee and beer only have taste because of the caffeine and alcohol used to make them.

"When I was a kid, Mom made pancakes every Sunday after Mass. Originally she made them before Mass, but then we kept falling asleep in church. She learned to use pancakes as a bribe to get us to behave there."

"Brilliant tactic."

"Then I got diabetes, so I couldn't always have them. Mom would make me eggs instead. And I could never have syrup."

"That sucks."

He nods. "So definitely pancakes."

"With syrup."

"With syrup."

The doorbell rings. Shane goes still for an instant, then looks at me. For a moment his eyes are tinged with sadness and anxiety. Then he smiles and says, "Speaking of breakfast . . ."

Dexter beats us to the door, forgetting the training session in his excitement. He knows how his favorite people knock, I guess, so he barks only at strangers, who tend to leave quickly upon hearing that sound. Jehovah's Witnesses are not a problem.

We open the door for David, who smells freshly showered. Unscented soap, of course, like all FOVs (Friends of Vampires).

"Hey." He lifts a six-pack of our favorite microbrew. "Is it weird that I brought beer?"

"It'd be weird if you didn't." Shane steps aside and lets him enter, giving him a warm shoulder pat.

"Good. It's been a long time, so I'm a little rusty on protocol."

David has always been the donor-of-last-resort for the DJs, opening a vein in an emergency, if a regular donor moved away or was sick.

"Thanks for coming," I say, as if he's here to sell us an insurance policy. "You want a drink?"

"Yeah." He grabs one of the beers and offers the six-pack to Shane, his hand shaking a little. I don't know whether to be relieved or concerned that he might be as nervous as we are. At least one of us should be sanguine about this. (Heh, sanguine.)

"We have some energy drink, too," I tell him. "Hydrate you."

"Wonderful. I'll double-fist."

I try to chuckle, even though what David said wasn't really funny. I'm starting to wish I'd insisted on a perfect stranger for my first bite, or one of Shane's donors. Someone laid-back like Rick, the bassist in Shane's nineties cover band, Vital Fluid. He'd probably jump at the chance.

But David's here now, when I need him.

"I heard the Control scheduled your tribunal for Friday night," he says to Shane. "That was fast."

"Might as well get it over with. If I have to be punished for staking Jim, I don't care." Shane looks at me. "It was worth it to know she's safe."

"Safe from having my head ripped off," I say with a nervous chuckle, "but not safe from fading."

"Right." David takes off his jacket. "Speaking of which, where do you want to do this?"

Shane gestures to the couch. "We could try here, but the living room's pretty dark. The guest bedroom has a good lamp on the headboard, so she can see what she's doing."

David shifts his jaw. "Actually, I meant, where, uh, on my body, did you want to do this?"

I am now official proof that vampires can blush.

"Oh." Shane rubs his nose self-consciously. "Arm? Easy to see the veins, and that way you can sit up if you want."

Right. Biting a human above the heart can give them an air embolism that could kill them instantly. Good way to ruin a meal.

Oops, I just made myself laugh, inappropriately. I turn it into a cough, which isn't believable, since vampires don't cough except to cover up inappropriate laughter.

"I'll go scrub up in the bathroom and meet you there." David takes a large swallow of beer, which I hope will help him stop fidgeting.

When he disappears, I look at everything in the living room except Shane.

"You sure you're okay with this?" he asks me.

"Are you? This is even weirder than I thought it'd be."

"It's for a good cause. The only cause I care about." He comes over and runs a soothing hand down my arm. "I know you've drunk from humans before, but there's nothing like biting. It'll give you strength like you wouldn't believe."

"That's like saying a protein shake gives you better nutrition by drinking it through a straw."

"Blood isn't a protein shake, and you know it." He grasps my shoulders gently. "I'm sorry. I've been trying to shield you all these months, make it seem like being a vampire isn't a big deal, that it's just like being human with a different diet and schedule, but it's not. It's magic." Shane runs his thumb over my lips. "And part of that magic is sinking your fangs into someone's skin, making life flow out of them and into you."

I think of my cousins. "The vampires who live with Travellers don't bite people. They're healthy enough."

"But they're tame. They wouldn't win a fight with a normal vampire."

"I'm not fighting vampires."

"No, you're fighting something much bigger. You're fighting time, and for that you need all the strength in the world." Shane leans over and kisses my cheek, right in front of my ear. "Let me give you that strength."

I slide my arms around his back. I want to stay in this life, just like we are, as long as I can.

Even if it means believing in magic.

13

Lust for Life

When we enter the guest room, David is waiting for us, propped with pillows against the headboard, wearing a black sleeveless undershirt. A stack of dark brown towels sits where the second pillow would be. The bedspread and carpet are also dark brown—not to make the room look masculine, though it does have that effect. It's to hide the bloodstains.

A spare, haunting tune comes from the MP3 docking station on the nightstand. "Found this new English band, The xx," David says. "Hope it's okay, Shane. I thought something minimalist would be soothing."

"It's fine." Shane sweeps off his own T-shirt, mussing his hair. He always does it before biting, to keep the blood off his clothes. As usual, my pulse speeds up at the sight of his bare chest. A weird thought flits through my brain: I'd like to see Shane and David with their shirts off, together. Maybe that's not such a weird thought.

I look down at my cami, wondering whether to keep it on. The low cut of the neckline means it'll stay clean, and if not, that's what a sink full of cold water is for.

"That shirt'll be fine," Shane says as he climbs onto the bed to David's right side. "Come here." He angles the reading light on the headboard toward David, who shades his eyes against the glare.

As I approach the bed, I can hear David's heartbeat. I crawl to kneel on his left side, wishing I could do this without thinking of the pain I'm causing.

"He's right-handed," Shane says, "so we'll use the left arm."

I nod politely and try not to lick my lips. Despite my hunger, my fangs aren't popping. In fact, it feels like they're shriveling back up into my skull.

Shane sits behind me and extends David's arm over a folded towel, flat at his side, so that his forearm is below his heart. Then he guides me to scoot down to put my face inches from the limb.

Shane's finger traces the vein that arcs over the edge of David's forearm, front to back. "This is the radial vein. It can be bitten in a lot of places, but his least painful spot is halfway down, where it crosses from the front to the back of the arm. Now, without biting—I repeat, without biting—run your tongue along the length of it so you can feel the heat. You won't always be biting under a bright light."

I do as he says, sliding my tongue along the vein. Shane's right: I can feel the heat in the vessel even through the skin.

"Got it?" he asks. I lift my head and nod at him, not looking at David. "You sure?" I nod again. "You ready?" I shake my head. "Why not?"

I open my mouth and point inside. "Nothing but blunt instruments in there. Performance anxiety?"

"Maybe if we—" David looks from me to Shane. "Can you give us a couple minutes?"

Shane goes very still, then seems to measure the distance between me and David. "Okay," he says, barely parting his lips. He slides off the bed. "Call me when you're ready, and don't start without me."

When he's gone, I can't take my eyes off the door, and I find myself wanting to run after him.

Instead I shift over to sit next to David. The headboard wobbles as I lean back against it. "So."

"So . . . I can't say I ever foresaw this event."

"Why would you? You're not clairvoyant. Not that I believe in clairvoyants."

"I know. I'm just making awkward conversation."

"Oh, good. I was afraid we would skip that. It's not like with you and Shane, when you could talk about football or music to ease the tension."

"You like football and music."

"Yeah, but when I'm crazy nervous like this, I can't think of any teams or bands but the Dallas Cowboys and Mötley Crüe."

"Hm. There must be a supermodel who's slept with both."

I laugh, much too donkeylike. "Yeah. Am I your first first?"

"First first what?"

"Were you ever someone else's first bite?"

"No, other than Elizabeth." It's the first time he's mentioned her since I've been a vampire. His voice doesn't catch on her name like it did years ago, and there's no change in his pulse or body temperature. Lori has turned his life around.

I hold up a hand to swear. "I promise I'll be gentler than Elizabeth was her first time."

"You better be, or Shane'll have to stake you."

"You think he'd choose you over me?"

"It's his responsibility as an Enforcement agent. Besides, I sign his paychecks."

"Duty and money versus love and sex. He won't have to think about it very hard."

"Hopefully it'll be a moot point."

"Especially if my fangs don't pop." I fumble in my mouth, feeling my gums for any sign. "Itsch like dey ran aray up in by head."

"Here. Try this." He takes my hand in his own warm, warm, holy-crap-so-warm one, then places it on his chest. "Feel that?"

I close my eyes and let my fingers curl, relaxed, their tips resting on his shirt. His heartbeat pounds straight through my palm, leaving a hot glow in the middle. "Uh-huh."

"That's for you tonight."

My elbow twitches in reflex to pull away, but he doesn't loosen his grip.

"Not metaphorically," he adds. "I'm not giving you my heart like in a song. That heart belongs to Lori. I mean, it beats for you literally. To save your body and hopefully your mind as well."

Tears sting my eyes before they squeeze out through my lashes. David reaches up with his other hand to wipe one away.

"I don't deserve you guys," I whisper.

"Bullshit." He pulls me close, resting my head against his shoulder, my nose to his neck. "Just listen to the music. Breathe me in. It always seemed to help Shane."

The first breath comes as a shallow sob, but I press my lips together and focus on inhaling only through my nose. His scent fills my head, clean and crisp like a forest after a hard rain, with a hint of citrus underneath. I let it bathe my brain.

I close my eyes and lose myself in this tiny universe. Another hypnotic song starts, one I've heard on the indie rock station. The man's flat, smoky voice curls around my brain, and the female harmony adds a comforting sweetness.

Oddly, lying here in David's arms, I feel closer to Shane than ever. Like I'm holding his place. Like I'm him. It makes me feel like a vampire, since that's all I've ever known him as. My fiancé has always had fangs, walked in the moonlight, and drunk the life force of humans to survive and thrive.

And now, so do I.

I lift my hand from David's chest and move it to his face, cupping his chin, then the edge of his jaw, imagining his skin flushing red from my superheated touch. My fingers trace the fine hairs of his eyebrows, then travel down his nose.

David tilts his chin to bring his open mouth to my palm. I gasp at the heat of his breath on my skin. He's so warm on the inside. I want to get there. Now.

Just like that, the fangs are out. I call Shane's name.

He finds us like this, my head on David's shoulder. I'm afraid to stop breathing the warm human scent for even a moment, in case I lose my nerve (and fangs).

"Ready?"

I sit up slowly. "Let's do this."

Shane situates me where I need to be, and quickly my tongue locates David's vein beneath his skin. My fangs ache.

"Remember," Shane says, "a human's skin is thinner than mine, so don't chomp on him the way you do me." He pulls my hair from my face, back over my shoulder. "Whenever you're ready, slide your fangs into the vein, slow and smooth, and when the blood comes, pull out, again slow and smooth."

I find the spot, close my eyes, and bite. My fangs break through. My mouth fills with liquid heat, like that of a jelly doughnut fresh from the oven.

David's breath doesn't catch—he must have made sure it wouldn't, must've known any change would startle me. He could be screaming for all I know or care. My ears and mind are full of sound, ocean waves and erupting volcanoes.

Shane was right: there is something different here, a vibration in my fangs that goes out to all corners of my body and back. This blood will be different.

"Pull out, Ciara," Shane whispers. "Nice and slow. Perfect." He strokes my hair. "You're perfect."

When my fangs withdraw, David draws in a long breath and lets out a contented sigh. I guess I did okay.

"Drink like you would from a water fountain," Shane says. "Don't suck."

I resist the urge to flash him an annoyed glance. I've been told that only a hundred and forty times.

As the blood flows into me, I let out a moan of surprise. It *is* different. More potent. My muscles are singing, urging me to run, leap, chase, pounce.

Bite. Bite again.

I tense all over. Shane pulls me away from David's skin, slowly. "You feel that?"

I meet his eyes and swallow. "Scary."

"Scary like a roller coaster? Not like an axe murderer."

"I've never been chased by an axe murderer, but—"

"No. I mean, do you feel like you are one."

I meet David's eyes. They hold no fear. My muscles relax a fraction, and my fangs retract.

Shane lets go of me. "Keep going. Carefully."

I lie between the two men and drink the slow, steady flow from David's arm. Shane strokes my back and murmurs quiet encouragement. When I take a break, he leans forward for his own quick taste. David stares at the ceiling with the donor's usual blissed-out expression—eyes soft, mouth half open, tongue stroking the back of his lower front teeth, side to side. I wonder why they all do that.

After fifteen glorious minutes, I lie back in Shane's arms. With my bloodlust sated, the other sort of lust pounds at my skin, wanting my clothes to melt off, replaced by hands against me.

Time for our guest to leave.

Shane looks into my eyes, which are probably dilated with desire. "David, let me get you cleaned up." He vaults over us onto the floor and, in one step, crosses to the desk where a roll of bandages and a box of wipes sit next to the remnants of David's energy drink.

I close my eyes and revel in this unbelievable buzz coursing through me. I don't dare move for fear of having a monumental orgasm on the spot.

"Ciara, I'll see you at the office." David's hand comes

close to my arm. The warmth of his skin radiates against mine, and he jerks back without touching me.

"Thanks. Really. Thanks." I can barely control my breath. "Sorry I'm not walking you out."

"I'll do it." Shane's voice is low and husky. "And then I'll be back."

The moment the door closes, I'm on my feet, peeling off my jeans. They're like a skin too tight, and they stand between me and the thing I want most.

I kick them off, along with my underwear. They fly onto the desk, where they hit—

David's energy drink.

A quick knock, then a creak of hinges. David says, "Ciara, I think I left my—"

With a yelp, I toss the bottle at the door and dive behind the desk. Luckily, the bottle is plastic, so it doesn't shatter when it hits him in the face.

"Ow!"

"Sorry. Thanks."

"You're welcome," he says. It sounds like he's holding his nose.

This time when he retreats, I slip under the covers before taking off my camisole and bra. The pillows and bedspread still smell like David. Not sure if that's a good or a bad thing.

Shane opens the door a crack. "Are you gonna throw something at me, too?"

"Just myself."

He swings the door wide. "Under the covers? Are we on a soap opera?"

"Huh?"

"On soap operas, they always show people in bed

with the sheets pulled up to their armpits like that. At least, they used to." He undoes his belt and his jeans, slowly enough to drive me mad.

"They can't show people naked on network television."

"When I was growing up, my mom used to watch soaps—she called them 'her stories'—and for years I thought people only had sex *in* bed, not *on* the bed. It didn't occur to me how sheets could get tangled in legs." He sweeps the covers off me, like a magician pulling aside a curtain to reveal a marvel within. "That's better."

I flex my toes, then curl them as his jeans fall to the floor. "Soaps are misleading in a lot of ways. People are always coming back from the dead. Oh, wait, never mind."

Shane hooks his thumbs into the waistband of his boxer shorts, tugs them down to the rise of his hip bones, then stops. "How do you feel?"

I spread my legs, reaching one foot to nudge his thigh. "You tell me."

He lets out a gasp, then runs his fingers along the arch of my foot, making me squirm. "You're so warm."

"Hot, even." I slide my foot out of his hand and up under the leg of his boxers. He groans at the touch of my toes, then closes his eyes for one long, savoring moment.

In the next, he's naked in my arms, kissing me hard. He tastes like David, tastes like I do. I know he needs to repossess me, cover the smell of another man, even a donor, on my body and in my mouth. I'll gladly let him.

He slips a hand down my side, caressing and clutching, then between my thighs. I press it close, already on the edge. With barely a touch, I'm soaring and spinning to the first of what feels like a hundred peaks.

My fangs are out again, and I reach forward to nip at his neck. He seizes in my arms, a growl rumbling in his throat beneath my lips. "Yes . . ."

I didn't need his affirmation, but I respond by sinking my fangs deep into his flesh. Shane cries out, louder, and with his blood flowing into me, moves between my legs. I arch my hips to meet his, the fullness ready to burst all over again.

For hours, we fuck joyously, recklessly, with no calculated movements or artful acts, just two bodies needing to consume each other. We caress, we suck, we come, we start again.

We live.

Near dawn, we're still making love, our limbs limp and languid. Shane is examining my face, maybe for signs of regret. "So you liked biting, then?"

"I loved it. Thank you." I run my hands down his back and over his hips. "I love being a vampire with you. I want to be as good at it as you are."

"It's like anything else." He lowers his head to kiss me. "Practice."

David's blood is still lighting me up from within, and every touch of Shane's hands or brush of his lips feels like a sunrise.

There's only one thing missing from this night, an absence I feel—we both feel, undoubtedly—every night. Maybe now that I've taken a big step toward being a real vampire, I can take the final one.

I arch my neck. "Bite me."

"You sure?" he murmurs, but his hesitation is belied by his sudden twitch inside me. He wants this.

"Positive." My blood is sparking at the thought of

it. "It's perfect timing. I'm totally relaxed and kinda numb."

He presses his mouth to my neck, and I feel his tongue search for the heat of my vein. I squirm and moan beneath him, though I know I should hold still.

He slides his hand behind my head, gripping the back of my neck. My eyes fly open as I plummet into my worst memory.

My lips form the "W—" of the word "Wait." Shane's fangs break my skin.

"No!" I shove against his chest hard and fast. Shane flies across the room, slamming his back against the door. He slumps to the floor with an agonized grunt.

"Oh my God!" I sit up, brain spinning from adrenaline. "Are you okay?"

Shane lowers his head into his hands, his legs twisted under him. "Yeah . . ." The word is full of wince.

"I'm so sorry." I get out of bed and kneel beside him. "I can't believe I threw you across the room."

"I can't believe I bit you."

"I told you to."

"I should've known you weren't ready."

"I *was* ready. I mean, I thought I was." I sit on the floor and curl my arms around my knees. "Will I ever be normal?"

"Your fear of being bitten is normal, or at least understandable, after what you've been through."

"But I was afraid before Jim bit me. He just made it worse." My breath comes faster. "I've never been normal."

"Shh. Come here." He takes me gently into his arms and leans back against the door. "We'll figure it all out, I promise."

The happy haze in my brain is long gone, and all I can feel is the fear. I don't want to fade. I don't want to die. Whatever it takes, I will be just like the rest of them.

The kitchen phone rings. Shane sighs. "Who the hell's calling this time of night?"

"Can we ignore it?"

"It's the landline, so it's probably one of the other DJs." He opens the door and hurries for the phone. I make my way to the bathroom to wash up. I may be a vampire, but that doesn't mean I enjoy being covered in blood—my own or someone else's—any more than humans enjoy being covered in food. Which is to say, I enjoy it a little, under the right circumstances.

"Deirdre, slow down."

Outside the bathroom, I stop. "What's her drama now?" I would eavesdrop, but I really need that shower.

Afterward, I leave the steaming bathroom, tucking the end of my towel under my armpit. Sitting at the kitchen table, Shane looks up at me, eyes full of dread.

"We've got problems."

14

He's in Town

Typically, Shane's statement turns out to be an understatement.

"*All* of Jim's progeny?" I ask him after he's started to explain. "Out for our heads?"

He points his pen at the legal pad in front of him. "Deirdre says that eight out of Jim's nineteen remaining progeny are here in the United States, not including her. The other ten are in England, though they're being encouraged to come help avenge Jim's death. But these days—"

"Wait. Back up. How do they know we killed him? We didn't tell anyone but the people at the station and the Control." I stomp a bare foot against the linoleum floor. "Shit, it could be anyone." Why did I tell Adrian? I barely know him. What if in his grief he told two friends, and they told two friends, and—

"It *could* be anyone, but it isn't." Shane grips his pen so hard, the plastic cracks. "Deirdre told them."

"Why? How did they find her?"

"Apparently Jim told them he'd go to her place for

sanctuary when he escaped. They were getting ready to go meet him there when he died. It took them a few days to recover from the pain."

"Then they came after her."

"First they accused *her* of staking him, and they threatened to kill her, then her son."

I sit down hard. "Oh my God. No wonder she ratted us out." I look at his notepad. "So how many and who are they?"

"Deirdre said six out of the eight came to her house. She didn't get all their names, but there's a Billy and a Bonnie. They seemed to be the top henchmen."

"Henchpeople, since one's a girl."

"Sorry." He covers his pained expression at my correction by rubbing his jaw stubble. "And of course there's their leader, who is Jim's firstborn, so to speak—

"—Kashmir," we say in unison.

"You know him?"

"Regina and Noah told me all about him. Hang on." I slide back my chair, making it squeak on the tile, then dash for the door.

"Where are you going?"

"Making sure this is locked."

Dexter follows, concerned by my urgency. Both dead bolts are turned, as well as the lock on the doorknob. Spencer once tested it to see if he could break in. He couldn't, so we figured the younger, weaker Jim would be unable to as well.

Now we have bigger problems than one vampire. Eight times bigger, to be exact.

"As I was saying," Shane continues, "there aren't many safe, affordable passenger ships across the Atlantic, so Deirdre doesn't think the rest of Jim's progeny will join up in time."

"In time for what?" I pat Dexter's head in an attempt to soothe him. Unconvinced, he adheres to my leg as I walk back to the kitchen.

"Thanksgiving. The ultimate vampire holiday. To Jim, T-Day was practically a religious occasion."

By tradition, modern American vampires get together with their fellow undead on Thanksgiving (or T-Day as they call it, though no one will tell me what *T* stands for—it's not "turkey" or "Thanksgiving"—and I'm starting to wonder if they even know). On T-Day, each vampire brings his or her favorite donor to the feast. A grand meal is had, with all the best human food. Then afterward, instead of eating pumpkin pie, the donors *become* the dessert. Whipped cream is optional.

Jim's progeny probably mean to attack us when we're understaffed. On T-Day, usually only one person is at the station, whichever DJ is on the air. The humans are with their families, and the vampires are with their donors.

"Deirdre says they plan to take a DJ hostage to draw the rest of us back to the station, at which point they kill us all."

The last three words strike me so hard, I sink back into the kitchen chair, tugging up my towel. "Maybe *they* set the Halloween bomb at the Smoking Pig. The FBI told us they had no solid leads yet."

"They might have set it. At least this time we'll have more than a few minutes' warning."

"Assuming Deirdre's telling the truth."

He holds up the notepad. "She gave me details about

all Jim's progeny that she knows. See if they match what's in those boxes under Jim's room."

"The best way to lie is to sprinkle in a liberal dose of truth. She might think when her details on these vampires check out, we'll be more likely to believe the part about when and where they're attacking."

"Why would she lie?"

"Because if she double-crosses us, we end up dead. If she double-crosses Kashmir, her kid ends up dead. Easy choice."

He grunts in acknowledgment, then goes totally still. "Wait."

I keep my mouth shut while he thinks.

After several seconds he speaks. "If she wants us dead, even just to save herself and her son, then why tell us anything at all? Why give us names? Why not let us get ambushed without even knowing they're out there?"

He has a point. What does Deirdre gain by betraying a man who makes Jim look like a Sunday school teacher? "Maybe she wants us to kill Kashmir and the rest of Jim's progeny." Besides her, of course.

Shane nods slowly. "Kashmir scares her. I could hear it in her voice. She wasn't faking it."

"Regina says he's a whole other level of bad." My mind seizes on a terrible possibility. "Kashmir could be feeding us disinformation through Deirdre. If he's threatening her son, she'll do anything."

"So maybe they'll attack sooner. Either way, we need to prepare." He rests his hand near his cell phone on the table but doesn't pick it up. "We should call in the Control."

My, how times have changed. In the old days I would've been the one to suggest it.

"Can we trust them? The Control might have let Jim go, knowing either he'd kill us, or that we'd kill him and start a cycle of vengeance."

"How could they know about Kashmir?"

"If they were working with him in the first place to set Jim free."

"I wonder if there's a record of who visited Jim in the nursing home. They do let outsiders visit, at least in the part that I was in. That's how David rescued me."

"Rescued" in a metaphorical sense. Shane was in a special ward reserved for young vampires who have trouble adjusting to their new life. Suicide watch, basically. When David started the radio station and hired Regina, she led him to her progeny Shane.

The rest is WVMP history. The station gave Shane something to live for. No way we'll let it be attacked.

"According to Deirdre," Shane says, "the progeny will move in right after sunset, once we all leave for T-Day, except for whoever has the first shift that night."

The DJs' three-hour shows go in chronological order on alternating nights. On nights that begin with odd-numbered dates, Monroe, Spencer, and Adrian play their forties, fifties, and sixties music, respectively. Noah, Regina, Shane, and Jeremy (seventies, eighties, etc.) play on even nights.

"What's the date for Thanksgiving?" I ask Shane.

"The twenty-fifth."

A cold fire burns in my chest. An odd night: Monroe will be there. They'll take him hostage, knowing I'd do almost anything to save my maker. Killing him would be the perfect revenge against me. "Tell me you have a plan."

"I do. We hold T-Day dinner at the station. We'll have Control Enforcement agents pose as donors."

I give an admiring nod. "So if Kashmir ambushes us, we'll be ready."

"We'll have the tactical advantage of being inside the building. We could modify the boarded-up windows, put little doors in them so we can shoot the vampires as they approach."

"Shoot them with holy water?"

"With crossbows."

"You want to kill them?"

"They want to kill us. Just like Jim. They're his progeny, so they won't stop. *He* wouldn't have stopped."

"What about his progeny's progeny? If we kill Kashmir and his blood siblings, we might have an even bigger fight on our hands in another month. I think we should go nonlethal, debilitate them with holy water and let the Control arrest them for attempted murder."

"Ciara, have you forgotten Halloween? They tried to blow us up just for putting Jim away. He wasn't even dead yet. It made no difference to Kashmir."

"It might make a difference to the next generation." I lean closer to him. "I can't believe you, of all people, want to just wipe them all out."

"It's self-defense, Ciara." He touches my shoulder. "I won't let anyone hurt you again. Ever."

"Is that what this is about? You feel guilty for what Jim did to me?"

"I shouldn't have let you meet him alone."

"If you hadn't, my cousin Cass would be dead. Jim gave us no choice."

"I should've found a third choice."

"We did the best we could with the time we had." I move onto his lap and press my cheek against his neck. "You can't stop all the bad things in the world. I wish you could. I'm not so proud that I'd rather be dead than have my man protect me."

"I would do anything, Ciara." He strokes my hair. "I've vowed on my soul to keep you safe. You have to let me keep that vow to myself, even if it means losing my own life."

"Stop it." I push against him, my throat wanting to rip open with tears. "I don't like you this way. I want the old Shane back, the one who was too cool to fight."

"Tough shit." He holds on to me, gently now, so that if I wanted to pull away, I could, but I don't. "That Shane is gone until this is all over. One way or the other."

15

Lawyers, Guns, and Money

The tile floor of the Control headquarters building was made to torture vampires like Noah.

His compulsion is symmetry, sort of. His feet follow the patterns in carpet, hardwood, sidewalks, whatever. He does what he can to avoid stepping on cracks, seams, tiles of a different color from the ones around them, even drops of paint or tufts of grass sticking up through concrete.

The floor outside Shane's hearing room is made of tiles with patterns that point forward and backward, alternating with tiles that point from side to side. One can align one's feet with the grain only by taking carefully spaced, awkwardly short steps. You'd think it'd make it hard to pace, but Noah manages, head down, watching his sandals mark the pattern. It's like a hopscotch game without the hop.

On my other side, Spencer is adjusting the rug outside the hearing room so that its edge is perfectly parallel with the threshold.

I've got no room to judge their compulsions—I had

to rotate the sign that said 2:15 AM, MCALLISTER TRIBUNAL so that I couldn't see it. It's the marquee-style sign that has white block letters on a black background, with no glass front. The temptation to physically rearrange them as well as mentally is almost overpowering.

Monroe sits on the bench beside me, reading an antique copy of *Life* magazine he picked out of the rack. It's from 1960, twenty years after he died. But for him it's the future.

It's not that they don't know what year it is or who's president or who won the World Series last week. They read the news out loud to their listeners every day. They're just happier and more stable when they can connect to their own "Life Times." The music does that for them. It's why the WVMP DJs are probably the sanest vampires in the country.

All of them but one. Even a seminightly psychedelic show couldn't keep Jim from riding the crazy train. That's what we've all been called here to testify. Regina, Jeremy, and Deirdre spoke last night, as well as Jim's necro-psychologist at the Control nursing home. Tonight it was me, Monroe, Spencer, Noah, and lastly Shane himself.

Before the tribunal, Lanham told us that he checked Jim's visitor list for the last month. No one outside the agency came to see Jim. Which is frustrating for our investigative purposes, not to mention sad for him.

The tribunal room is soundproof even for vampire hearing, like most rooms in this building. We've taken turns pressing our ears to the center of the door and every crack, straining for a scrap of conversation among the five tribunal members. There's one from each major division: Enforcement, Command, Recruitment, Logistics, and VHR (Vampire-Human Relations). The Immanence Corps is the semisecret sixth division, a jagged line and shaded triangle on the Control organizational chart.

When I testified, I watched each member's eyes for signs of sympathy. I watched the way they looked at Shane while I spoke. I tried to find some clue on which to hang my hope or despair.

Nothing. I am never playing them in poker.

The hour drags on, until finally I can't take it anymore. I cross to the sign, turn it around, and start rearranging.

BAR MCALLISTER, UNTIL 2:15 AM. No, they might take that suggestion literally.

I raise the comma and create *RUB'N MCALLISTER TAIL, 2:15 AM*. "Yeah, baby."

Still no sounds from the hearing room. I pace a few more times, then add Shane's last name to the remix. This'll keep me occupied for a while.

Fifteen minutes later I have *I'LL SCAM A BURNER TIL 2:15 AM*, but I can't find a place for the second *T*.

The door suddenly opens. To a very quiet room.

I slip the white plastic *T* in my pocket and turn to see Shane walking out, chin high and jaw set. His entire black-uniformed body is rigid.

"It's done." He sweeps past us, obviously eager to leave the building.

"What's done?" Spencer and I say simultaneously. Noah and Monroe flank us as if in protection, though no one else seems to be in a hurry to follow Shane.

"Suspended for sixty days without pay. Plus I have to repeat my nonlethal methods training with the January Indoc class." Shane sighs. "That'll be humiliating."

"You'll teach those newbies a thing or two." I glance back down the hall into the hearing room, where everyone looks as creepily neutral as they were when I was testifying. "I guess it could've been worse, huh?"

"Yes." He makes a crisp turn toward the stairs. "They could've suspended me longer, even thrown me in prison."

"They shoulda given you a medal," Monroe murmurs.

"One of the tribunal members argued for that." Shane takes the stairs two at a time, and we have to hurry to keep up. "But in this political climate, they had to make an example of me."

"'Political climate'?" Noah asks.

"With the Project Blood Leash investigation going on, the Control is extrasensitive about any anti-vampire violence."

Spencer scoffs. "Don't it matter that you're a vampire yourself?"

"Colonel Petrea was a vampire," I point out, "and he was the head of Project Blood Leash." I want to take Shane's hand, but it's forbidden when either of us is in uniform. "So why didn't they punish you worse?"

"Because of the circumstances. Jim had a history of violence against both of us, especially you. The tribunal said they believe I acted correctly to preserve our lives."

"Then why punish you at all?"

Shane sighs as he shoves open the outer door and stalks down the marble stairs that gleam in the moonlight. "Remember when I told Deirdre how I'd run that scenario over and over in my mind, so that if I ever saw Jim, I could act without thinking? So that killing him would be a reflex?"

"Yeah."

"Saying that was a moment of supreme stupidity. It made it sound like it was premeditated, like I had a grudge."

"You did." Monroe stops at the bottom of the stairs to light his cigarette. "We all did."

Shane turns on his heel, impatient at the brief delay. "The tribunal board said that it hampered my ability to adhere to the Control's first precept: 'Cooperation before coercion.'"

"If you'd cooperated before you coerced," I point out, "we'd be corpses."

He looks at the others, then drops his gaze to the ground. "We'll never know that for sure."

"*I* know it. Jim broke my wrist. He tore out half my throat. He was faster, stronger, and more ruthless than you." I wrap my arms around Shane's waist and press my face to his chest. "I don't care what they say. I'll always know you saved me."

"That's all that matters." He kisses the top of my head, in total violation of the no-PDA-in-uniform rule. "And I'd do it again in a heartbeat."

We prepare the station for battle, without looking like we're preparing the station for battle.

When Shane and I arrive Friday night, David and Franklin have just finished installing hinged doors in the two boarded-up windows of the main office.

"Check this out." David swings open the square door in the window behind Lori's desk. Then he rests the nozzle of a holy-water pistol in a little notch at the bottom. "For greater shooting stability."

Shane strides forward. "Close that thing, it's after dark! Someone might see it." He slams it shut. "I mean, it's great. Thank you."

"You're welcome." David points to the window. "You couldn't see them from outside when they're closed, could you?"

"No, they're completely seamless." It's a little weird, I admit, being in the office with Shane and David after having been sandwiched between them. But I'll get used to it. I run my fingers over the wrought-iron handle of the other "turret door." "Nice style, too."

"Got the handles on sale at Lowe's." Franklin unplugs the electric drill and starts to wrap the cord around the grip.

I notice they've moved our coatrack, which is currently a heavy cardboard cutout of Eric Clapton. I put it back in place. "So, Franklin, big date tonight. Will it be *Hair* today, gone tomorrow?"

The others cover their ears, too late to escape my bad pun. Franklin turns to me, drill poised as if to shoot me with it. "Excuse me?"

"You're going to see a musical. Are you feeling okay?"

"I'm great. No, wait." He sets down the drill and makes exaggerated jazz hands. "I'm faaaaabulous! Is that better?"

"If by 'better' you mean scarier than *Saw* and its four hundred sequels put together, then yes."

David and Shane go into David's office for another tactical meeting. Just because David is retired and Shane is suspended doesn't mean they can stop being Enforcement agents when our lives are on the line.

"So this thing with Adrian . . ." I begin.

"This thing with Adrian," Franklin says, "will either kill me or complete me. Or completely kill me."

I take a moment to absorb Franklin's combination of sanguinity and cynicism. Sanguinicism.

How long before I think of nothing but words? How long before I can't relate to humans at all, and then finally not even other vampires? How long before I retreat into my own head?

How many more years do I have?

I follow Franklin into his office and watch him sift through his drawers. He's still got Aaron's picture on his desk, off to the left of his desktop computer.

They probably thought they had years left to them, but Aaron was stolen away. At least I came back, so I could spend whatever time I have left with Shane. It's better than nothing.

"Why are you staring at me?" he says.

I lean against his doorjamb. "Did you ever know anyone with Alzheimer's?"

"Why?" He looks up, concerned. "Not your mom."

"Nah, she's sharper than your stash of pencil stakes. You'll see when you meet her next month at our wedding. Plus she's too young for Alzheimer's."

"People can get it younger. I had an aunt who wasn't even sixty when she died of it." He shakes his head. "It was horrible. She disappeared little by little. You know when your DVR is on the fritz and the picture gets all pixilated and sometimes it even freezes? And then it's normal again?"

"Yeah?"

"It was like that. At the beginning, anyway. Then the pixilation would last longer and longer, until one day there was no normal picture anymore. It was all frozen."

I feel that way right now, staring at him, thinking of those moments when everything stops and my mind seizes on some little thing. I was never an absentminded human. In fact, I was present-minded. My mind was always—oh, crap, I'm doing it right now.

"That's terrible," I say, because I have a vague recollection that what Franklin said was, in fact, terrible.

He gives me a strange look. "Why do you ask?"

"It's my turn to pick the charity for next year's Rock-athon." It's like a telethon, but with rock. "I thought of Alzheimer's, and it'd be great if one of us had a personal connection to it." That sounds bad. "Not 'great' like 'fortunate,' but 'great' like . . . 'useful.'"

Franklin gives a gruff chuckle. "Every one of those DJs seems like highly functioning Alzheimer's patients some days, the way their minds are all going." He looks up suddenly. "I don't mean you or Shane. Sorry."

"It's okay. I'm young. I've got years and years and years of fun before the decay starts." I imitate his bad jazz hands, then turn away so he doesn't see how fast my smile disappears.

"This place is a glorified shack," Shane is telling David in his office. "Only two windows, and they face the same direction."

"Right, north. It cuts down on the sunlight."

"It also makes it really hard to defend. We can't see anyone coming from other directions."

I walk over to David's office as he says, "We could station someone outside."

"They could be killed or taken hostage." Shane

points to the ceiling. "I'm telling you, we need the attic. Cut holes to make windows."

The door at the bottom of the stairs opens, and Jeremy saunters up.

"It's not a real attic," David tells Shane. "That floor wouldn't hold a chipmunk, much less a pair of Enforcement agents."

I imagine a chipmunk dressed from head to toe in black and wielding a crossbow. It doesn't cheer me up as much as one would think.

"Besides," David says, "it'll cause flooding."

"What are they talking about?" Jeremy asks me.

"How to see and shoot our approaching enemy from on high without them seeing and shooting us."

"I don't know about the shooting, but a security camera'll take care of the seeing."

"That's an idea," David says. "We should've had some installed years ago."

"When people started trying to kill us," I add, then ask Jeremy, "How much do one of those things cost?"

"For the whole system? It depends. Anywhere from several hundred to several thousand."

"Can you install one in a single day, oh, A/V god supreme of ours?"

He blushes a little and adjusts his glasses. "Sure. I can try to get the really small cameras that no one'll see. Otherwise these vampires can just knock them out with a rock or their fists."

I hadn't thought about how high a vampire can jump. I fold my arms over my chest, more to hug myself than anything. "We're sitting ducks here."

"But we're making preparations," Shane protests.

"We're stockpiling weapons, setting a perimeter, gathering personnel. We'll have at least two Control Enforcement agents here at all times, not including me."

"Against eight vengeful vampires. Maybe more. It's not enough, and you know it."

"What else can we do?"

"I don't know." I shove my hands in my pockets. My middle finger scrapes against a small, hard plastic object. I pull it out and almost laugh.

It's the *T* from the sign outside Shane's tribunal hearing room. I never found a place for it on the sign when I turned 2:15 AM, MCALLISTER TRIBUNAL into . . . what was it again? *I'LL SCAM A BURNER TIL 2:15 AM?*

That sentence makes a weird sort of sense. I was, after all, a scam artist in my younger years. "Burner" could be short for "burnout," what Regina would call a "waste-oid." Or it could just mean "one who burns." But "burns" as in "They burn other things," or do they themselves burn up? Heh, like a vampire.

I'm peripherally aware of the conversation continuing around me: how to fight off the horde of Jim's progeny who'll soon be coming for us. How to solve the uncertainty of when they'll attack, and the problem of their greater numbers.

I'LL SCAM BURNERS . . .

But how?

My con artist's brain says, soothingly, *Start with their weakness. Start with something they love, something they want more than anything in the world.*

Jim.

I can't give them Jim. He's dead. They felt him die, so I can't pretend he's still alive.

What's the next best thing to having someone you love back in your arms? I imagine Shane dying—no, that's too painful. I imagine my father dying without my ever seeing him again. What would I want most, other than to go back in time and tell him I loved him? (I really need to write myself a note to do that.)

I'd want to honor his memory. Pay my respects. Share my grief with both my mom's and his families. I'd want a—

"Funeral."

David, Jeremy, and Shane stop talking and stare at me. Shane comes to me. "What'd you say?"

"Jim needs a funeral. Or at least, a memorial service or a wake. For all his fans and friends, and for his progeny."

"Why would we want his progeny to—oh." Shane breaks into a grin. "You want to flush them out."

"I want to know when and where they'll appear. If they really love Jim—and based on the stuff he kept, they do, very much—they'll jump at the chance to pay tribute."

"What if paying tribute means killing everyone in the building?" David's face is full of dread (dreadful? No, not really). "You'd be endangering the public. At the very least, you'd risk exposing the truth about vampires."

"Then we don't tell the public." Jeremy pats the sleeve covering his inner forearm, something he does when a new tattoo itches but he can't scratch it. "We could put the word out through vampire channels only."

David contemplates this for a moment. "With enough Control presence, no one would get hurt."

"This is perfect." I pull out my phone. "The Control

can't dispatch enough agents to the station every day to keep us safe, but I bet they can do it for one night."

Jeremy goes to Lori's desk and wakes up her computer. "I'll write the invitation now."

"Send me the draft when you're done. I'll approve final wording once I get the go-ahead from the Control. This is brilliant." I dial Colonel Lanham, not caring that it's my own idea I just praised.

I reach Lanham's voice mail and ask him to call me, with no specifics. His line is supposedly secure, but I don't know who checks his messages.

As I hang up, I realize that's not all I don't know about Lieutenant Colonel Winston Lanham. I don't know if he's married or has kids, whether he loves or hates his job, or even where he lives when he's not at work. For all I know, he sleeps on the couch in his office.

Shane picks up the holy-water pistol from Lori's desk. They're made from top-of-the-line children's toys, the summer yellows and pinks painted over with a dull black lacquer for nighttime camouflage. But in Shane's careful, expert hands, it becomes as sexy as a Glock.

I can't believe I'm getting turned on by weapons. What's happening to me? Am I so desperate to survive that I'm reverting to cavewoman mode?

"Shane, can I bring my laptop into the studio tonight and hang out with you?"

"Sure." He sets down the pistol and gives me a smile. "You know you're welcome anytime."

"I also know it's crowded in there with two people, and sometimes I distract you."

He takes a step forward, bringing his body close and

sliding his fingers between mine. "I like when you distract me."

"Get a room!" Franklin yells from his office. "And I don't mean the studio. We could hear you guys the last time."

Shane looks toward Franklin. "Did I leave the mic on?"

"Yes," say Jeremy, David, and Franklin in unison. Then Franklin adds, "I can't wait until you're a boring old married couple like Lori and David."

"Hey," David says. "We're not old."

"You will be." Jeremy talks while typing. "Babies make people age faster."

Once it was obvious that the older vampires could detect Lori's pregnancy, she decided to let Jeremy and Franklin in on the not-so-secret secret.

"I thought kids are supposed to keep you young." David looks among us. "Right?"

I shake my head. "Stress, lack of sleep, Chuck E. Cheese's–induced malnutrition. Not to mention brain rot from children's music."

Jeremy starts singing a Teletubbies song (I assume that's what it is, based on the high-pitched baby voice and bad British accent).

"Our kids won't be listening to that crap," David tells Jeremy.

"No, they'll be listening to They Might Be Giants' children's albums, so you and Lori can pretend you're still cool while you drive around in your beige minivan with the DVD player and four million cup holders."

"Don't forget stain-resistant seats," Franklin adds.

David raises his voice. "We won't have a minivan, and for the record, They Might Be Giants are very cool."

"They *were* very cool," Jeremy says, "until they started making minivan music." Without looking at me, he casually holds up his hand for a high-five, which I dispense posthaste.

Then I notice that Shane hasn't joined the jocularity. He's leaning over my desk, going over our weapons inventory for the fortieth time.

"No point in obsessing over that list now," I tell him. "The Control will give us more once they approve our new plan."

"After my suspension, I can't touch a Control-issued weapon, so I need to see what's ours."

I've been putting his tribunal out of my mind as much as possible. Since we left Control headquarters the other night, he's spoken very little about his sentencing. When Shane clams up, it usually means he's upset.

"They were making an example out of you," I remind him. "They have to punish every instance of anti-vampire violence, even when it's justified."

"And they should. If someone whacked me the way I whacked—" His chin twitches as he tries to force out Jim's name. "The way I—the way it happened, I'd want that person put on trial."

"Even if you were a homicidal maniac who deserved to die?"

"Yep." He picks up the holy-water pistol, then aims along the sight at our two-dimensional Eric Clapton. "Justice isn't only for the good guys."

16

New Slang

The following Monday evening (Tuesday morning, really) I'm heading toward the DJs' apartment for a quick snack, when I see Adrian in the booth. I wave to him through the glass and he beckons me inside.

Entering the studio always gives me a thrill. Most of the DJs other than Shane are territorial about the space.

Golden Earring's "Radar Love" is thumping out of the speaker. "I love this song," I tell him. "But wait, it didn't come out until nineteen . . . seventy-three, was it?"

He beams at me. "Good call. Yeah, it's harder for me to play the newer stuff, but I had to learn. Classic rock stations insist on lots of seventies music, sometimes even early eighties these days."

"That's great that you could adapt. A lot of vampires can't."

"We do what we must to survive."

"Hmph." That's a line I've told myself a lot the last several months. "Hey, how was *Hair*? Did Franklin love it?"

"He hated every minute. The food was terrible, too."

"That sucks."

He shrugs. "We left early and went back to my place."

"Oh, that doesn't suck."

Adrian lets out a warm, melodious laugh. "It's not what you think. A long talk and a kiss good night is all we had."

"That's a start. I guess he told you about Aaron."

"Yeah. I can relate. After almost fifty years as a vampire, I've had to watch a lot of loved ones die."

"I'm sorry." I think about this for a moment, wondering if I'll even outlive my parents, much less Lori and David and other friends my age.

"Speaking of passing on," Adrian says, "Regina told me that Jim's memorial service is a week from tonight."

"Yep, the twenty-second." We thought the anniversary of JFK's assassination would add a macabre appeal that Kashmir and Company couldn't resist. "We're holding it at Crosetti's Monuments, the headstone maker off Raleigh Avenue."

"The place with the little fake graveyard, across from the church with the little real graveyard?"

I nod. "Mr. Crosetti used to be one of Jim's donors. He's probably looking for a new vampire to donate to. You should talk to him while you're there."

"I don't know if I'm going." He traces the stack of LPs on the table, which I just realized are Jim's. "It might be too painful."

"I think it'll be a good way for us all to get closure. I'm sure there'll be lots of music, especially the psychedelic stuff he loved so much."

"That music was a lot like him." Adrian's brown eyes droop at the corners. "He was always on the edge of madness. That's why he was so brilliant."

"No. He was brilliant in spite of his madness. Think of

what he would've accomplished if he hadn't had to battle that." My ire rises at the thought of Jim's instability. "I can tell you, his so-called madness wasn't inspiring or romantic. It was terrifying and destructive. And annoying. That's the reality of crazy. You can dress it up any way you want, but in the end it's a sickness, and most sicknesses are gross."

Adrian stares at me, looking much younger than his twenty-seven years. I've struck something soft inside.

"I'm sorry," I tell him. "Sort of."

"It's all right." He lowers his gaze to the Jefferson Airplane record in his hands. "I hadn't thought of it that way. I guess we all want to believe that our heroes are better than perfect."

Better than perfect. I've never heard that phrase before. I think I like it. Either that or it frightens me.

"Yeah" is the best I can offer. "So, do you have a signature sign-off song? Monroe's is 'Never Get Out of These Blues Alive.'" I don't mention that Jim's was "It's Only Rock 'n Roll (But I Like It)" until the very end, when he changed it to "Gimme Shelter," the song I can never hear again.

Adrian nods. "I do have a signature sign-off song."

"What is it?"

"You'll see, at five of six." Adrian gives me a sweet, gentle smile. "It's a message."

"For who?"

"Everybody. It's one we all need to hear these days."

The cynic in me wants to roll my eyes, but he's so earnest. I never got the feeling that Jim believed in the hippie philosophy. Like the temporary sixties' DJs we've had working over the summer and fall, he was more infatuated with the trappings of the times. The openhearted acceptance was an excuse for excess and hedonism.

But Adrian really believes. Either that, or he's a better actor than all the others combined.

I wish him luck and head to the apartment for breakfast.

That night I keep the radio turned up while I work at my desk, studying market share reports and choosing a new merchandise producer. (Sometimes I wonder if they wonder why all our swag orders are placed in the middle of the night. They must think we are very dedicated workers.)

Adrian's show shares none of Jim's lurking, psychedelic darkness. It's all peace, love, and flowers in rifle barrels. The music has a purity of belief and faith in the goodness of human nature and the future of the world. How can a vampire be the source of such sunshine and delight?

At 5:55 a.m. he signs off his show with a farewell message: "Thanks for hanging out with me on this beautiful November morning. I appreciate all the calls with your requests and good wishes. It's nice to know I'm not just talking to myself. So, everyone out there: Today, be good to each other. 'Cause we're all we've got."

A distinctive, languorous guitar and soft drum trickle from the speaker. The gentle harmonies of the Youngbloods' "Get Together" implore us all to love one another, not tomorrow or next week, but right now.

Can it be that simple? Can a bunch of mutual smiles change the world? My twenty-first-century sensibility says no way.

But I know the power of music in all its forms. It's sustained me and so many others in our darkest hours. Shane's voice singing my song brought me back from the dead, and it kept me free when Colonel Petrea tried to control my mind.

So I suppose, for five measly minutes every other day, I can believe.

"Now, to send a text, simply open your flip phone . . ."

I stare at my Contemporary Awareness instructor, then at the sample phone on the desk in front of me.

"This has to be a joke." I pick up the phone, feeling whisked back to 2001. Admittedly, it is nice and light compared to my current phone, a portable computer that doubles as a people-calling device and can triple as a blunt weapon, especially with the oversize long-life battery strapped to the back.

Agent Detwiler has us open a new message to her. Then she demonstrates how to press the phone-pad keys multiple times until we find the letter we want. It takes most of the class nearly a minute to write *Hi!*

I raise my hand. She calls on me.

"Yes, Agent, um . . ."

"Griffin. I'm new. Really new. I just wanted to point out that most smartphones these days have QWERTY keyboards." I hold up my own and slide out the hard keyboard. "See, it's like a mini-typewriter for your thumbs. Faster and more accurate than scrolling through three letters, then pausing before going to the next."

"Ooh, can I see that?" asks the teenage-looking agent next to me. I hand it to her, wondering which decade she's from. It's hard to tell with Control vampires, since CAD training keeps them current on today's fashion and slang. "Wow, that's, like, totally gnarly!"

Current, except when they get excited.

The other six vampires in the class gather around. Agent Detwiler tries to control the chaos.

"This is, of course, the latest in technology," she calls out, "but I thought we'd start with something more basic for training purposes."

"Why, if this is easier?" asks Valley Girl Vamp. "Oops, I think I just messaged a text." She hands the phone back to me. "Sorry."

I check my screen to discover she just sent *duuuuuuuuuuude* to Colonel Lanham. Fabulous. "You guys should know, a pullout keyboard like this is getting rarer. Most phones now have it only on the screen. But they'll have to pry my hard keyboard out of my cold, dead hands."

That sounded funnier in my head. Also, less pathetic. Only six months old and already I'm attached to the technology I've been using for the past two years. I resolve to start using the touch-screen keyboard.

The class finally ends, after much thumbing and clicking and cussing.

"That's all the time we have." Agent Detwiler slaps shut her ancient phone. "For homework, I want you to text me once a day telling me about a story you heard on the news. This will enhance not only your technical skills but your comprehension of current events. Next week we'll continue our discussions of twenty-first-century technologies. I'll also introduce you to something called 'reality television.' And yes, it's as oxymoronic as it sounds."

I'm the first one out the door, and not just because the class is causing me physical pain from all my eye rolling. I don't want to be late for coffee with Anca Codreanu-Petrea.

This time of night, the café in the Control headquarters building is always crowded. The human agents working night shift need the caffeine to keep going, and the vampire agents starting their own "day shift" need the camaraderie to remind them why they work here (and the caffeine doesn't hurt).

I find Anca near the coffee's condiment stand. She's coating the foam of her cappuccino with cinnamon that matches the color of her hair.

"Agent Griffin!" She sets down the shaker, then reaches for the nutmeg. "I was worried you wouldn't come."

Way to set me on edge from the beginning. "I'm not late, am I?" I take a cup from the dispenser and pour myself a large French roast. I drink it black, since I can no longer taste milk and sugar.

"No, I just worried you wouldn't accept my invitation, after . . ."

I keep my face impassive. Does she mean "after my daughter raised the zombies who spread the disease that killed you"? Or does she mean "after you staked my husband"?

"I know you had nothing to do with Tina's wayward behavior." That's a lie—I don't know that, and in fact I suspect the opposite. "How is she, by the way?"

"Penitent." Anca heads for the cashier and I follow. "She'd like to see you and your friend Lori."

"I didn't know she was allowed visitors."

"Short, supervised visits are permitted."

We fall silent as we pay for our drinks. No need for the cashier to hear any more than she already has.

Heading for an open table next to the wall, I stay a

step ahead of Anca so I can sit facing the door. She looks disappointed when I take that seat.

"Do you think I should go see Tina?" I have no intention of doing so, and I'm sure Lori feels the same way, but I want Anca to keep talking about Project Blood Leash in an oblique, nonthreatening way that doesn't implicate herself. And by doing so, maybe she'll implicate herself.

Anca pats the top of her foam with the bowl of her spoon, testing its thickness. "It would mean a lot to her. She never intended to hurt anyone."

"Maybe not explicitly, but raising the dead? Tends to have negative consequences. Which you as a necromancer would probably know."

"My work is strictly limited to speaking with the dead, not bringing them back to life. It is against the laws of God and nature for a human like me to undo death."

But it's okay for vampires, I guess.

Anca continues. "Tina was distraught when the Control assigned her to Enforcement instead of letting her join us in the Immanence Corps. And angry that her father and I couldn't pull strings to give her the placement she wanted. But she is mundane, and IC is only for those with paranormal abilities."

"Which can be faked." By psychic-hotline workers, for instance, or my parents and their "faith healing."

"They can be faked to fool civilians, but not the IC."

"Do you have supernatural detection tools? Like a wand you wave through someone's aura or whatnot? If it beeps a happy tune, they're paranormal, but if it buzzes, they're mundane?"

Anca laughs. "I wish we did. It would make our jobs so much easier." Her smile fades. "Tina's anger, I think, was what drove her to speak so awfully of her father."

"That, and she got a reduced sentence for being so cooperative." She's not the only one. Rumor has it that Anca herself threw her late husband under the bus, so to speak, to protect her own hide. "Do you think she told the truth?"

"Sadly, yes." Anca sips her cappuccino, staring through the wall next to us as if it's a window. "Stefan always hated the demon inside, as he called his vampire aspect. I think he thought if he could control other vampires, he could control the monster within."

I remember Petrea telling me how his maker took him home after he turned him, how they slaughtered Petrea's own parents, wife, and daughter. How he staked his own maker and barely survived. Assuming all that was true—a vampire never tells the complete story of his turning—I could understand his self-hatred. But it doesn't excuse creating zombies to use as guinea pigs for vampire-control methods.

I voice my sympathy to lead her on. "After what happened when he was turned, I could see why he'd want a way to corral rogue vampires. They're dangerous, not just to humans, but to our whole way of life. They risk getting us discovered with their reckless behavior." That sounded a little too party line–ish, so I add a personal touch. "I was almost killed by one."

"I heard, and that Agent McAllister was suspended for protecting you." She puts her hand over mine. "No one doubts that he did the right thing. But the Control has its first precept for a reason. We've moved beyond what we once were: a band of bloodthirsty vampire hunters, obsessed with ridding the earth of the undead scourge."

Not even a crack in her façade, if that's what it is. I

come at the subject from a different angle. "Colonel Lanham has a tough job keeping us vampires in line. I think he gets in trouble for being too sympathetic. Which is a weird word to use to describe an emotional robot like him."

She gives a gentle laugh. "You don't know him the way I do." Her voice is almost tender. "There's much beneath the surface with that man."

Huh. "Do you know him well?"

"We've worked together since we joined the Control. We were in the same Indoc class." She holds the corners of the sugar container with her immaculately manicured thumb and forefinger, but takes nothing from it. "There was a time when Winston and I thought we might . . ."

I hold my breath. Her and Colonel Lanham? No wonder he hated Colonel Petrea so much. Or maybe I'm assuming.

I keep forgetting that, as a vampire, I can smell a human lie. "You and Lanham were involved?"

Her heart rate increases, but the flush of her face tells me it's from embarrassment or excitement, not deception. "We were. We thought we might marry, but we were young and stupid."

"Stupid? But you were both human. You worked in the same field, so there'd be no lying about your work. If you were both unattached—"

Her eyes shift to the side. Oh.

"Was Lanham married?"

"He never married anything but his job." Her eyes soften as she sighs.

"Were you already married to Colonel Petrea?"

"Not married, but we'd been engaged. I dated Winston while Stefan and I were, er . . ."

"On a break?"

"Yes. My relationship with Stefan was tempestuous, to say the least. I suppose that's typical of human-vampire romances. Eventually I went back to him and we married, then adopted Tina, since obviously we couldn't have our own children."

To me, that was one of the bonuses of getting engaged to a vampire. But one's mileage may vary.

"Anyway"—she seems eager to change the subject—"how are you enjoying your Contemporary Awareness course?"

"It's fascinating stuff. I can't wait to learn all about 'digital video discs' and how to join 'the Myspace.'" I employ liberal use of air quotes.

She laughs. "Sounds like you have your own ideas on how CAD should be run."

"I do, but they'll never listen to a vampire. I'm inherently unhip. They were my first choice of assignment, along with the Anonymity Department."

"I think you'll love Immanence Corps," Anca says. "It will never be dull."

"After all I've been through, I'd be okay with dull."

She shakes her head, making the waves of dyed dark-red hair dance about her face. "I've read your record. Your life has been full of adventure, always in motion."

I appreciate her use of the present perfect tense "has been" instead of the simple past "was" to describe my life. Despite the change, it does feel like one life interrupted by a moment of death, rather than two lives.

"Just the words 'Immanence Corps' open doors around here." She surveys the rest of the cafeteria with a mixture of disdain and amusement. "You'll see. They fear us."

I notice no one has taken seats at any of the adjacent tables. Is it her reputation or the indigo patch on her shoulder?

"I wonder if you might be able to help me." I take a sip of coffee to give her a chance to respond.

"Of course! Anything for a fellow IC-er."

"See, that's the thing. I think there are elements within the Corps that aren't happy about my abilities. When I was originally assigned to IC, I was human. I was anti-magic."

"And now you're not either. I don't see why anyone should have a problem with you. No offense, but you're just a vampire."

I sense no unease about her, no deception. The only people who know I've undone magic with the power of my mind *since* I became a vampire are those who were there when I killed her husband.

"There are rumors," I state simply.

She sighs, her eyes drooping. "I was once a conduit for rumors. I had my ear to the ground, as they say. But after Project Blood Leash, I hear nothing. No one trusts me. No one!" Anca gestures with her spoon, unwittingly flicking foam into her hair. "I am not my daughter or my husband. To me, necromancy is a sacred duty. We owe it to the dead to let them speak."

Her words give me an idea. If I can get her and Kashmir in the same place, I can see if they know each other.

"Speaking of the dead, what are you doing the night of November twenty-second?"

17

Bargain

"Hey, guys, thanks for coming."

I resist the urge to laugh at Jeremy's words as Shane and I glide into his dimly lit living room. I should be thanking *him*, not the other way around. But it would offend him to say so.

For a bachelor pad, Jeremy's new studio apartment is big on style, even if that style could be described as *Arabian Nights* meets *Underworld*. In the far corner, his queen-size bed is surrounded by a cascade of draperies of a nearly black crimson, suspended by a single fixture in the ceiling above the center of the bed.

"The drapes set off the bedroom area from the living room," he points out. "Plus it keeps out the sun so I can sleep during the day."

Jeremy's show runs from three to six a.m. every other morning, so he keeps a nocturnal schedule. He's also practicing for the day he thinks he's going to be a vampire.

"Neat." I check out the coal-black living room furniture and the two-by-three framed print of Edvard

Munch's *The Scream* between the windows. "What does Lea think of this place? She seems so girl-next-door-y."

"She thinks it's cool. She gets me, even though she's nothing like me."

"Do you get her?"

"Trying." Jeremy points the stereo remote at the receiver. As the music clicks on, I hear Shane sigh with disapproval.

"Is this that band without guitars?" he asks Jeremy.

"One of them." Jeremy sets down the remote, not offering to turn off Keane's *Under the Iron Sea*. The opening track, "Atlantic," used to remind me of Shane before I was a vampire, when I worried he would grow "old" alone after I died. Now I worry he'll grow old alone while I'm still alive.

I set my bag on the counter. "Jer, I've been dying to see your new ink. Can you show us now?"

"Yeah, it's small, not much shading, so it's healed already." He joins us in the kitchen and heads for the stove, where the light by the exhaust fan is switched on.

Jeremy removes his glasses, then tugs off his My Chemical Romance black-sleeved white raglan shirt. "I got the tattoo for you, but I guess it'll help Deirdre, too, if you're okay with sharing me."

I don't answer, because I'm not okay with it. But we can discuss that later.

Jeremy puts his arm under the light, revealing a dark blue line on his inner forearm. My mouth waters as I realize the line traces the vein we like to sink our teeth into.

An arrow points to the middle of the line, along with two words in a bold, narrow typeface: BITE HERE.

"Aww, that's really sweet." I have an overwhelming urge to buy him an ice cream cone.

"It's in your favorite font."

"I have a favorite font?" I peer at the tattoo again, then gasp.

"Haettenschweiler!" we shout together in an exaggerated German accent, then laugh like goofballs. I don't know if I've ever actually used that typeface, but I could never resist the urge to say it loud and commandingly, Colonel Klink style.

"What did your tattoo artist think of it?"

"Amber wanted to know why I didn't want it on my neck. I had to explain the whole air embolism thing, which of course made me dizzy, so I had to lie down."

"I know, right? It still queases me out. Did she think you were talking about real vampires?"

He rolls his eyes as he shakes his head. "I might as well have been asking for unicorn-related body art. Don't worry, she thinks the vampire thing is just a gimmick I'm into. I mean, look at me."

True. Jeremy has that break-me-I'm-emo aura about him.

Shane examines the new tattoo, which blends in nicely with his arm's other designs. "It looks healed, but we always wait a month just to be safe. You hydrated?"

"Come on, I've done this a hundred times." To placate Shane, Jeremy grabs a blue Gatorade from the fridge.

The sight of the bottle flashes me back to my own death. Spencer gave me the same drink before Monroe drained me, so that I'd be easier to bite. The fever from the chicken pox had sucked the fluids from my body like a Shop-Vac.

Shane comes to my side. "Ciara, you okay?"

I jerk my head to look up at him. "Yeah, why?"

"You went completely still there for a second, like you'd had a short circuit."

"Just zoning out."

Shane's hand lightly brushes the back of my shoulders in a comforting gesture that in my worst moments feels like pity.

Jeremy goes to the sink and cranks up the hot water. I notice something for the first time. "How come you don't have any tattoos on your back? Isn't that where most people start?"

"Never saw the point." He scrubs his arm to help prevent infection, the steam rising around him. "Why should I put them where I can't see them?"

"Other people could see them."

"I don't get inked for other people. I do it for myself. That's what separates me from the poseurs." He rinses and dries his arm with a fresh tea towel from the drawer.

"Ready?" Shane says from the living room area.

"Ready!" Jeremy hops over the back of the sofa and onto the cushions like a little kid about to get a birthday present. For a moment I think of how our birthdays are so close together, how this past May he turned twenty-seven. I didn't and never will.

Shane folds a clean, threadbare towel and inserts it between Jeremy's right arm and the sofa cushion beneath. "Ciara, you want to try on your own without me coaching you?"

My stomach flutters as I sit on the floor next to the couch. "It's hard to see in here."

Shane sits beside me. "Some donors prefer to leave

the lights off completely, so you have to learn to bite without your eyes. Use smell and touch. Those are a predator's best senses."

"Right." I look at Jeremy's position, leaned up against the throw pillow at the end of the couch, then make sure his arm is even with the cushion.

I close my eyes and run my nose along the length of his forearm. When I smell the place where his blood is closest to his skin, I use my tongue, pinpointing the curve of the vein.

"Don't be shy," Jeremy says. "You can't hurt me. I mean, you can, but I like it."

I glance at Shane, who shrugs. "Listen to him, Ciara. The donor is always right."

I press Jeremy's arm to my lips and sink my fangs, puncturing the smooth, cool skin.

His body seizes, and through the pounding of blood in my ears, I hear him cry out in what sounds like a mix of agony and ecstasy. The noise makes me want to tear deeper, rip muscle from bone, but I hold on to my control. My other hand grips the bottom of the sofa until I hear wood splinter. I force my fingers apart—all of them—dropping his arm.

Taking that as an invitation, Shane dips his head forward and drinks his fill. I watch Jeremy's face as his blood becomes part of us. He gazes at the ceiling like he's watching an angel descend from heaven. He could be in a medieval painting, if it weren't for the piercings and bleached hair.

When Shane moves back to let me drink again, his eyes burn into mine with an unmistakable lust. I keep my gaze locked with his as I slake my thirst.

I understand now. This need for blood is about more than just survival. It's about living. And I desperately want to, um, live with Shane. Maybe in the car right here in Jeremy's parking lot.

"That's enough," Shane says finally. My thirst agrees. It's quiet now, ready to sleep while my other appetites take over.

Though he's shown me a dozen times before, Shane goes through the aftercare procedures again. "First, gauze." He tears off the pad's white cover, his hands looking steadier than mine feel. "Since he washed up beforehand, we don't need iodine. Our saliva has no bacteria."

Right. Nothing lives inside us.

Jeremy is still staring at the ceiling, but his expression has changed. A tear trickles from the corner of one eye.

"What's wrong?" I ask him.

He wipes away the tear with a knuckle. "I miss Jim."

"Sorry, I forgot to tie you up and torture you first." My harsh words reflect my bitter hurt.

"You were fine. I guess I expected to feel some kind of bond between us, like what I had with Jim from the start. This felt good but not . . . sacred."

"Understandable." Shane checks the gauze to see if Jeremy's stopped bleeding, then opens a butterfly bandage. "You never forget your first. You got some vitamins with iron?"

"I know the drill by now," Jeremy snaps, then takes a sip from his Gatorade bottle.

While Shane carries the bloodstained towel and gauze pads to the kitchen for disposal, I smooth out the splintered wood along the bottom of the couch. It's just a hairline crack, no permanent damage.

Jeremy's phone rings on the coffee table behind me. I give it to him, noticing the number on the caller ID. "Deirdre."

Jeremy thumbs the screen and puts the phone to his ear. "Hey."

Shane seizes the remote and shuts off the music. He gestures to Jeremy with his thumb straight up, then points to his own ear. Jeremy nods and raises the volume on his cell phone.

"Slow down," he says shakily. "What do you want?"

"It's been two weeks," Deirdre answers. "I'm thirsty."

"Sorry, I just fed Ciara."

"What!? I thought you were mine now."

"Uh, no, I never said—"

"You saved my life!" Her voice is clogged with tears, and probably rum.

"I was happy to, but we never made a deal where I'd be your new donor."

Deirdre's whimper hurts my ears. "Is she there now? Are they both there?"

He looks at us. Shane reaches out, offering to take the phone, but Jeremy shakes his head.

"I don't know where they are." Jeremy winces as Deirdre raises her voice, calling him a liar. Vampires can not only smell a lie, we can also hear it in the timbre of voices we know well. "I thought the DJs were giving you a couple of Jim's donors, plus all the bank blood you need."

"They are, but I want you. I like you." Her voice goes low and seductive. "If you want, we could just hang out, see what happens. No biting."

"Are you asking me on a date?"

"Is that so bad?" she shrieks. "Am I too old for you?"

He holds the phone away from his ear. "Jeez, no! I have a girlfriend."

"I've seen your girlfriend. I know where she works. Does she know what you do with Ciara?"

His face freezes. "Um—"

"She doesn't know the truth about vampires, does she? Maybe it's time she found out the hard way."

"Don't you dare touch Lea."

"Silly, I don't mean *I'd* show her the hard way. I meant *you* would. Jeremy, I could give you what you want," she purrs. "I could turn you."

Jeremy's face goes blank, his eyes vacant. I've seen that look on game-show contestants, the moment before the reality of their megabucks-win sinks into their brains.

I grab the phone, barely beating Shane. "Deirdre, this is way out of line. You can't take care of a fledgling. You can barely feed yourself."

"You're not Jeremy's mother. He can do what he wants."

I look at my friend sitting in front of me. Though we're the same age, I've always considered him kind of a teenager, the way he dwells in fantasy and experiences every emotion at such great heights and depths. But Deirdre's right: Jeremy's a man who can make decisions for himself.

"Don't do this," I tell her. "You'll both regret it."

She lets out a drunken cackle. "We'll see." She hangs up.

Jeremy hunches over, his whole body folding in on itself. He looks exhausted and beaten.

"We can't stop you," Shane says. "But you need to

wait at least two weeks from tonight. If you try to change before that, you won't have enough blood to finish. You'll die for good."

Jeremy nods slowly as he raises his hazel eyes to meet Shane's. "Two weeks, then." He lets out a sigh, then picks up the remote from the coffee table and turns the stereo volume up. "I'll walk you guys out."

I laugh a little, since the door is only ten feet away. "Thanks for, you know." I give Jeremy my hand to help him stand, my muscles singing with new strength.

"You're welcome. And thank you." He manages a crooked smile as he walks us to the door and undoes the dead bolt.

I follow Shane out, then stop and turn to Jeremy. "When you said, 'Two weeks, then,' did you mean two weeks to make your decision?"

He answers as he swings the door shut. "Two weeks to tell life good-bye."

18

True Faith

Deirdre's phone call has not only killed Jeremy's blood buzz but Shane's and mine, too. The mood on our drive home is tense and sad.

"You think she'll really turn Jeremy?" I ask him.

"She was impulsive and reckless even before she had Jim's blood in her, so yeah. Then she'll regret it later."

A jolt of empathy hits me. "I wonder if she wants another kid, now that she's lost Ben. Someone who needs her."

Shane's fingers twitch on the steering wheel. "I hadn't thought of that, but you're probably right."

His phone rings. I can see its screen where it sits on the console in front of the gearshift. Deirdre. He hits Ignore, then shuts the power off.

I think about my own turning, exchanging my blood for Monroe's. Moments of peace interspersed with long periods of agony. "I could never do it, not even to save someone's life."

"You think that now," Shane says, "but when the time comes—when Lori or one of your parents gets hurt or sick—the decision will tear you apart."

I look at his face in the soft blue glow of the satellite radio screen. Regina's weekly three-hour show on the punk channel is playing, but the volume is turned down to nearly zero. "When you knew I would die, did you consider turning me?"

"Every moment."

"Even though you thought it'd make you a murderer, and me a suicide, and we'd both go to hell."

"Yep." His lips go toothpick straight, then soften again. "Even though," he whispers.

I feel a pang in my chest, as if my heart has literally expanded from the incremental but sudden increase in my love for Shane.

He stops at the traffic light a block from our house, then turns his head to look at me full on. When his eyes meet mine, his pupils dilate and his mouth opens half an inch. I want to gaze into the darkness of one and fill the other.

He takes my hand and pulls it to his lips. I slip one finger inside. And just like that, the blood is flowing again.

The light turns green, the tires squeal.

In less than a minute we're in our apartment. From the sofa, Dexter quickly raises his head and wags his tail, then returns to his nap. Miracle.

I shut the door behind us and go to turn the top dead bolt. Shane's hand covers mine, his skin burning hot.

By the time the locks click shut, his other hand is under my shirt, his mouth at my neck. He slides against me, hard against my ass, making me squirm.

Part of me wants to take him right here, right now, against the door. I hate waiting.

But knowing someone wants to kill us, knowing what the days ahead might bring, gives me one certainty.

"Shane . . ." I can barely get his name out between gasps. "I want you to bite me."

"What? Huh? What?" He pushes himself away from me and steps back. "What if you're not ready?"

"I *am* ready. I want to try again."

Shane gives me a sidelong look. "I don't feel like getting punched tonight."

"I promise I won't punch you, or throw you against a wall." I take his hand and lead him toward our bedroom.

"You can't promise. You can't stop a reflex." He drags his feet as we cross the threshold. "And if you break the wall with my head, we won't get our security deposit back."

"I know." Reaching our bed, I open the bottom drawer of our nightstand. "So you'll have to tie me up."

His gaze freezes on the set of handcuffs I'm displaying. "Oh."

I shake the cuffs, jingling the chain. "We know they're strong enough to hold me. Heck, they're strong enough to hold *you*."

"It's not that." Shane is clearly having trouble breathing. "I just—after what happened to you . . ."

With Jim, he means. Having my throat half torn out. "It was bad. But since then, I've bitten David, I've bitten Jeremy, I've bitten you. I didn't hurt any of you. It was nice. With you, better than nice."

He takes a tentative step closer. "Do you really want to be bitten, or do you just think you *should* want to be bitten?"

"I won't lie and say I'm not afraid. But that doesn't

mean I don't want it." I lay the cuffs in his palm. "It doesn't mean it's not worth it."

He swallows, then touches my face with warm, trembling fingers. "I promise I'll make it worth it."

I sit on the bed, then pull off my shirt and bra. "You take off the rest after you tie me up. Our usual safe word?"

"Yeah." He clears his throat. "Lie down."

I don't say the safe word, "Ravens," out loud, because nothing snaps Steelers fanatic Shane out of a sexual reverie like the name of his least favorite football team.

I lie on my back, but when he slips one cuff over my wrist, something feels wrong.

"Wait. This'll be better." I turn to lie on my stomach.

"You sure?"

"This way it'll be different than, you know, before." When Jim bit me. "Plus, easier access to the best part of my neck."

Shane leans over me, loops the handcuff's long chain around the reinforced-steel bed frame (specially built for vampires), then fastens the other cuff over my left wrist. "How's that?"

"Perfect."

He lies next to me and brushes the hair out of my face, smoothing it back over the curve of my shoulder. "What's this about?"

I meet his eyes, the pale blue barely visible in the low light. "We might die soon. That's what this is about."

His eyes narrow with a new ferocity. "No way I'll let that happen."

He leaps out of bed, so quickly I wonder if he's gotten mad and changed his mind. Instead he jerks open his belt buckle and jeans. He shoves them to the floor along with his boxers, then tears off his shirt.

Shane climbs atop me, then kisses a trail down my spine until my back is arched with need. His hand slips around the front of my own jeans, and I sigh at the feel of his fingers between my legs, even through the thick denim. He unzips me and slips a hand inside, over my panties.

"Tell me when to do everything," he whispers.

I groan at his command. It gives me a sense of power, even as I relinquish that power to him. "Take it all off me."

In a few moments I'm naked.

"Your mouth, everywhere."

He starts at my toes and moves up, his hands a few inches ahead of his lips. Shane's human teeth scrape and bite at the backs of my knees, then my thighs, and then . . . he lifts my hips, spreads my legs, and gives me his mouth and fingers.

I writhe and moan, jerking at the chain that binds me. He takes me close to the edge but lets me hold on. I want to come later, with him inside me and his mouth at my neck, tasting me at my fullest.

Maybe not too much later, though.

"Fuck me. Now."

Obeying immediately, Shane moves forward and above me, sliding his hot, smooth chest against my back, and then finally himself inside me.

For a moment I forget about the biting and savor the feel of every inch of him, meeting his long, slow thrusts with my own. For a moment, this is enough. For a moment, this is everything.

Shane's hand slips around my waist and down. He strokes me, inside and out, in a perfect rhythm, but I can't come, not yet, because when I do, he'll sink his teeth into me. And yes, I'm still afraid.

He stops, sensing my hesitation. "Ciara," he whispers behind my ear. "I don't want to hurt you."

He's giving me one last chance to back out, avoid the pain, pretend I'm still human, still fragile.

But I'm not. I'll never be a real vampire—at least in my own mind—until I can do this.

I turn my head to the side, wishing I could touch his face. But my hands are bound, so I slowly lift my hips, grinding them against his. "You'll never hurt me."

Shane pulls in an unsteady breath, maybe overwhelmed at the trust I've put in him. He sweeps my hair off my neck, then inches forward, filling me up, deep and sweet. I let out a moan.

The next breath I draw is cut short by the feel of his fangs on my skin.

"Breathe," he whispers. "Keep breathing, no matter what."

I do as he says.

"Good." He runs his tongue, hot and wet, over my skin. "And remember I love you."

The pain spikes into me. I cry out, jerking my arms to punch, but I'm trapped here, under him. Shane goes deeper, and not just with his teeth. He seems to expand inside me, stretching me mercilessly with his unyielding hardness.

The pain shoots out from the back of my neck, burning toward the tips of my fingers and toes, like lines of gunpowder leading to bundles of dynamite.

It arrives, and explodes, everywhere at once.

My mind turns pure white with fire. I've lost the breath to scream. Yet somehow, I manage to choke out a strangled, pleading "Yes . . ."

Shane groans in assent, sinking his teeth to the hilt. My body convulses with wave after wave of delirium. I hear him gasp when I come.

"Oh God, you taste . . . oh God." His voice is muffled with the flow of my life into him.

The world bursts apart at the seams and all my senses collide. I see sounds and hear smells and taste light. My mind flashes and spins like a carousel out of control.

Slowly, inexorably, it all fades, and the world returns to normal. Normal, but never the same again.

Shane rests on top of me, holding his weight on his hands. He licks the back of my neck, collecting the last few drops, or maybe just soothing me like a cat grooming its mate. His tongue trembles, as does the rest of both of us.

Finally he collapses beside me. I turn my head to gaze at him.

His eyes half-closed, he sweeps his fingertips over my shoulder. "If you never want to do that again, I understand. Even this once has been more than I could ever ask for."

"Are you kidding? That was literally out of this world. I now believe in astral planes, because I'm pretty sure I wasn't here for about a minute."

His eyes open wide, shining into mine. "Really?"

"Really. Now uncuff me."

"Oh, right. Sorry." Shane grabs the key from the nightstand.

"I promise, no retroactive punching."

"After that, you can punch me all you want. You can do anything to me." He frees my right wrist, then the left, then lies beside me again with a heavy sigh. "Are you okay?"

"I think you already know the answer." I reach out and trace the line of his collarbone. "It's weird: tied up and held down and bitten, I've never felt so powerful. I wish we hadn't waited so long."

"I'm glad we waited." Shane pulls me into his arms. "It was . . ." He doesn't finish the sentence, and he doesn't have to. For once I don't need words.

We lie together, letting our breath slow, falling into the same rhythm, finally the same.

19

A Murder of One

An hour before dawn, Shane and I decide to go to the station so we can spend part of the day planning Monday's wake for Jim. Two of the main Control operatives, Agent Rosso and Captain Henley, along with our combat trainer, Captain Elijah Fox, have been guarding the place all night and have some thoughts on how best to protect the station from an attack.

So we pack up Dexter and head for WVMP. With Kashmir on the loose, we can't bear the thought of leaving the dog alone.

I enter the lounge and walk past the other vampires, a secret triumph humming through my veins. I finally conquered my fear of being bitten. Lori will be thrilled. In fact, she probably won't even mind if I call to tell her.

I pull out my phone as we enter the DJs' apartment, but as usual I'm getting a spotty signal here. Sometimes Shane has better luck.

"Can I try your phone to call Lori?" I ask him.

"Why, whatever could you have to tell her?" He smiles at me as he hands me his phone.

"You forgot to turn it back on last night." I watch the screen while it searches for a signal. His bedroom often has the best reception, so I open his door.

As I step across the threshold, his phone buzzes in my hand.

10 VOICE MAILS, the screen flashes.

Oh, crap. I hit Play.

"Shane!" Deirdre's terror comes through on the first word.

Shane drops his duffel bag and zips to my side.

"They're coming for me," she says through the speaker. "I'm at home, but I don't know if it's safe to stay." A long pause. "Call me." Click.

He goes completely still, his eyes frozen on mine. I skip to the next message, from an hour later.

"Shane? It's me, Deirdre. Ignore my other voice mail. Sorry if I sounded panicky. Everything's okay." The tension in her voice belies her words. "I was just being paranoid. Hey, we should get together for lunch like we talked about."

"We never said we'd meet for lunch." Shane takes the phone and steps farther into his room, leaving the door open. "It's gotta be a signal that something's wrong."

He plays the message again, louder. As he listens, he cocks his head and peers intently at the wall. "I hear someone breathing in the background. Clothes shifting."

I can't hear it, but he's got fifteen vampire years on me.

"The next one's from her number, too," he says as he hits a button on the phone.

Her number, but not her voice.

"Shane, Shane, Shane." The man lets out a long

sigh. "I don't know how these phone message mails work, but I think you do. So I can't understand why you'd ignore one from your old lover. Is it because of that new girl, Ciara?" He pronounces it See-AIR-ah. "I pity you, being too young to experience free love. Things became so uptight in the eighties, when you finally got laid. By then, sex killed. And not just sex with vampires."

"Kashmir."

We turn to see Noah, his light-brown eyes going round and wide behind his glasses. His mouth hangs open after saying the name.

The caller sighs again, but the noise can't cover Deirdre's muffled voice in the background. It sounds like she's wearing a gag. My heart races faster.

"Where was I?" Kashmir sounds genuinely distracted. "Oh, right. I'm taking Deirdre for a walk, a little gift for my blood sister. See, I remember being her age. As a human, I was a surfer, and I used to love to get up before dawn and hit those early waves. During my first year as a vampire, the thing I missed most was sunrises. So I want to give Deirdre that gift of one last sunrise."

My stomach plummets. I grab the edge of the dresser for support. Shane's head whips around to look at the clock: 6:09—fifteen minutes until morning twilight.

Unless she's right around the corner, we can't save her without burning up ourselves.

"Don't worry," Kashmir continues. "You'll be able to say good-bye. To Deirdre and to Ciara." This time he pronounces my name right. "Shane, I'll be seeing you."

The phone rings and vibrates in Shane's hands, making

him jump and almost drop it. He hits the Answer button.

Deirdre screams his name, then "Please help me. Oh God, it's coming. The sun is coming."

"Where are you?"

"I don't know. They put me in a trunk and then on one of those things that goes through the woods."

"Who did?" he blurts.

"Kashmir and Billy, and two other blood brothers. Bruce and Leon, I think they're called." She takes in a shaky breath. "They tied me to—I don't know what it is. Cold and metal. Then they put my phone in my shirt pocket and dialed your number."

"Are they still there?"

In the background comes the whine of what sounds like all-terrain vehicle engines. Gears grind and the engine noise fades quickly.

"Not anymore," she says softly.

Shane starts to pace, two of his long strides covering the tiny room. "Describe where you are. Take a breath—listen, look, smell, everything."

"Um . . . trees. Grass."

"Is there a road nearby? Can you hear cars?"

She pauses while I dare to hope.

"No. Just birds."

I cover my mouth with both hands, holding back a groan of dismay. Shane takes his makeshift rosary beads from the closet doorknob. He crosses slowly to the bed, then sinks to his knees on the floor.

"I didn't know birds sang before dawn this time of year." Deirdre's voice sounds far away now, like she's realized we can't help her if she's not even near a road. "It's pretty here. Ben would love it."

I look over to see Regina has joined Noah. One hand grips his while the other clutches the doorjamb.

Shane shakes his head hard. "Deirdre, what else do you hear and see and smell? Tell me everything."

"There's a hum. Power lines, maybe?" Her voice goes tight like her head is turning. "Yeah, I can see them over my shoulder. Those big high-tension lines with the giant towers. Does that help?"

No. No one lives near high-tension power lines. People think they cause cancer.

But there must be a safe place to hide somewhere close. Kashmir and the others would be headed there. If Deirdre can get free and follow their tracks . . .

"What about my cell phone?" she says. "Can you trace my location from it if I stay on the line? My GPS should be on."

"Give me her number," I tell him. "I'll call the Control."

He scribbles it on a sheet of paper. I grab it and run out of Shane's room, heading for the landline near the kitchen. There I dial 777, the Control version of 911. The dispatcher answers.

"Yes, what is your emergency?"

"This is Agent Griffin."

"Yes?"

"From Immanence Corps."

"Oh! Good evening, Agent Griffin."

Huh. Anca was right. I need to name-drop my division more often.

"There's a vampire somewhere about to burn up at sunrise. Can we put a trace on her cell phone number? She says her GPS locator is on."

"Oh dear, I'm sorry, that'll take hours."

"Hours? Why?"

"The signal would have to be triangulated and even once we find it, unless she's near one of our agents with a vampire safe van . . ."

My heart sinks. "She's being murdered. Her killers are holed up close by. If we can locate the phone with her GPS, maybe they can be found."

"We'll do our best. What's the number?"

I rattle it off, then have her read it back to me.

"I'll put this through to Enforcement immediately. Can I be of any other assistance, Agent Griffin?"

"No." Her obsequiousness is a little creepy. Now I see why all the IC agents I've known are so full of themselves. "Thank you."

I hurry back to the room, pushing past Regina and Noah.

Shane is trying to keep Deirdre calm. "They're doing everything they can. Just hang in there."

I sit next to him on the bed and listen to her voice from the speaker.

"What time is it, Shane?" she whispers. "How long do I have?"

"Let me check the clock. I think you've got—"

"Don't bullshit me. I want the truth. You owe me that much."

Elbow on his knee, Shane rests his forehead against his fingertips, like an agonized version of Rodin's *Thinker*. "Twelve minutes until twilight. Forty-two minutes until sunrise."

Deirdre is silent. "I won't see the sunrise, will I?"

I wrap my arms around myself. The indirect light

will turn her to ash long before the golden orb peeks over the horizon.

"I can feel it coming," she says. "Starting to get tingly under my skin." Her voice is detached now. "Will it be quick?"

Shane closes his eyes. "I don't know. But I'll be here until the end. I promise."

"Thanks," she whispers. Then she clears her throat. "Can you do a few things for me when I'm gone?"

Still holding the paper with her phone number, I click on the pen. From the corner of my eye I see Adrian appear behind Regina and Noah.

"Of course," Shane says. "Go ahead."

"I don't want my son, Ben, to spend the rest of his life thinking I abandoned him. Can you find a way to tell him, someday, what happened? He won't understand now, but maybe when he's older. Please tell him I love him so very much."

"I will."

"Then there's my house. If people go in there, they'll wonder why I have blood in the fridge and why I was sleeping in the storeroom."

"We'll take care of it."

Under *Tell Ben*, I write: *Code White Deirdre's House*, my handwriting shaky.

"I was way behind in my mortgage, so you better hurry. The bank people'll be coming soon."

"I promise, we'll take care of it all."

"Shane, I'm sorry I told Kashmir who killed Jim. I might end up getting you and Ciara killed."

"I forgive you."

I don't, I think, but stay quiet. Forgiveness is a big deal to Shane. Maybe to Deirdre, too.

I wave my hand to get his attention. "Ask her if she can tell us anything about Kashmir. What he looks like now, what kind of car he drives, anything he said to her."

"I can hear you, Ciara, you can ask me directly." Her breath is coming faster now. "He's got dark hair, straight, silky, past his shoulder. Eyes like amber. Eyes that'll make you do anything. It's why I let him into my house. Stupid, stupid."

Sounds like he hasn't changed his appearance much since that photo of him and Jim was taken.

"What else, Deirdre?" I don't mean to snap, but we're running out of time.

"He's got a holy-water scar, just one drop's worth, on his right cheek. He tells people it's a birthmark or a tattoo. It looks like a teardrop, so—augh!"

Her yelp of pain jolts me, and I almost ask, by reflex, if she's all right. But of course she's not. Noah and Regina huddle together, as if they're in the line of the sun's fire themselves.

"What about his car?" Shane asks. "New, old, what?"

"Old. Black. Some kind of sports car, big engine, but I don't know what kind. Couldn't tell from the inside of the trunk." She whimpers. "Oh God, the sun's getting closer. Shane, will you pray for me?"

"Of course I will."

"Two doors or four?" I ask. When he looks up at me incredulously, I continue. "A sedan or coupe?"

"She said it's a sports car," he says through gritted teeth. "So two doors."

"Sorry." I lower my voice to the softest whisper. "Ask her if he said anything else. Anything. Save our lives, then pray."

"Shane, are you there?"

He angles his shoulder away from me. "I'm here, Deirdre. Are you ready?"

"No." She's sobbing now, almost hiccuping, but her voice is dry, with no tears. She's in pure fear mode. "I don't want to die. Please, please help me."

"Just breathe, okay? Focus on my voice."

"I'm trying."

"Is there something nearby that's beautiful? A tree, a rock, anything?"

"There's a tree. Still has leaves. Orange at the top, yellow at the . . . at the bottom . . . of the tree."

David has a tree like that in his backyard. A red maple, I think he said it was.

"That sounds pretty," Shane whispers.

"Everything's pretty here. Shane . . ."

"Deirdre, look at the tree. Don't take your eyes off it, okay? Don't look at the sky. Just watch the tree while I talk."

She sniffles. "'Kay."

He bows his head and starts to recite the novena for the souls of the departed, the same he said for me when I died and came back to life. He was praying for my soul, and for those who'd helped make me a vampire, and for his own soul, because he was happy they did.

For the first minute or two, Deirdre is silent except for her quickening breath. Even here beneath the earth, with no windows or doors, I can feel the sun coming. At the doorway, Regina and Noah have their eyes squeezed

shut, but Adrian stares at Shane hard, as if he can pull
Deirdre through the phone itself into safety.

Shane is now halfway through the novena for the
second time, his magic voice lulling my mind again.
Like Orpheus, he once pulled me back from the realm of
death. But now his role is different—he's leading Deirdre *into* that realm, and she'll never return.

Just as I close my own eyes, Deirdre starts to
scream.

Shane goes rigid, pausing for three seconds. Then he
keeps going. She needs him.

And he needs me. I kneel beside him and wrap my
arms around his chest from behind. I lay my head on his
shoulder and feel his body quake as he prays.

Her last words are "I'm sorry." She screams them
again and again as she burns.

Why does the sun hate vampires? Are we so, so
wrong that light itself wants to crush us into nothing?

My tears flow onto Shane's shirt, every blink releasing another flood. Could we have saved her if we'd gotten the call in time? Would I have saved her if it meant
risking our lives? I'll never know.

Deirdre's screams streak into my brain, down my
neck into my body, where they wrap around every organ,
sending lightning bolts through every vessel. I'm shot
through with her pain as if it's my own.

A crackling sound begins. Her flesh is dissolving. It's
almost over. Her voice pitches up, and she draws in a
breath for one last—

No. Not one last scream.

Silence.

Shane keeps whispering, faster now, racing to reach

the end of the novena. I hold him tighter, letting him know he's not alone.

"Amen." The word echoes, though it's just a whisper.

Shane stays as still as the silence itself, then turns and lets me take him in my arms. Behind me, I hear the other three DJs retreat into the common room. One of them—Adrian?—is crying.

"I'm sorry," I whisper to Shane.

He holds me so hard, even my vampire ribs threaten to crack and crumble. "Why didn't I answer? Why didn't I answer?"

Shane repeats this line again and again, until I pull away.

"Because she was a traitor and you didn't trust her, that's why. It would've been a trap, anyway. If we'd gone to rescue her, Kashmir would've killed us, too."

"I'm the one who killed Jim." Shane's eyes are a cloudy blue sky. "It's me Kashmir wants, not us. Maybe if I give myself up, he'll leave you alone."

I snatch Shane's shirt in my fists so fast, it even startles him. "No! You are not sacrificing yourself for me."

He moves to swipe my hands off his shirt, then changes his mind and folds his fingers around them. "I can't listen to him do that to you, too. I can't let you die."

I shake Shane hard. "And I can't live without you."

"That's not true, and you know it." He strokes his palms over the backs of my hands. "Ciara, my first death was meaningless. I want my final one to be for something."

I shove him away. "Why? So you can go to heaven? You think you can martyr your way into God's arms?"

"Maybe. I don't know."

"If you leave me on purpose," I choke out, "I hope you burn in hell."

He stares at me, and it's like I can see his soul die. The light in his eyes goes dim.

"No. I'm sorry." I reach for him, but he slips away, rocking back on his heels. "I didn't mean it."

"Yes, you did."

"I don't even believe in hell. Why would I wish anyone would go there?"

"You didn't mean that exactly, but you meant something low and vicious."

"What do you expect? You're saying you want to leave me."

"I don't want to leave you, I want to save you!"

"Then stay with me." Tears pour down my cheeks as I force myself into his arms. "We'll find another way, all of us together. Please."

He buries his face in my neck, his body shuddering with tearless sobs. I cling to his back and wish I could watch Kashmir himself writhe and burn for what he's done to Deirdre, and what he might do to us.

Shane finally pulls away and wipes his dry cheeks, then his forehead. "Okay." He takes a deep breath. "We stick with the plan. Hold Jim's wake on Monday and hope his progeny can't resist coming."

I return to logic mode, where I'm happiest. "Until then, we should hunker down here. They probably know by now that Deirdre warned us about their Thanksgiving attack."

"Assuming that was ever their real plan to begin with."

"Somehow they found out she told us. Either she confessed or they saw us preparing."

"Or both."

"So we can assume they won't wait until Thanksgiving to attack." An unpleasant tingle worms up my spine. "They might not even wait for Jim's funeral."

"They will," says a voice from the doorway. Adrian.

He steps inside the room and shuts the door behind him. His face is red from crying, and his hands twist around each other. "It should've been me out there in the sunrise."

"Why?" Shane asks him.

"Deirdre was a good kid. She wasn't the only one who betrayed Kashmir." He meets my eyes. "I did, too."

20

You Don't Know Me

Shane gets to his feet, slowly, as if Adrian's a wild animal he might scare away. "What do you mean, you betrayed Kashmir?"

"I called the police the night of the bombing. You can check the 911 tapes—they're public record." He clutches his hands together. "I didn't want revenge. I just wanted Jim's freedom. Ciara, I didn't know what he'd done to you. I thought the Control captured him because he was too much of a free spirit. I'm so naïve."

I shake my head hard, trying to dispel the confusion. It feels like time is tying itself in a knot. "Wait, wait, wait. Start from the beginning."

Shane steps closer to Adrian. "Yeah, like, who the hell are you?"

"These days I'm Adrian Donovan. But when I was alive, I went by Carl Keller."

I remember the name from Jim's box of progeny paraphernalia. He went to a Dead show in San Francisco with Carl and Bonnie. But that was, what, the mid-seventies? "How could Jim be your maker when you were turned in 1965? He didn't even turn until 1970."

"My turning wasn't until 1975." He gestures to his wool poncho. "I prefer the early sixties, though."

His ease with seventies music makes sense now. He didn't have to learn it to survive at a classic rock station. He'd lived through it, with Jim as his maker.

"You lying sack of shit." Shane grabs the front of Adrian's poncho, opens the door, and drags him out into the common room. I follow quickly, worried that in his rage, Shane will toss Adrian out into the sunlight, which he can't do without burning up himself.

Regina and Noah are on the couch together. Her tear-soaked face is pressed against his chest. I remember that her other progeny, Shane's blood sister Sara, died the same way as Deirdre, though by accident instead of murder.

Shane shoves Adrian into the armchair and turns to them. "He's one of Jim's. All this time and he didn't tell us. He's Carl Keller."

They sit stunned for a moment, then Noah simply says, "You shaved your beard."

"A spy for Kashmir? Motherfucker!" Regina leaps up, claws out, and Noah barely grabs her in time. "We let you stay under our own roof, and you sold us out!" She twists and writhes in Noah's grip. "Let me go, I need to kill him."

Adrian watches her carefully. Despite his peace-loving demeanor, he'd surely defend himself with lethal means. Vampires don't live almost fifty years—crap, I mean forty years—without learning how to fight.

"Regina." I almost step between them, but my own sense of self-preservation keeps me out of the way. "If you kill him, he can't answer our questions."

"If I kill him, he can't betray us again."

"I haven't betrayed you!" Adrian raises his hands. "That's what I've been trying to say. I didn't come here to spy on you. I came here because this is a dream job. Living with other vampires, having fans who adore us, getting to sit in the same chair, sleep in the same bed, as one of my idols—"

"That idol of yours killed my cousins." This new fact shuts Adrian up. "You already know he nearly killed me. So stop romanticizing him."

"I stopped romanticizing him about a day after I turned. I've seen him do more nasty things than you can possibly imagine. But the blood bond can never be broken, not even by death."

Shane and Regina share a look, and in the brief silence Noah speaks.

"I know what you mean." His voice is soft but commanding. "My maker was a monster by any standard. He abandoned me when I refused to kill. But I know that when his death comes, I will feel the same tear in my heart as I would if we were best friends."

Regina goes limp in his arms. After a moment he lets her go, and she stalks back to the couch. "Start talking, you bastard." Noah sits beside her, and I sit on his other side.

Only Shane stays standing, blocking the path between Adrian's chair and the exit. "You were turned in '75. By Jim alone?"

Adrian lowers his head. "By Jim and Kashmir, in California. I was the first of what they called the Magnificent Seven."

"After the movie?"

"It was Jim's favorite when he was growing up." Adrian's light-brown eyes skip over us. "Kashmir would find the fledglings. He'd befriend us, promise adventures, then hand us over to Jim, and the two of them would turn us together. If we fought back, we died for good. And sometimes, even if we didn't fight back, we died for good. Sometimes Jim and Kashmir overdrank."

"Were you really in medical school when they found you?" I ask Adrian. "Or was that a lie, too?"

"It was the truth. Sometimes I'd patch up the humans they left for dead and get them to a hospital." His gaze drifts slowly to the floor like a falling leaf. "Sometimes I was too late."

"Why didn't you finish school?" Regina asks.

"Day classes, obviously. Jim said he was giving me a long future, but really, he took my future away when he made me this." He gestures to his body with disgust.

"Did you leave them," Noah asks, "or did they leave you?"

"Both. Jim wanted to take the Magnificent Seven back to England, find his own makers, and show them what he'd become. They wouldn't let him turn anyone, because they thought he was too crazy."

"He *was* too crazy," I interject.

Adrian nods. "I wouldn't go with them. So they left me behind. I heard that on their way across America they created a new vampire so they could still go by the Magnificent Seven."

That would bug me, too. It was an excellent movie, after all.

"We met Kashmir eleven years ago," Regina tells him. "Jim seemed to blow him off. Do you know why?"

"I only know that Kashmir hates this radio station for what he calls Jim's 'domestication.'"

I scoff. "'Domestication'? He went crazy here."

"Not as fast as he would've out there." Adrian looks toward the door that leads to the studio. "There's something about this place. It's a haven, and not just for good music. I feel safe here. Places like WVMP threaten everything Kashmir stands for. He thinks you destroyed what made Jim special."

"Do you agree?"

"Just the opposite. I've heard Jim's shows. This station brought out the best in him. He knew music inside and out. Not just the notes, but the people and the society. He could tell you the exact length of any song, the day the record was printed and how many copies, which recording label executives pushed it, which stations supported it. All that knowledge died with him two weeks ago."

Shane shifts his stance as if to step back, but stays where he is. "I didn't kill Jim the DJ or Jim the musical historian. I killed Jim the monster, who would've killed me and Ciara and maybe even you one day."

"I know." Adrian slumps forward, elbows on his knees and face in his hands. "Vampires are supposed to live forever. What good is this kind of forever? We fade and go crazy, and people pity or fear us, and then they kill us so we don't kill them. If I'd known what a curse this was, I would've said no."

"They would've turned you anyway." Regina twists her chain-link bracelet. "Jim never cared about what anyone else wanted, only what made him happy for a brief moment before he lost interest and moved on to something else."

I force my mind back to the fact-finding mission. It's a solace amid all this death and doom. "How did you end up back with Kashmir?"

"He wrote to me in Albuquerque a few months ago saying Jim was in custody and did I want to help break him out before the Control killed him? Of course I came."

"But before you guys sprang Jim, Kashmir set the bomb under the Smoking Pig to try to kill us. How did he pull that off?"

"It was in an empty keg. The bartender had left it outside for pickup. Kashmir stole it, inserted the bomb, then snuck it back into the basement dressed as a beer delivery guy."

"Do we want to know what happened to the real beer delivery guy?"

"He's one of Kashmir's donors now."

At least he's still alive.

Adrian continues. "Kashmir didn't tell me until half an hour before the bomb was meant to go off. I managed to get away to phone the police in time."

I watch him carefully as I utter the next sentence. "You probably saved Franklin's life."

Adrian's shoulders droop at the sound of the name.

"Was that real?" I ask him.

"Franklin was part of what changed my mind about the station. But I expect he'll hate me now."

"He should. With me you get points for coming forward and confessing, but all Franklin will see are the lies you told him and the way you made him feel." Anger boils inside me at the thought of Franklin's imminent hurt. "After what he went through with Aaron, he was finally starting to live again." My voice catches, which fills me with even more rage. I want to pummel Adrian's face until his perfect nose is pointed sideways. "And now you're some kind of scummy double agent."

"I thought I was being neutral. I thought that was the path to peace. But I was wrong. I was a coward."

"So now what?"

"After what happened to Deirdre, I'm on your side all the way."

"Why should we believe you?"

"You shouldn't. If you want, you can follow me everywhere, monitor all my phone calls. I'll only tell him what you want me to tell him."

"Kashmir trusts you?"

Adrian considers this for a moment. "No, but he needs me. I'm his only connection to you, now that he's gotten rid of Deirdre."

"You can tell us where to find him? How to get rid of him?"

"On one condition: you don't kill him." Adrian puts a hand to his chest. "I don't know if I'd survive having my other maker die so soon after the first. Not sure if any of us would. So, by killing him, you might kill ten of us, maybe more."

I think of Franklin. He'll break up with Adrian the moment he finds out the truth, yet it would still hurt him to see the death of another man he cares about.

"We can't promise not to kill him," Shane says. "But I'll let the Control know that they should use nonlethal methods when possible. If you cooperate with them fully, they'll protect you."

"Thank you." He puts his hands on the chair's armrests and stands slowly.

Shane steps in front of him. "Where are you going?"

Adrian has the look of a man on his way to the gallows. "To tell Franklin what I really am."

21

Our House

When informed of this latest development, the Control lends us resources we could never get on our own.

First they procure the 911 tapes from Halloween to confirm that it was in fact Adrian who called in the warning. Though the Control is a secret agency, they work with law enforcement at all levels in every nation. Local cops think they're with the FBI or Department of Homeland Security, and the top officials at those agencies are happy to "confirm" their identities.

The fact that Adrian warned us about the bombing doesn't prove he's on our side. It may have been part of the plan all along. Maybe no one was meant to be killed at the Smoking Pig.

He still has to prove himself to us, and that means putting the Magnificent Seven into our hands. Deirdre said that it was Kashmir and three others who had kidnapped her, so the other three must be somewhere else—somewhere they can be taken before Kashmir can return to town tonight.

But where? They don't carry cell phones, so it's not

as if Adrian can just ring them up and be like, "Hey, man, where you guys hangin' today?" He's called every motel they've stayed at since arriving in Sherwood, with no luck. Teams of human Control Enforcement agents turn up nothing.

By midafternoon, Shane insists I get some sleep. Every time I close my eyes, I see Deirdre burning from the inside out, her beautiful skin turning to flames, then ash. I stare at Shane's bedroom ceiling, putting myself in her place, playing out alternative scenarios to avert that fate. But with so many captors, how could she have escaped or resisted? They all came for her, and then three took her away, so she had no chance to—

Suddenly it hits me. I sit up in bed. "Duh!"

Out in the lounge, I find Shane going over the layout of Crosetti's Monuments with Captains Fox and Henley, in preparation for Monday's memorial service. Spencer and Noah are watching the four security-camera monitors mounted on the wall. Adrian sits at the other end of the table, talking to Agent Rosso.

"Any news?" I ask them.

"None good, I'm afraid," Captain Henley says in his clipped British accent. "Ms. Falk's phone burned before it could give us its location. So we've no idea where Kashmir and Billy and the other two have gone to ground, only that it's within a three-hour radius of Sherwood."

"That's based on the time stamps of the messages she left on my cell phone," Shane says. "But she didn't give us much more to go on."

Elijah scoffs. "Yeah, 'on a hill near power lines and maple trees' doesn't exactly narrow it down."

I hate when clues add up to nothing. Why can't real

life be more like TV? "So now we wait for them to come to us?"

"It seems unlikely they'd attack the station now," Captain Henley says. "They know we know they're coming."

"But you can't just leave us here unprotected."

"We won't." He adds under his breath, "Not for the next few days, at least."

Great. Kashmir only has to wait for the Control's budget on Operation Rock-and-Roll-Can-Never-Die to run out.

"I think I know where the others might be," I tell them, "the ones who didn't go with Kashmir. Deirdre's house is their last known location. She had a safe room there, the storeroom under the stairs."

Agent Rosso plops the lounge phone's cordless handset in front of Adrian. "Call the house. Remember, it oughta sound like you're doing it in secret. Everyone else, complete silence." He distributes a warning glare that he's clearly been practicing for years.

I sit on the sofa so I don't fidget. The rest of the room goes totally still.

Adrian dials, then gets up suddenly and starts to pace. That's good—it'll help him sound nervous and maybe cover up any of our own noises.

He stops. "Bonnie, it's Adrian." He gives us a thumbs-up and speaks to her in a loud whisper. "I've been looking everywhere for you guys!"

"How'd you know we were here?" asks a woman with a high-pitched voice. "Is Deirdre with you?"

"Bonnie, Deirdre's dead. Kashmir left her to burn in the sun."

"What?" she shrieks. "He said they were taking her to a safe place. Why did they kill her? And how do you know?"

"She called Shane here while she was dying. I heard it all."

"Oh my God." She sobs. "Are you okay?"

"No, I'm scared to death. You should be, too. Any of us could be next."

"Why would he kill her? She's our sister."

"She told Shane about Kashmir and all of you guys—that you were out to kill him and Ciara. She even told them about Thanksgiving."

"Ugh, fledgling bitch! But still, she didn't deserve to die. Not quickly, anyway."

I curl my lip at Bonnie's words.

"Are you at the station now?" she asks Adrian.

"Yeah, I'm in my room. They've got Control agents swarming all over, but not our apartment."

"I wish you were here. It sucks, three of us in her teeny little storeroom. Wesley and Oscar both snore. By the way, Kashmir wants to move again."

"Where?" Adrian asks.

"I don't know. Not far. We have to stick around for Jim's wake Monday night and the bloodbath we're having in his honor."

"Have Kashmir call me when he gets in. I want to talk to him about Deirdre."

"A little advice, Adrian? Kashmir's had it up to here with your lectures. You better watch out, or you'll be the next one greeting the sunrise."

She hangs up, and Adrian slowly puts down the phone.

"Either she's a really good actor," I tell him, "or they don't suspect your loyalty."

"Didn't you hear what she just said?"

"You don't threaten someone you're about to off," Shane says. "It scares them away, sends them running into the arms of your enemy."

Elijah picks up the phone. "I'll call in their location. We'll have a team there at sunset to take them into custody."

"But no one dies, right?" Adrian asks Elijah.

"They'll wait until after dark, then go in, holy-water pistols a-blazin'."

"Wait," Shane says. "If the Control takes out three of the Magnificent Seven, that still leaves Kashmir and the other three on the loose. And Adrian's cover'll be blown. They'll know he ratted them out."

"Good point." Elijah starts to dial. "I'll tell them to keep one vampire at Deirdre's to answer the phone in case Kashmir calls and gives a rendezvous point. But since they don't carry cell phones, they'll probably just show up, straight into our arms. Bada bing, bada boom."

I wish I shared his optimism, though I'm sure much of it is a façade.

To occupy my mind until sunset, I ask Jeremy to help me finish addressing and stamping our wedding invitations, since David made Lori stay at home today with a Control bodyguard stationed outside. This simple task feels irresistibly bold. It asserts that *yes, we will be alive on Monday to mail these things*. And alive next month to get married.

We sit on opposite sides of my desk. David's in his office with the door open. Behind Jeremy, Franklin's door is closed and locked, the way it's been ever since he found out the truth about Adrian.

Jeremy picks up a fresh sheet of violet-adorned "Love" stamps. "My girlfriend Lea went to a bridal shower last weekend. When they walked in, the guests had envelopes on their plates. Turned out to be the bride's thank-you notes for them to write their addresses on, so she wouldn't have to do it herself."

"I'm an etiquette idiot, and even I know you have to address everything yourself. I would've written inside: 'Dear Ciara, Thank you for the blank. What a blank gift! It will come in handy when we blank.'"

"Like Mad Libs. You could even fill in the part of speech. Noun here, adjective here, verb here."

"I would. I'm courteous that way."

Jeremy picks up the next envelope and stops. "I guess we don't need a stamp for this one." He puts it in front of me. *Deirdre Falk.* "You invited your fiancé's former blood-donor-slash-lover to your wedding?"

"We needed to fill the vampire side of the church. Shane's Irish-Catholic, so his human family is huge."

He takes the invitation and traces the outline of her name. "I can't believe she's dead."

"Sorry." I put my hand on his arm. His dreams of being a vampire died with her. "I know you had a bond with Deirdre. You saved her life."

He sets the invitation aside and picks up the next. "I hadn't decided yet whether I wanted her to turn me. After you and Shane left last night, I thought about it for a long time."

"It's a scary thing to have to plan." I should know.

"In college I worked on a suicide hotline. They told us to ask the callers if they'd figured out how they would kill themselves."

"You'd just ask them straight out?"

"Yeah, they're used to everyone in their life beating around the bush about it. People worry that if they say the word 'suicide,' it'll make it real. It'll make it happen."

"Like saying 'Beetlejuice' three times makes Michael Keaton appear in wacky makeup."

Jeremy blinks. "Kinda. Anyway, on the hotline we knew it was serious if the caller had a method in mind. I guess at that point it becomes about more than just wanting to escape life. It becomes about wanting to die."

I think of Shane before Regina turned him. He wanted eternal death, and instead she gave him eternal life. "What about you? Are you making plans?"

"I've got those blackout curtains in my apartment."

"But you need them to do your job. You work the night shift."

"I know which song I want playing when I die: 'Asleep' by the Smiths. I've told Shane and Regina."

Sometimes he reminds me a bit of that band's lead singer, Morrissey. But to say that would encourage his fantasy.

"What about Lea?"

He raises an eyebrow. "I like Lea, but I'm not ready to make life-or-death decisions based on her."

I go to the next address on the list, for one of Shane's aunts in Ohio. "I don't think Deirdre would've been a very good maker. You should stay away from anyone with Jim's blood in them."

"You're probably right." He peels off another stamp from the sheet. "You'd be a good—"

"Nooooo, la la la la la, can't hear you!" I put my hands over my ears and sing "Mary Had a Little Lamb" off-key at the top of my lungs until Jeremy throws up his hands in surrender.

"Okay, okay, sorry. You'd be a terrible maker."

"Thank you. Can I get that in writing, with your signature?"

"Yeah, but I get to sign it in blood."

The station phone rings. I reach to answer it, then notice it's an internal call from the lounge to Franklin's office. It rings five times before he answers it. With my sensitive hearing I can usually pick up on his every word, even with the door closed, but his side of the conversation is nothing but a series of monosyllabic grunts.

Then a roared "NO!" and he slams down the receiver. Ten seconds later, the phone rings again. Franklin yanks open his door, pulling on his coat.

I stand up. "Franklin, can I—"

"No." He heads for the front door, then stops and looks at me, realizing he can't open it. "Fucking vampires." He pulls his coat shut like it's a suit of armor, then tromps down the stairs. I hear doors slam, and in less than a minute Franklin's car outside roars, squeals, and departs.

"Do you think he'll ever forgive Adrian?" Jeremy asks me.

"Should he?"

"Not until he earns it by giving us Kashmir's head on a platter. Of course, it wouldn't stay on the platter, since vampires' heads get sucked back into . . ." His voice trails off as he looks at me. "Sorry."

I shrug as I sit behind my desk again. "That's reality."

"You think vampires feel it when their bodies go through the hole?"

I think of Jim folding into himself. "I hope not."

"Maybe it's better to burn, like Deirdre."

"That didn't sound too fun, either. It took longer than I thought it would." Her screams still echo in my memory.

"Maybe because it was indirect sunlight. I bet it'd be faster if you just jumped out into a sunny day at noon."

"Then it'd be like jumping into flames, which is fast." I think of Lori's old boyfriend Travis, who died saving me from a fire. He was gone in less than ten seconds. "Yeah, that'd be the way to go."

"Guys?" David calls from his office. "Can you take your morbid conversation elsewhere?"

"Sorry." I lower my voice toward Jeremy. "Expectant father."

"We need to talk about your wedding video, anyway. I had an idea: put a five-minute edited version on the station Web site."

"That'd be great PR. The listeners will love seeing Shane in a tux. Maybe they'll even send gifts." I jot a note on a Post-it: "Add wedding registry link to WVMPradio .com." It seems silly, but these small acts of defiance remind me that *yes, goddamn it, I have a future, and no undead fashion-criminal glam rocker is taking it away from me.*

When we're finished, Jeremy and I join Shane and the other Control agents in the lounge. Monroe and Spencer are there, too, as well as Dexter, lying next to the sofa.

Shane stands, watching the security-camera monitors on the wall. Spencer and Monroe flank him, the three of them as still as cats waiting for prey.

I join them. "How's it going?"

"Uneventful, except when Regina was here. She couldn't stop counting the cars going by on that one." He points to the far right monitor, connected via satellite to a camera mounted on a tree at the end of our quarter-mile-long driveway. It was by far the most expensive part of the security system, but well worth it. The driveway is full of ruts and bumps, which means drivers have to take it slow. With the camera, we'd have more than a minute's warning if any vehicle entered our property. Assuming they came via the road.

Elijah's speaking quietly on his phone, while Henley and Rosso are drinking coffee and studying a map of Maryland power lines, no doubt trying to narrow down Kashmir's daytime location.

"You think they'll wait until Monday and come for us all?" Jeremy asks me. "Maybe they'll try to call you and Shane out by yourselves. Maybe they'll give one last warning, like a 'Surrender Dorothy' written in the sky."

Most of us offer a nervous chuckle at the *Wizard of Oz* reference. But something about the Wicked Witch of the West skywriting those words with her broomstick gives me pause.

"Was she saying, 'Surrender, Dorothy,' telling Dorothy to surrender? Or was she telling the people of Oz that they had to 'Surrender Dorothy,' meaning 'Give her up'?"

After a long silence of maximum awkwardness, Jeremy says, "I assumed it was the first."

I know the timing of this discussion is weird, yet I

can't stop myself. "But there's no comma after 'Surrender.' Right?"

"I'll do an image search." Jeremy pulls out his phone and brings up a Web browser. "You're right."

"Probably hard to skywrite a comma," Elijah says.

"It could've been done." Jeremy touches his screen to zoom in on the image. "This pic shows where the witch finished the Y in Dorothy. She was perfectly positioned to add the comma after the R."

The room takes a moment to absorb this, or maybe to figure out how to change the subject. Finally Shane speaks without looking over at me:

"What if 'Surrender Dorothy' was meant to have two meanings?"

Usually that would please me. But now it just pisses me off. It feels like my life depends on knowing which it is.

Jeremy's still examining his phone screen. "Huh. There are several bands named 'Surrender Dorothy.'"

"Folks."

Spencer speaks quietly, but his voice commands attention, as always.

"It's five twenty-one," he says. "Twilight."

Twilight. Half an hour after sunset. Wherever Kashmir and his pals are, it's safe for them to come out.

Monroe steps closer to me, our shoulders almost touching. Instinct makes me lean into him before I can stop myself. Slowly he puts a sheltering arm around my shoulder.

"We won't surrender you to no one," he says. "Not nobody, not no how."

• • •

At five thirty-four, Captain Henley's phone rings. Though we were expecting it, all of us here in the lounge jump like a firecracker just went off.

"Sir," says the voice on the other end. "Reporting in from Ms. Falk's house. We've got them."

"All three?"

"Yes, sir. Two have been taken into custody, and we're staying with the third in the event Kashmir calls."

"Good work, Beckett. Let us know the moment you hear from any of the targets or the other operatives."

He hangs up, and we let out a collective sigh of relief.

Such bright early progress, unfortunately, is no sign of how the rest of the night goes. Hours drift by. Henley checks in with Beckett, who is equally bored sitting with Bonnie at Deirdre's house. Midnight passes with not a peep from Kashmir.

Shane does his radio show at midnight, then Jeremy at three a.m. Eventually Monroe and Spencer join the other DJs back in the apartment. Shane and I keep the volume low as we watch the monitors and listen carefully for any sounds outside.

Just after five a.m. the station phone rings. My direct line.

As I answer, I take a breath to keep my voice smooth so I can pretend it's just a regular night.

"WVMP, the Lifeblood of Rock 'n' Roll. This is Ciara."

"Good evening. It's your nemesis."

Kashmir's voice pokes a hundred cold needles into my spine. "Sorry, you'll have to be more specific." I mouth Kashmir's name to Shane and the Control agents.

"I paid a visit to your apartment last night," Kashmir purrs. "Looks like I missed you."

I shiver at the thought of him lurking outside our home, and am ecstatically happy that we brought Dexter with us to the station. "You must've also missed our sign that says *Absolutely No Solicitors or Assassins.*"

He actually chuckles. "That's a good one. But before your charm completely distracts me, I should mention that we found someone there. Someone you love very much."

I run through the list of loved ones as fast as my panicky mind will allow. Lori's at her own home, and everyone else is here. Wait: Where did Franklin go?

Another voice comes on the phone. "Ciara? Sweet pea?" The woman is breathing hard and fast, making her words shake. "Are you really there?"

My own words drown in my throat as the ice in my gut rises, then melts in the hot wash of fury. *Kashmir, I will kill you.*

I force out the only comfort I can give. "I'm here, Mom."

22

Bullet with Butterfly Wings

"Who are these people?" Marjorie's voice rises and falls with her breath. "They're so strong and they move so fast, faster than I can—aaah! Oh my goodness."

I fix my gaze on Shane. "Mom, did they hurt you?"

"No, not yet. They told me they worked with you. That's why I went with them, even though I knew I shouldn't. Their eyes made me stupid."

"But why are you even here?" It's an irrelevant question, but I'm still getting a handle on this horrific new reality.

"I'm sorry, I fibbed to you about when I was being released. I wanted it to be a surprise when I showed up on your doorstep. Honey, I'm so scared."

Her words are coming almost faster than I can process them. Kashmir must have found her waiting outside my door. "Where are you now?"

"I don't know. They made me lie down in the back-seat." She lets out a sob. My hands curl into fists so hard and fast, my middle fingernail breaks.

Kashmir comes back on the phone. "So here we have

a puzzle for you to solve: how to get your mom out of here alive."

"Tell me what you want." My con-artist caginess has fled me. I'm ready to trade myself for her, no tricks or double crosses. Just life for life. "Tell me when and where. I'll come."

"We're at Crosetti's Monuments off Raleigh Avenue. But I don't—"

"I know where that is. The headstone makers." Damn it, Johnny Crosetti's a double agent, or maybe just in thrall to Kashmir. "The place with the fake graveyard out front."

"Not entirely fake, from what I'm told. As I was trying to say, I don't want you to come here. I want you and Shane to send Monroe and Regina in the next hour. Or we'll kill your mother."

In the background, Mom's voice rises high and sharp. It cuts off suddenly as Kashmir hangs up.

I take the phone slowly from my ear and look at the time on its screen: less than an hour until sunrise. Kashmir's not the only enemy we have to face.

I whisper to Shane, "Did you hear what he wants?"

He nods slowly. "I'm not giving up our makers."

Luckily they're not in the room to protest. "What do we do? We don't have time to send trained hostage negotiators."

"There's the Control Enforcement team at Deirdre's house."

"If they bust in there, he'll kill my mom. Humans can't be quiet enough."

"We'll go," says a deep voice behind me.

I turn to see Elijah standing with Henley and Rosso.

"I'm coming with you," Shane says, grabbing a stake from the table.

"Me, too." I go to grab a stake and realize there are none left.

"No way," Elijah says. "McAllister, you're suspended, not to mention unqualified for this kind of operation. Griffin, you're not even Enforcement-trained."

"But this is my mom!"

"Which makes it an even worse idea for you to go," Henley offers. "You're too emotionally entangled."

"The three of you against four of them, with a hostage?" Shane says. "I don't like those odds. You need us."

Elijah throws up his hands. "What part of 'unqualified' do you not get, boy? You're not trained in these tactics."

"What if we don't go as Control agents?" I take the stake out of Shane's hand and lay it back on the table. "What if we go as us? We walk through the front door and offer ourselves as ransom. While he's distracted, you rescue my mom."

Elijah shakes his head. "What makes you think he won't up and kill your stupid asses in one second?"

"The fact that he hates us." I look up at Shane. "He'll want to hurt us first, especially since he can't do it by killing Monroe and Regina."

Captain Henley widens his stance, arms crossed. "I don't like it. Not at all."

"Dammit, we're running out of time!" Shane grabs his phone and car keys from the side table. "Let's quit jaggin' around and get moving. You can fire us if you want, but we're saving her mom. This is the best plan we have right now, and you know it."

The taciturn Agent Rosso finally speaks. "Sirs, they're correct. The more we talk, the more time slips away. There's a human life to save."

"Yeah, well, no one asked your opinion." Elijah pulls on his uniform jacket. "Even if it's the right one. Let's go."

The three of them walk out the door into the back corridor. Elijah sticks his head back in the doorway. "I said, let's go!"

Shane and I drive in my car, while the Enforcement agents take off in their own. Jeremy and Noah keep an eye on the monitors and promise to call if they see anyone following us away from the station. But we get no phone call.

Sitting in the passenger seat, I take Shane's hand. "Want to hear something funny? I'm more afraid of the sun than I am of Kashmir."

"With any luck the Enforcement guys will kill Kashmir and the Not-So-Magnificent Three, and then we can all stay in the room below Crosetti's for the day." He squeezes my hand. "I'm glad we didn't tell our makers that they're the ones Kashmir wants. They would've wanted to go in our places."

"Monroe would. Not sure about Regina."

He lets out a soft guffaw. "She would, too."

"In a heartbeat?" I ask him, calling back to his own declaration.

Shane tilts his head, considering. "Maybe two or three heartbeats."

We review the plan once more. Shane and I will enter unarmed through the front door, ostensibly surrendering. Adrian said their weapons are few and unsophisticated: no crossbows, only a stake or two among them. With their strength, they don't need weapons. Any of them could probably rip off our heads in a split second. We'll need every minute of our hand-to-hand combat training, if it comes to that.

The X factor is Mr. Crosetti. If he's in thrall to Kashmir, he might fight on their side. Or maybe he just gave them the keys and went home, deciding to look the other way and figuring any blood spilled would flow from dead vampires, which are self-cleaning.

As we wait at the light to turn left on the road to Crosetti's, Shane simply says, "I love you." The finality in his voice snaps my heart in two.

"Don't tell me that now. It sounds too much like good-bye."

His silence says, *Maybe it is good-bye.*

We pull into the parking lot, where the white concrete glows a deep violet, reflecting the sky above. I check my watch again. Half an hour until morning twilight. It's a ten-minute drive back to the station, so unless we can solve this problem quickly, we'll be staying here tonight.

We get out of the car and the yellow porch light pops on. As Shane steps in front of me, I take his arm. "I love you, too."

He stops, turns, then brings his mouth to mine. Our kiss is hard, brief, and open-eyed.

The front door creaks. "You forgot a someone or two."

Kashmir stands with arms spanning the doorway, the top of which nearly brushes the crown of his head. Though the porch light is the gold of the supposedly bug-free variety, no warmth touches Kashmir's visage. His hair is an unbroken waterfall of black flowing just past his shoulders and covering his forehead with perfectly straight bangs. His sharp cheekbones seem to slice the air around him. From here I can barely see the holy-water scar Deirdre spoke of. It truly is the size of a teardrop.

In almost brutal contrast to his ink-black tresses, his body is clothed in an all-white suit, not unlike the famous Elvis-in-Vegas outfit. But it lacks adornment, so with his height and slimness he doesn't appear ridiculous. Stick a pair of wings on his back and he'd look like a fallen angel still using heaven's wardrobe.

"I asked you to send your makers. I asked rather nicely, if I recall."

"Ciara?" comes Marjorie's voice behind him. "Ciara, are you there?"

Perfect, Mom. Make tons of noise so they don't hear the Control agents who pulled to the side of the road a half mile away and are hopefully booking it over here right now.

"I'm here, Mom!" I want to say something soothing, but I'm afraid it'll work too well and she'll quiet. "It's me they want, not you."

"You can't have her, you fucking bastards!"

I've never heard my mother say so much as "hell." I guess prison has changed her more than I thought.

Despite her yelling, Kashmir's gaze doesn't shift from our faces. It's as if we're the only three people in the world.

Mom's protest pitches up, then muffles, as if she's been gagged. Damn it.

"Shane's here, too, Mom," I tell her. "He won't let them hurt me, and he won't let them hurt you."

"That's right," Shane says. "We're here to get everyone out safely."

She says something that sounds like "I'm sorry" but without consonants.

"Have you showed her your fangs yet?" I ask Kashmir softly.

He shakes his head. "Not necessary. All I needed to convince her to get in the car were these." He points to his amber-colored eyes. Even on me, a fellow vampire, they have a mesmerizing effect. I focus on the bridge of his nose instead.

"Please, come in." He steps back, bowing slightly.

We stride down the walk, passing sample headstones of every size, shape, and shade, all engraved with MILLER (the most common surname in this county, on account of all the mills). We're too close to the small brick building now to see if Captains Fox and Henley and Agent Rosso have arrived. We'll have to trust them.

Shane crosses the threshold first, stopping to check for an ambush behind the door. But everyone's inside: Kashmir, Billy, Bruce, and Leon.

And my mom, gagged and bound to a chair by her arms and ankles.

I run toward her. I can't help it.

Kashmir grabs me by the throat, in a movement so deft, it was as if he were picking up a saltshaker. He swings me backward, into Billy's arms. Bruce and Leon seize Shane, and just like that, Kashmir and the Magnificent Seven Minus Four have three hostages.

This is part of the plan, I remind myself. I force my breath to stay steady.

But that breath brings one distinct scent that floods my brain and sears my veins.

Blood.

Not from my mother, though the rope is scraping her ankles. This is from a wound that must have flowed like a waterfall. It's all over Billy behind me—his mouth and neck.

In the far corner of the shop lies a shadow. A hand pokes out of the shadow, palm up, fingers curled limply. As my eyes adjust, I see a dark-haired middle-aged human man. A mustache, a checkered shirt.

Johnny Crosetti.

Billy killed him in front of my mother. By the pool spread around Crosetti, already drying, it looks like he did it by tearing out his throat.

"Mom, I'm sorry."

"She didn't know about vampires, did she?" Kashmir goes to the worktable to her left, where a large stone slab is sitting faceup. "Shame she had to find out this way."

"Why'd you have to kill him?"

"Once he let us in and showed us how to work the equipment, we didn't need him anymore. With him here, it was too many people to keep track of. A tactical risk." He smiles past me. "Besides, Billy was thirsty."

Billy chuckles into my hair. It tickles and makes me want to shove an elbow through his solar plexus. But it's too soon to start a fight.

Shane speaks first. "Jim was my friend, too. I didn't want to kill him. I had to."

"You don't know anything about Jim." Kashmir caresses the smooth granite slab. I strain to see the name engraved on it.

JAMES ESPOSITO, JR. Below his name are three dates: his birth, his turning, and his final death.

Kashmir's face is reflected in the shining gray stone, but the dark mottled surface of the slab erases the reflection of his teardrop scar, as if it doesn't exist in more than one reality. "Did you know that graphite and diamonds are chemically identical?" he asks me.

"Graphite is like coal, right?" I remember the line from that '80s movie *Ferris Bueller's Day Off*, something about Cameron, one of the characters, being "so tight, if you shoved a lump of coal up his ass, in two weeks you'd have a diamond." Shane is probably thinking the same thing, since it's one of his favorite movies, and *why am I thinking about this now?* The vampiric compulsions are not serving me well at the moment.

"The word 'graphite' comes from the Latin *graph*, meaning to draw," Kashmir continues. "These days, only four percent of graphite is used to make the thing we draw with most." He slides open a shallow drawer in the small table nearby and pulls out . . .

. . . a single, sharpened pencil.

"Funny thing about graphite. It's so very soft. To keep it in one piece, it must be encased in wood." He gazes at the tip in wonder, eyes softening. "Such a simple implement, to cause so much pain. Shane McAllister, did you ever wonder why wood through the heart can kill a vampire?"

Shane remains still and silent, held tight by his two captors. Only his chest rises and falls with his steady, rapid breath.

Finally he says, "It's life. Literally."

Kashmir blinks slowly. "That's my guess as well.

When our hearts are pierced by life, they cry out in joy, recognizing all they've lost. And a moment later the wood leaves us, and our hearts shriek. We turn inside out with sorrow. But for that one beautiful moment"—he taps the pencil point against his own chest—"our hearts are home."

He's dropped the Big Bad Villain façade and looks like any other sad, vulnerable young man who's lost the most important person in the world.

"But Jim didn't have that beauty for just one moment. Six months he lived with wood inside him. It was agony, he said in his letters. Every time his heart beat, he'd feel the press of the earth's life."

His words weave a sticky web of melancholy around my mind, like an early Leonard Cohen album played on repeat.

"One other thing you don't know." Kashmir turns the pencil over and over in his fingers. "That life and pain in his heart changed him. It changed him for good."

23

No Sunlight

A chill runs over my entire body, like someone's drawing a chalk outline around my corpse. "'Changed him'?"

"Not metaphysically. It's not as if he became alive and human again. But it made him what you would call a better man."

"What are you talking about?" Shane says, low and threatening. The vampires holding him tighten their grips.

"Adrian told me you wondered how Jim escaped a maximum-security facility. You thought someone in the Control must have helped us get him out. Adrian didn't have the heart to tell you the truth." Kashmir twirls the pencil among his fingers as he speaks, faster and faster. "Jim was still in custody as punishment for what he'd done to you, Ciara. But he was making progress. He'd earned his way to minimum security. Breaking him out was a piece of cake."

"Are you saying Jim was being rehabilitated? That when he got out, he wasn't coming for us?"

"Oh, he was coming for you, all right. To make

amends." He says the last word with a curl in his lips. "Rather weak of him, if you ask me. Between your stupid radio station and his time with the Control, he'd become a shadow of himself. But your boyfriend didn't save you by killing Jim. He didn't save anything at all."

His eyes slide over to meet Shane's, and they share a long look of grief. Then Kashmir's harden to flint. In a flash he flings the pencil across the room. My strangled shriek mixes with my mom's.

Shane gapes down at his chest, where the pencil protrudes just below his collarbone. Too high.

Kashmir opens the drawer wider and withdraws an entire handful of pencils. "Maybe I'll take better aim this time." He throws another pencil, plunging the orange spear two inches deep into the flesh near Shane's armpit. "Or the next."

Shane grunts as each pencil strikes his chest. When it's all over, they form a heart-shaped ring around his heart. From here I can't tell if any struck home.

Kashmir turns to the wide, empty table beside him, its surface made of metal rollers instead of flat wood. A blue steel beam arches over the table, leaving a clearance of at least a foot, enough room for a headstone to lie underneath. An object extends from the beam, covered by a dust-resistant tarp.

"As I was saying before, graphite is soft, a one or a two on the hardness scale. But its chemical twin, the diamond, is a ten. Diamonds are the only stone that can cut every other stone." He switches on a work light above the machine, then gently takes off the cover to reveal what looks like a rotary saw. The teeth of its blade glisten in the light. "Diamond can cut granite, marble, slate.

Even vampire flesh, which sometimes feels as tough as stone."

He reaches for the machine's switch. The blade shrieks to life. Kashmir grips the handle and looks at my mother.

"No!" I slam my heel into Billy's shin and twist my body. He curses in pain, almost letting go. To my left, my mother screams, and to my right, Shane shouts and curses, held tight by Bruce and Leon.

Billy secures his grip again and walks me forward toward Kashmir. He forces me to my knees in front of the table, then grasps my wrist and extends my right arm. I gasp with relief when I realize it's me who'll get cut and not Mom, and it'll be my hand instead of my head. For now, at least.

Kashmir takes my hand in his, binding my four fingers together. "You'd be better off holding still."

"Mom, don't look!" I slam my own eyes shut as she screams.

"Noooooooooo!"

The blade is so sharp, I don't feel it sever my thumb. There's just a slight tug, then the splatter of blood on my forehead and the bridge of my nose. Shane's roar of anger turns to a gurgle as someone chokes him.

Mom shrieks and bangs her feet against the chair. Kashmir holds up my hand for her to see. A few seconds later, when my blood stops flowing and the skin heals over my wound, she goes deathly silent. There's no sound but the whir of the diamond-bladed stonecutter as she looks at my hand, then at me.

"Ciara?"

She faints, thankfully, before he starts on my other

fingers. Before my endorphin rush expends itself and the bone-rippling pain sets in. Before I start to scream.

At least we were right: he wanted to torture us first. He wouldn't give us the mercy of a quick death like Shane gave Jim last week. Though even that may not have been mercy. If Kashmir was telling the truth, Shane killed a repentant man.

Through the red haze of agony I see a shadow move over the floor of the back room. Under the shouts of Shane, I hear the click of a loaded crossbow.

Kashmir hears it, too, but too late.

An arrow whistles above my head, shot by Agent Rosso from the rear doorway. Billy seizes and shudders, then drops my arm. When he falls beside me, I yank the arrow from his chest with my left hand. I don't wait to see if he's been hit in the heart but instead launch to my feet, flinging blood over the machine and Kashmir and the wall behind him.

Elijah picks up my unconscious mother, chair and all. "Come on, Griffin."

Kashmir jumps between us, but Elijah shoves him away with the legs of Mom's chair. Her limbs flop at the impact, but she seems otherwise unharmed.

Henley has reached Shane already, and the two of them are fighting with Bruce and Leon.

"Griffin, move out!" Agent Rosso holds Kashmir at bay with a holy-water pistol. "You and Fox take your mom. We'll follow!"

I can't bear to leave Shane, but Kashmir's severed all but my pinky from my right hand. I can't hold a weapon, much less throw a punch.

I lurch out the door after Elijah, then pass him on

the walkway, leaping over headstones like hurdles so I can get to the car first and open the back door for him.

Somehow he angles Mom's chair to fit her in. The sky is getting scary light now.

I point to it with my intact left hand. "What do we do?"

He checks his watch as he opens the driver's-side door. "Plenty of time to get to the station. Too dangerous to stay here."

We climb into the car, which still has the keys in the ignition, and peel out of the parking lot. I feel like I'm leaving my own heart behind with Shane, but we have to save my mom.

I watch Crosetti's Monuments disappear in my side-view mirror, then awkwardly pull my cell phone out of my right jacket pocket with my left hand. "Come on, baby. Call me."

"He will."

"If he's alive."

"Henley and Rosso got it in hand. Speaking of which . . ." He nods at the bloody mess at the end of my right wrist. "How's that feel?"

"Better than it did a few minutes ago, when I thought I'd lose all ten." The adrenaline surge is starting to fade, and the chills are beginning. "I guess you know how it feels, after that zombie ripped your arm off."

My mother moans in the backseat, tipped over on her side. I probably shouldn't have mentioned that in front of her.

"Mom, just hang in there. We'll untie you when we get to the station."

"Are you okay, honey?"

"I'm fine. Ish. Fine-ish." I wipe as much blood as I can from my hand, but smearing it on my jeans doesn't help my claims of fine-ishness.

Just as our car turns onto the long gravel driveway to the station, my phone rings. Shane's number.

Please be him and not Kashmir calling to gloat over his death. "Shane?"

"We made it."

"Oh, thank God." I put the phone to my chest and yell at Elijah. "Slow down! If you go too fast on this driveway, you'll break the car and we'll be stuck."

"Okay, okay."

I put the phone back to my ear. "All three of you are safe?"

"Yeah," Shane pants. "But dammit, we were only able to stake Bruce. Kashmir and Leon got away with Billy. It looked like his wound wasn't fatal."

"What about yours? The pencils in your chest?"

"Gone. Hurt like a motherfucker, but they all missed. On purpose, I guess. Anyway, I gotta drive. I'll see you in a minute."

We hang up. After a moment of no sound but the gravel banging on the undercarriage and the squeak of shock absorbers, my mother says one word softly.

"Surprise."

A few minutes later, we're safely indoors with my mother untied. David's applying an ice pack to her swollen, bruised ankle, while Monroe wraps my disaster of a hand with a bandage. Regina's pacing by the front door, muttering, "Drive faster, Shane."

I wonder how many months or years it'll take for my fingers to grow back. At least they left me the hand that holds my engagement ring, and someday soon a wedding band. Assuming Shane survives the next ten minutes.

"Will someone please tell me what's going on?" Marjorie yells.

"Mom, I promise I'll explain everything once we get past this. But the short version is, everyone in this room except David is a vampire, including me."

Her jaw looks permanently agape. "Which one is David again?"

The door to the lounge jerks open and Elijah pounds up the stairs. "No sign of Shane and the others on the security camera."

My heart lurches. "They should've pulled into the driveway by now." I jerk my hand out of Monroe's and rush for the door.

"They're not answering their phones," Elijah says as he follows. "Unless it's a cloudy day, they're—"

I turn the key and yank open the door. The sky is perfectly clear, a gorgeous azure blue.

I finish Elijah's sentence in my head. *They're screwed.*

He puts his hand on my shoulder. "They still got time. And they can take that driveway faster than we could. Control cars got cop shocks, cop suspension, cop—"

"Shut that door!" David orders. "Five minutes to twilight. I want all vampires downstairs now." He strides out of his office with a three-foot-high stack of dark material in his arms. "Elijah, send Jeremy up. We'll use these blackout curtains to get Shane and the agents into the station when they pull up. The car'll shelter them a little. They'll still burn, but not as fast."

"There's only two humans in the station right now, and three vampires that need covering." I curse Franklin for running away.

"*I'm* human," my mom says.

"You can't walk on that ankle, much less leap on a burning vampire." My voice crushes the last two words, thinking of them describing Shane.

"I'll do it."

Adrian's standing at the top of the stairs to the lounge. He looks like he means it. Would he really sacrifice his life?

"If you want to help," I tell him, "carry my mom downstairs and . . . take care of her."

His eyes tell me he catches my meaning: *Console her if I die.*

While Adrian carries away my protesting mother, Regina comes to stand behind me at the door. I still haven't closed it, despite David's order. It feels too final.

"I want you to know," she whispers, "I will knock you unconscious to keep you from killing yourself."

"Shane's not yours to save anymore."

"I'm his maker. He'll always be mine." She looks out into the front yard, where the gravel reflects the pale blue glow of the lightening sky. "I'd last longer than you in the sun."

"Maybe five seconds longer."

"Maybe that's all we need."

"I can't believe we're having this discussion."

"You're not." Monroe steps between us. "Shane made me promise not to let anyone else get hurt, not even to save him. So get yourselves down into that lounge right now. Or I will carry you."

Regina juts out her bottom lip. "I could take you if I wanted," she grumbles as she obeys.

I start to follow her, then wait with Monroe at the top of the stairs until she disappears. "You're lying," I whisper to him. "You didn't promise Shane anything. You're just saying that to protect us."

"Maybe." He opens his arm to gesture to the stairs. "Go on."

I shake my head slowly. "Promise you won't stop me."

He takes a deep sigh and closes his eyes. "In all my years as a vampire, I ain't never had no one like you and Shane have each other. I can't take that away from nobody."

I put my hand on his arm. "If I burn, you'll feel the pain. I'm sorry."

He places his hand over mine. "I'll be all right. You do what you gotta do."

Shouting comes from the lounge. Jeremy opens the door and runs up the stairs. "Some guys blocked off the Control agents' car at the end of the driveway. Shane and them got away, but they have to make a run for it."

I put my hands to the sides of my head. Now they don't even have the car to protect them. Now there's nothing but the trees on either side of the driveway, with their leaves nearly gone. And once they get near the station, the trees end and the last hundred yards are in the wide-open clearing.

Jeremy tugs my arm. "What can I do to help?"

"Get a blackout curtain from David. You're saving a vampire from the sun."

My phone rings again. It's Shane.

"Ciara!" His voice is being forced out, and I hear

the pounding of feet. "They cut us off at the top of the driveway."

"I know." I look at the clock: 6:33 a.m. One minute past twilight. They must already be heating up inside. "Come to the front door—and don't talk, just run!"

His breath comes fast, from fear, not exertion. "Ciara . . . if I don't make it—"

"You will! Now shut up and run."

"I love you. I love you so much."

"Hang up and run!"

"Okay."

Except he doesn't hang up. Maybe his finger missed the End Call button. But I can still hear his feet strike the gravel, and I can hear his labored breath.

Then I hear his screams.

I shove the phone into Monroe's chest. "Go downstairs. No vampire follows me."

I don't wait for his response. I grab the extra blackout curtain from David's hands, pull the key from my pocket, and dash for the exit before anyone can stop me.

The moment I open the door, the pale morning light singes me from the inside out.

I don't care, because three flaming figures are running toward me. Shane is burning. Dying.

I leap. Hoping to save him, but ready to join him.

24

Follow You Down

Our bodies meet in flame. I feel Shane's disintegration, his agony, as much as my own. The blackout curtain is a useless shield against such heat. We burn beneath it, flesh becoming ash and smoke.

Shane groans, his mouth too melted to form words. I hold him close and tell him it's okay.

My last thought is: *I'll never live without him.*

25

Into the Mystic

It's dark here. Not a tunnel, like when I died before. This darkness is a shapeless void that stretches forever.

But I'm not alone. Shane's here. I can't feel my hand—or any other part of me—but I know he's holding it.

Was Shane right when he said he'd never be allowed into the light because he'd once asked for death? If I can move into the light without him, will I?

No. I'd rather spend an eternity in darkness with him than in the light with the rest of the universe. I won't let him be alone.

I love you, I try thinking at him.

I get a warm feeling in return, wordless but unmistakable.

A white light appears in the distance, a pinprick in black velvet, just like when I died before. It comes closer, and I can feel Shane's wonder and disbelief and resistance. He thinks the light's coming only for me.

I won't let it.

This man and I are a package deal. Take me and you get him, too.

I imagine my soul wrapping itself around his until it's as if the boundaries between us never existed. Like Shane has never been Shane and I have never been me. We've only ever been us.

As the light moves closer, the surrounding darkness sinks into me until I feel nothing but . . . nothing. I claw and clamber at the void, wishing for pain, anguish, anything to make me feel alive again.

That's when I realize: Shane is gone.

The light comes faster. I try to run away, search the darkness for him.

Come back! I plead. *I won't go without you. I died to be with you, so don't let me move on alone. Please . . .*

The light is almost upon me. It reaches out with greedy tendrils, promising peace. I push it away.

No surrender, not even to this. No surrender. The Bruce Springsteen song by that name plays in my head, but I can't remember any of the words, just the part where he and Steven Van Zandt sing, "Lay lay lay lay lay lay laaaay, lay lay lay LAY LAY."

The light hesitates, then pulls back in a great wave, like a tsunami before it crashes onto shore.

I won't go without him. Lay lay lay lay lay lay lay laaaay, lay lay lay LAY LAY.

The light shoots forward, pulling me under, drowning me in a peace I don't want.

Shane! I call out as the wave sweeps me into another realm. *I will find you. I promise.*

Heaven—or whatever this is—has changed a bit from my first brief death. Now it has furniture.

I'm in some kind of waiting room, like in a doctor's office, but there are no magazines and no receptionist pretending to file things so she doesn't have to make eye contact.

The white walls don't stand solid but rather pulse and sway like curtains. I'm made of light, too, iridescent instead of white, as is the furniture beneath me.

The entire room zigzags in different colors and at different angles to form shapes. It's like "Laser Floyd" without the Pink Floyd music.

In fact, there's no music at all. How can this be heaven?

"You can't hear the music?" rasps a familiar voice.

I turn to see a woman lying on a bed, her bare feet pointed toward me. The bed's legs are the flimsy steel of a foldout couch, but at least they're not made of light like the thing I'm sitting—

Wait. I'm not sitting on anything now. The walls have gone wispy, and the only clear thing is the bed and the woman with tawny hair. Her limbs stretch and shift like she's in pain.

She *is* in pain, as I recall.

"Hey." I walk over and sit on the mattress next to a sweaty, red-faced, pustule-marked version of myself. "You look like crap."

She stares up at me with bleary blue eyes. Blood seeps from the side of her neck. "Your highlights look amazing. New colorist?"

"No, I'm a—we're a—we were a vampire."

Human Ciara gives me a weak smile. "It worked, then."

"Sort of."

Her brows dip in confusion, but then weakness over-takes her and she lets her eyes close. I realize that I *can* hear music now, soft as if it's coming from a distance. It's Shane on the guitar. But no words, only the chords of Luka Bloom's "Ciara," the song he played as I died. I look past the bed for Shane or Spencer or anyone else who was in the room at the time, but the bed meets the mist of the white wall a few feet away.

Her breathing turns shallow and pained, like the air is full of daggers. "Now what?"

"No clue. Have you seen Shane? We sort of came here together, but I lost him."

She nods without opening her eyes. "He's right here."

The mist on one side dissolves into another room ad-joining this one. It's darker there, and instead of "Ciara" a desolate old Cure tune is playing. An empty bottle of whiskey sits on the nightstand.

Shane lies on his back, eyes vacant. Blood soaks the pillow and sheets.

I utter his name and crawl over Human Ciara's body to enter the other room.

"Take me with you," she says.

I stop, one hand in his world and the rest of me in hers. "Fine, come on." I reach back my other hand.

With her fingers an inch from mine, she says, "Do you know what this means?"

"Not really. I'm fumbling my way through and hop-ing for the best."

Human Ciara smiles. Her feverish fingers grasp mine, and she and her world disappear.

I'm on Shane's bed now, where the walls aren't misty

white but an inky black. Under the bloodstained sheet, his body is pale and so, so thin. I listen as the breath rattles in his lungs, uneven and slowing.

I reach to swipe the limp hair off his forehead, but something stops my hand. It's not time yet.

So I lie next to him, as close as I can get without touching, while the blackness presses in. The pupils in his pale-blue eyes expand with each blink.

"I don't know what I'm doing," I whisper, "but I know who I am. And I know I'm not leaving without you."

His next blink lasts an eternity, and when his lashes part, that's exactly what I see. Forever. It's dark there—the blue of his irises has been swallowed by a black mirror—but I'm not alone.

It's time.

I touch his cheek, turn his head, and bring my burning mouth to his freezing one.

The light of this world dies with us.

Before my eyes open, I hear a distant voice, more familiar and intimate than a DJ's or a lover's or even a mother's. A voice I've heard in headphones and earbuds my whole life.

Jim Morrison wants us to break on through.

It's nighttime here, and down the hill, even the stage is shrouded in darkness, broken only by the flash of camera bulbs from an invisible audience. We're at the Isle of Wight Festival, the English Woodstock of August 1970. Among the tents surrounding us, blankets are spread and bottles are strewn, but I see only one person, lying on the ground between me and Shane.

Shane kneels next to his former friend. Jim's naked body bleeds from three wounds where his arm, thigh, and neck have been bitten. No, four wounds. The blood on his mouth comes from his lower lip pierced with fangs.

But his chest is whole and clean. No stake wounds, no pencil wounds.

Where Shane's pale eyes were full of darkness, Jim's dark eyes are full of light. He's blissed-out, from drugs or music or death or all three.

But he blinks and focuses on Shane. "Hey, man." His voice is casual, like they just ran into each other at the 7-Eleven. "What's up?"

"We're dead, all of us. Like, really dead."

"Besides that, what's up?"

"I'm sorry I killed you."

Jim twitches his shoulder in a semi-shrug. "Can't say I blame you."

I kneel on his other side. "Kashmir said you rehabilitated yourself in jail. The wood stuck inside your heart made you good?" It sounds ridiculous out of my mouth.

Jim chuckles. "Babe, nothing could ever make me good. But it hurt like hell, and it made me think of all the pain I'd caused. You and Jeremy and Deirdre. Everyone." He swipes a languorous hand over his neck, looks at the blood. "Hey, whatever happened to your cousin? That blond chick?"

"Cass. She's fine, I guess. She left town when she got out of the hospital. She was pissed I didn't tell her about you killing her mom and stepdad."

"Yeah, sorry." He stares at the sky. "I probably deserve to just lie here forever."

I look around at the Isle of Wight's hills and valleys. Unlike the rooms where the dying Ciara and Shane lay, the walls of Jim's turning place appear far away, a gray mist near the English Channel. "Could be worse."

"You can stay if you want. The Who is up next. You like them."

"We can't stay." Shane is already getting to his feet. "But you can come with us."

With some effort, Jim turns his head to me. "Where are you going?"

"I don't know." I reach over his body to take Shane's hand. "But I'm going with him."

"Cool." Jim focuses on the sky beyond us. "I like it here."

I look up and gasp. The stars are every color, close enough to touch. The black velvet tapestry they dance upon rotates like a sped-up film of the night sky, with the Milky Way stretching and rippling purple and white. It's almost like being on another planet, but it doesn't need to be. This one is beautiful enough, especially through Jim's eyes.

I join Shane and lean back against his chest. Together the three of us watch the sky and listen to the Doors. It's not heaven, but it's damn close.

And it's not for us. "We have to go," I tell Shane. "Now."

"Last chance, man." Shane's voice is close to breaking. "I put you here, but she can get you out. I think."

"Nah. This is good. When I get sick of it, I'll go there." He points to the brightest part of the Milky Way's arm, where a blinding white light pulses. "If Kashmir asks, tell him everything is groovy with me."

"I doubt he'll believe us."

"Then tell him I found Lemuria. He'll know what that means."

Jim is still laughing when I take Shane's hand. But as we step away, Jim closes his eyes, stealing the light.

I am nowhere.

I am nothing.

I reach out with formless hands, call out with a silent voice, but Shane is gone.

What have I done?

I teeter on the edge of despair, doubting every choice of my life, my unlife, and both brief, foolish afterlives. It would take just one step to fall into that comforting eternity of regret.

And then I hear . . . a voice? Music?

It grows louder, until I can hear the raw, aching tones I'd recognize anywhere.

Shane is singing my song. The one he wrote for me as an engagement gift, even though vampires supposedly can't write songs, can't create anything new. He did it for me.

He's still here.

Unless it's a cruel trick. If I'm actually in hell, there'd be no worse torment than to hear my lover's voice only to lose it. I think of Orpheus, the Greek hero Lori told me about, who sang his beloved wife Eurydice out of the underworld.

Well, almost. At the last second, he disobeyed Hades's terms of release and looked back at Eurydice, either in fear or joy. She fell back into the land of death, this time for good.

I'm not Eurydice, and I don't believe in hell.

• • •

"Ciara!"

I see nothing but black. "Shane, where are you? Where are we?"

"Just follow me. This way." He starts to sing again, this time the second verse.

"How do you know?"

"I've been here before."

He continues the song, and suddenly I *see* his voice, streaming out in bright, dancing dots, guiding my way like airport runway lights at night.

But I'm falling behind. Shane is on the third verse, the one that talks about our future. He wrote it when I was still human, so it speaks of me growing old and him staying by my side until I die.

What happens if I don't find him before the end of the song? I want to call to him to wait for me, but what if that means dragging him back into the darkness? I can't do that to him. If he can find a way out without me—

"Almost there." His voice is so close now, like it's coming from inside my head. "Can you feel this?"

A hand slips around mine, warm and solid. I gasp.

"How . . ."

"I don't know. I don't know where we are, but I know one thing." Shane moves closer, and now his entire body is against mine. He pulls me into his arms. "No place without you should have the balls to call itself heaven."

I burrow my face into his chest, afraid to speak and break the spell. Soon death will part us. Nothing lasts forever, not even this.

Suddenly I feel heavy as a sandbag. I fall to my knees

(I have knees!), which meet something that feels like the ground (there's ground!). I reach down to feel dirt and a few sprigs of cold, dry grass.

If these are the Elysian fields, they've been oversold.

"Shane?"

"Shh. Do you hear that?"

I shut my mouth and listen. Voices are screaming in terror. Oh, crap, we *are* on our way to hell. Sucks that I was wrong about that.

His whisper is taut with fear. "It's coming."

"*What's* coming?"

"The sun. Ciara, get down!" Shane throws his body on top of mine as the world turns white.

26

Now We're Getting Somewhere

I scream at the searing heat on my arms and scalp and feet, the only parts Shane isn't covering. The sun must've burned out my lungs, because I can't breathe.

Is this what we have to look forward to for an eternity? Burning again and again? I promise, next time I'll stay on the Isle of Wight with the Milky Way and the Doors.

The morning sun pierces my eyes, so I shut them and wait to catch fire.

And then, I don't. The sun is warm, but only compared to the hard ground beneath me. The hard ground my hand is on. Totally not burning.

"Ciara!" Shane's voice rasps in my ear. He grabs my hand, trying to cover it. He's also not on fire.

Lori is screaming—that's who I heard in the other place. A thick black blanket is thrown over us. I cough from the heavy coating of dust.

"Your foot!" Lori yanks the blanket to cover my toes. "Ciara, Shane. Where were you? Where'd you come from?"

Shane and I stare at each other under the blanket. I can see him because one of the edges is lifted slightly, letting in the morning sun. Which, again, is not burning us.

"Where were we?" he whispers, echoing Lori's question. "And what are we?"

My body feels different yet familiar. It's the way I felt seven months ago. Warm. Weak. "Alive."

"Human?" He cups my face with one hand. "How?"

"Who cares?" I whip off the blanket, making Lori shriek. "See?"

David gapes at us, and I realize we're both naked. I pull the blanket back over us and tug it up to my armpits. Lori hands Shane one of the other blackout curtains. It wafts a strong scent of smoke.

David points to the scorched grass beneath us. "You guys went up in flames. You disappeared."

"How long were we gone?" I ask him.

"Half an hour at least."

I look at Lori's face, soaked with tears. "I'm alive."

"It's a miracle." She drops to her knees and hugs me hard. "I thought I'd lost you forever this time, but instead you're back. You're back for good."

"I thought you were at home."

"David called and told me. I came right away. So did Franklin." She tightens her grip. "Now you can have babies, too!"

"Whoa, whoa, we don't know that." I disentangle myself from her embrace and send Shane a nervous glance. But he's not looking my way.

He's looking at the world. Turning his head slowly, he sets his gaze on one mundane object after another: the Dumpster, Lori's compact sedan pasted with wet leaves, the radio tower reaching for the clear blue sky.

After six months without sunlight, I have to admit it

looks amazing—everything in full color, nothing a shade of gray.

But for Shane it's been sixteen years of night.

We stand up together, still wrapped in the curtains. I touch his hand, speak his name. He lowers his chin and gazes at me.

"Your hair," he whispers. He pulls it forward in front of my shoulder. "Look."

The sunlight glimmers on the golden strands. I have to admit, it's gorgeous. I gasp and look at my right hand. It has every finger *and* a thumb.

His eyes meet mine. "You know what I want to do? More than anything in the world?"

I give him a wicked grin. "What?"

"Eat pancakes."

I laugh long and obnoxiously loud, then throw myself into his arms. Our future just got shorter but potentially much, much sweeter.

Shane cries out in pain suddenly, dropping me. I stumble back. "What's wrong?"

Lori and David shout as he bends in half, grasping for the ground. His knees buckle and he collapses.

"Shane!" I reach for him, then feel something twist and stretch inside me. "Ow!" I put a hand to my temple.

Lori turns from Shane to me. "Ciara, you okay?"

"Yeah. Nasty headache for a few seconds." I look at David kneeling beside Shane. "What's wrong with him?"

"No idea."

I take Shane's shuddering body into my arms. He gasps and writhes, clutching at me. Did we come all the way back from death and beyond just to disintegrate in agony?

Shane stops convulsing, then goes limp in my arms for a moment, his heart pounding. He sucks in a quick, deep breath and lets out another grunt of pain.

"What's happening?" He puts a hand to his chest. "Am I dying? It feels like I'm dying."

I put my fingers under his chin and examine his face. Tiny wrinkles have formed outside each eye, and—are those gray hairs?

"Oh, wow."

"What? What's wrong with me? Am I sick?"

"No." I try not to laugh. "You're forty-two."

His grimace fades. He puts a hand to his face, then looks at his arm. All of the hair there is still light brown. No age spots, naturally, since he hasn't been in the sun in sixteen years.

"Amazing," David whispers.

"Understatement of the universe!" Lori bounces on her toes. "Not only are they not dead, they're alive." She points at me. "Next summer you'll be tan."

David gets to his feet and brushes the dust off his knees. "You should both have a physical exam, make sure everything's in working order. The Control's physicians can take care of that."

"Shit. The Control." Shane looks around. "What happened to Captain Henley and Agent Rosso?"

David shakes his head. "They didn't make it. Jeremy and I put the blankets on them, but they burned up just like you did."

Shane's face turns hard with anguish. "Son of a bitch."

"Elijah's already notified Colonel Lanham. We got the license plates off the security camera and a pretty good look at the guys who blocked your way."

Thinking of the driveway reminds me of the last time I was on it, and who I was with.

"Mom!"

I turn for the front door, tripping over the blackout curtain but regaining my balance, even with my new/old human lack of coordination.

The stairs are trickier. I let out a frustrated grunt as I lift the hem of the curtain. Finally I get to the top step.

The door opens and my mother's standing there, looking like a bedraggled angel. Her red-blond hair is mussed, and her face is streaked with mascara, making her look even worse than when she was a hostage. She's still the most beautiful thing I've ever seen.

She puts a hand to her mouth, fingertips barely touching her lower lip. "You . . ."

"Mom."

I fall into her arms, home at last.

Once we're all inside, with the door safely shut, the main office floods with joyous vampires. They were watching it all on the security monitors downstairs. They raged as we burned, then mourned after we disappeared. Most of the DJs went back to their apartment to weep and drink. Only Adrian and Franklin remained in the lounge, watching the monitors in silent vigil, though they had no reason to hope.

All six DJs gather around us now, hugging and cheering, their faces tearstained and their breath reeking of booze. I hold my elbows tight against my sides to keep my blackout curtain from falling.

Jeremy pinches the skin on my forearm. "You're

totally human." He examines Shane's face. "And you're old!"

"Gee, thanks," Shane says with a laugh.

"I mean, you're older. How the hell did this happen?"

"If we ever figure it out," Shane says, "we'll let you know. Thanks for trying to save Captain Henley."

"I'm sorry we were too late." Jeremy folds his arms and winces, and I realize they're burned, as is his neck. He still smells of smoke.

"You should go to the hospital," I tell him.

"I was just about to take him," David says, "and your mom, to get that ankle checked out."

I look at my mother's foot, which is turning a nasty shade of purple. "I want to come with you."

"Are you kidding?" she says. "Someone just tried to kill you. You're not going out in public and letting them know they failed."

She's right. I want to be out in the sunshine and go to all the places I used to go. But we have to hole up for our own safety.

I turn to Adrian. "Has Kashmir called?"

"No, but when he does, I'll tell him you're dead. Those two guys who cut you off ran after Shane and the Control agents. They may have seen you burn."

"Good," Shane says, "so he won't just be taking your word for it." He turns to the rest of them, looking like a badass Roman in his thick black toga. "As far as everyone here is concerned, Ciara and I are dead."

"We can fake tears pretty well," Regina says. "And we'll put the word out to the other vampires in the area."

"This might be outta line"—Monroe puts his hands

in his pockets—"but could we give y'all a funeral, too? Maybe with Jim's Monday night?"

My jubilation fades, replaced by something calmer and purer, as I remember Jim lying on his back at the Isle of Wight. At peace.

"That's a brilliant idea," I tell Monroe. "Did I give you some of my con-artist savvy when you made me?" I start toward him to give him a hug, but he takes a step back. Right. I *am* almost naked.

"You know what this means, though?" Shane frowns. "No going out for pancakes."

Franklin holds up a hand. "If it's pancakes you want, I can make you better ones than you'd get at IHOP."

The humans and younger vamps gasp at this hubristic claim.

"But first, Ciara, you should put some clothes on." Lori tugs my arm. "You look cold."

She's right. An odd sensation, chilliness.

"Come on." Shane nudges me. "Let's go get dressed and be where it's quiet for two minutes."

"Hang on." David looks at Regina. "Take Dexter into your room until Shane and Ciara are ready to meet him again."

My heart twists. What if our own dog doesn't recognize us? He knew me as a human not long ago, but he's never smelled this version of Shane.

One thing at a time, I tell myself. One thing at a time.

Inside Shane's room, we close the door and let our curtains fall.

No kisses, no caresses, just a long, hard embrace, as if only our arms can stop us from slipping into that other world again. I marvel at how strong Shane still is, even in mortal form.

"You wouldn't leave me," he whispers.

"Never." I turn my head so he can hear me clearly. "And you called me out of the darkness. Just like when I died before." I splay my hand on his chest. "Like Orpheus, only successful, remember? You saved me."

"You saved me first. I would've been stuck in that first void if you hadn't pulled me in."

"I didn't. The light did."

"But you convinced it, Ciara. You took me to heaven."

He bends down and kisses me. His lips feel full and soft and completely, utterly Shane. I don't know if we'll ever understand what happened, or where we were. But we're here, and we're together, and for now, that's all that matters.

That, and pancakes.

We return to the DJs' common room, where the five of them—Monroe, Spencer, Adrian, Noah, and Regina—plus Elijah are clustered near the center, speaking in hushed voices.

They fall silent at our approach. I've never felt like such a stranger to them, not even the night we first met. If I were them, I'd be freaked, now that reality is sinking in.

Surprisingly, Monroe is the first to speak. "Tell us what it was like."

We sit on the foldout sofa, which I try not to think of as the place where I died, though less than an hour ago I was sitting on it with Human Ciara 1.0.

Shane nods at me, and I start. "We burned up in the sunlight, which hurt about as much as you'd imagine. And then we—"

My voice is lost in the sudden roar coming from Regina's room. Dexter is barking his head off.

I raise my voice. "We went through a dark place, and then—"

Dexter barks louder, and now his claws are scrabbling against the door. There's a crash of glass, a yelp, then silence. Before we can react, he starts barking again as if nothing happened.

"Shit, I bet he broke my full-length mirror." Regina stalks over to her bedroom. "Might as well get this over with."

"Hold on." Elijah catches up to her. "I'll grab him while you open the door."

Too late. With a growl, Dexter slips past the former linebacker and races toward me. For a moment, terror fills my veins. I can see the monster in my pupper's eyes.

I crouch down. "Dexter, come!" It seems like a superfluous command, since he's running toward us. But maybe he'll know my voice.

Dexter slows just before he reaches me, then stops, one paw raised. He extends his neck as far as it will go, pointing his nose like a bird dog. I keep still, avoiding eye contact. "Good boy."

Another step. He sniffs my wrist, soaking it in slobber, his soft, loose jowls draping over my skin.

Dexter lifts his head, his eyes meeting mine. Then his mouth opens in a doggie smile.

My vision blurs with tears. "Come here, baby guy."

He steps forward, butting his head into my chest, the doggie version of a hug.

"That's right. Smushy Face." I resist the urge to throw my arms around him, in case he still feels threatened by my newness. He shoves his snout into my armpit, breathing deep. His tail waves slowly, then moves into full-out wag.

"Dexter."

The dog freezes at the sound of Shane's voice behind me. I wrap my hand around his leather collar as a low growl begins deep in his chest.

"It's all right, buddy." Shane kneels beside me, showing none of the caution he exhorted me to show. "It's me. It's Daddy."

Dexter backs away, whimpering. He casts anxious looks at Shane, then away, like he's shaking his head in denial.

"Come on, Dexter." Heartache bends Shane's whisper. "Don't be afraid."

Elijah steps forward with Dexter's leash. "Let me. Just in case."

I bite my lip and nod. I'm not strong enough anymore to hold on to Dexter if he goes into full attack mode because he thinks I'm being threatened.

Shane rubs his face, clearly upset at this development. Does he really smell or sound that different?

I sit at one end of the couch. Elijah sits at the other end, and Dexter lies on the floor at his feet, since that's as far as the leash will reach. Shane moves to sit beside me, and Dexter raises his head, giving a low growl as the fur rises along his spine.

"Sorry." Shane backs away toward the table.

"Maybe if you fed him," I suggest. "We have dog blood in the fridge here."

"Good idea."

Monroe stands and puts out a hand. "I'll do it."

"Thanks." Shane sits at the table. I go over to join him, and he gives me a surprised look.

"What?" I say. "You're shocked I'd choose you over a dog?"

"Over that dog? Yeah, a little. Go on. Start where you left off."

I turn to the others. "We went through a dark place. And then a light place where I saw my dying human self as I became a vampire, and Shane's dying self, and . . . Jim's dying self."

They make astonished noises of varying pitch and volume. Adrian sinks into one of the armchairs. "How was he? *Where* was he?"

"On the Isle of Wight, where his makers turned him." Shane glances at Monroe, who's heating up a serving of dog blood in the kitchen. "My guess is that when vampires die, we go back to the place we were last human."

"Oh, hell." Spencer looks horrified.

"But I think we can leave when we're ready," I tell them. "We can move on. He showed us a place in the sky. It was beautiful."

"Then why didn't you go there?" Regina asks me.

"I don't know. All I know is that we ended up in darkness again. But Shane led me out. He said he'd been there before."

Monroe comes over with a cereal bowl, which he hands to Shane. Dexter sits up quickly, nose in the air. He smells dog blood.

Elijah takes up the slack in the leash. "Go ahead, McAllister. Set it on the coffee table there."

Shane get ups and approaches Dexter slowly but casually. "Here you go, boy." He sets the bowl in front of Dexter, atop a *Guitar World* magazine.

Without blinking, the dog shoves his snout into the bowl. His ears pull back and lift slightly in happy-hound configuration.

As usual, Dexter finishes his meal in seconds flat. Then he looks up at Shane and gives a booming bark.

"Good boy!" Shane says with gusto. Dexter wags his tail, and when Shane reaches to take the bowl, the dog lunges—to lick his hand.

"That was easy," Regina remarks.

I shrug, though I want to cha-cha with joy. "It's how David won Dexter over, too, way back when they first met."

"Just to be safe," Shane says, "let's sit over here for a while." He returns to the seat beside me at the table.

"You look the same as you did before you turned," Noah tells me, "but Shane has aged."

"I've aged, too, I think. But only seven months."

Shane runs a self-conscious hand over his face. "Something happened after I came back. It hurt like hell, but now I feel normal. Well, normal for a forty-two-year-old human." He blinks hard and shakes his head. "Fuck, I'm forty-two."

"And I'm twenty-seven." I lighten my tone. "But what we both are right now is really, really hungry. Can Franklin come make us breakfast while we finish talking?"

They pass a look among themselves. "We don't usually let humans in here," Spencer says, "except Jeremy in an extreme emergency."

"What about me and Shane?"

"You could stay at David's," Regina suggests. "If you hunker down in the backseat and leave during the day, no one'll see you."

"You've gotta be kidding me." Shane advances on them. "All these years I was one of you. Now you're kicking us out of *my* room?"

"No. We ain't." Monroe comes to stand between us, facing the other DJs. "Human or vampire, they're us, and they stay."

"Thank you." I resist the urge to hug him. "What about Franklin?"

He gives me a warning glare. "Little girl, don't push your luck."

27

Pretend We're Dead

Still hungry, Shane and I go upstairs in search of take-out menus. Lori is at her desk, typing madly.

"I'm writing a press release about your deaths," she says, with way more glee than she should.

"I was just about to ask you to do that." I pull out the chair next to her desk. "Were they heroic? Did we die while saving a blind orphan and a three-legged puppy from terrorists?"

"Officially you took a leave of absence. Like Jim supposedly did after the Control took him away. So Kashmir will see the announcement and think we're covering up for your deaths. Especially with the quote, unquote 'secret funeral.'" She takes a sip of her stinky herbal pregnancy tea, which I'm glad I can no longer smell as much. "Shane is leaving to study guitar with a Tibetan monk, and Ciara, you're going with him because you convinced him to elope."

"A Himalayan honeymoon. I like it."

"I have something else you'll like." She scoots her chair back, almost running over Shane's toe, and opens her middle desk drawer. "I've been keeping them since you died. The other time."

Lori hands me a package about half the size of a tissue box. I tug off its red ribbon and lift the lid.

For the first time in my third life, I start to cry.

"I don't know why I kept them, but they reminded me of you the way you were when you . . ." She chokes up herself.

I lift the tortoiseshell-framed sunglasses out of the box, gripping the white tissue paper in my other hand. "I tried to give these to you after I died."

"You tried to give me a whole box of stuff. And I cried, and then I told you we couldn't be friends, because I was scared. And you got mad and broke everything in the box, which I totally deserved. But I dug these out of the trash and had them repaired."

I go to put on the shades, but she grabs my hand. "Do it outside."

She gets up and moves for the front door. Shane beats her there—fast now from enthusiasm instead of preternatural speed.

"I've always wanted to do this." He takes a deep breath, turns the key, then swings the door wide.

Soft light pours in, bathing his body and upturned face. He stretches his arms and examines them. They aren't flaming even a little bit.

I step into the doorway beside him, my tears acting like prisms to bend the sunbeams. Hand in hand, we walk down the stairs onto the grass, where the full sunlight from the southern horizon behind the station can reach us. I lift the sunglasses to my face and put them on, then turn to wave at Lori.

"How do they look?"

"*YAAAAAY!*" Lori jumps up and down at the top of the stairs. Then the phone rings behind her. She dashes back inside.

I gaze up at Shane, drinking in the sight of him in the sun. His eyes are bluer than ever, and the way the breeze tosses his hair over his forehead and cheekbones makes me want to do something other than eat food.

"You still look hot in those." He gives me a bewildered smile. "I'm trying to focus on all the minor stuff, so my head doesn't explode trying to figure out what it all means. Why it happened, what we do now. What does our future look like, now that we can do anything?"

Part of me warms with anticipation—of trips to the beach, pizza and nachos shared during football games, waking to see his face in the morning light.

Another part grows cold with fear. What if I'm not what he wants as a human? Now that he can have anyone—not just someone who understands and tolerates the vamp thing—why would he choose me?

I press my left thumb against my ring finger, like I always do when I get nervous about the future.

"Oh, no." I jerk my hand to my face. "My engagement ring is gone."

"It's probably on the ground over here."

We go to the patch of scorched grass, which still smells of smoke. I try not to look at the smaller patches to my left and right, where Agent Rosso and Captain Henley died.

"Got it!" Shane digs his index finger into the dirt. He holds up a marquise-cut diamond. "Where's the rest?"

I put my face near the ground, supporting my weight

with my elbows. "Here's the two little sapphires. And this blob of gold I guess used to be the band." I place the blue stones and the yellow lump in Shane's outstretched palm. "Nice work, Frodo."

He laughs, then kisses me. I move in closer, deepening the kiss, snaking my arms around his back, which is still lean and hard with muscle, and the warmth I feel is real, not relative.

Lori calls from the porch. "Elijah says to get your damn fool asses inside. His words, not mine. Also, he says you're avoiding something really important."

This is not the hardest call I've ever had to make to Colonel Lanham, but it's certainly the weirdest.

"Who is this?" he snaps, no doubt thinking I'm dead and someone is using my phone.

"Sir, it's me." I shift a pen from one side of my desk to the other and give Shane and Lori a nervous glance. "Agent Griffin."

A long pause. "Who is this, really?" His voice is hollow and hoarse. Was he . . . no, he couldn't have been crying.

"It's Ciara." I take a deep breath, then rush out the rest before he can hang up. "Shane and I burned to death in the sun, which you probably already know. But then we went through a few different, um, realms? And eventually came back to the same place where we'd burned, except we were—we are—alive. Human. And Shane is forty-two."

Lanham remains silent for several seconds. "I thought you were dead."

"Yeah, not so much."

"I—" He clears his throat, twice short, once long. "This is unprecedented."

"I'm not surprised."

"How do you know you're human and not just vampires who can be in the sun?"

"Is there such a thing? A real-life Gem of Amara?"

Lori's mouth pops open. Shane shakes his head in amusement.

"Excuse me?" Lanham says.

"Never mind." I'm proud and surprised that I've waited this long to throw a Buffy/Angel reference into one of our conversations. "Are there vampires who can be in the sun?"

"Not that I've heard of, but it seems more plausible than a reversion to humanity. Who else knows you're alive? Assuming you are."

"Everyone who works here, plus Elijah. Oh, and my mom. Not my biological mom, but the one who raised me. Marjorie."

"You must keep it a secret for your own safety until we can solve the Kashmir problem. And you and Agent McAllister must undergo a complete physical examination first thing in the morning."

"You're not going to lock us in a laboratory forever, are you?"

"No, probably only a decade or two."

"What?"

"It was a joke."

"It's creepy when you joke. Sir."

"An agent will pick you up tomorrow morning to bring you to the Research Division's facility."

"We'll be at Lori and David's house, as part of that whole staying-underground thing."

"Good idea. I'll meet you at the facility after you've had your tests."

"Okay." I notice Shane and Lori have disappeared into David's office, giving me the privacy to ask Lanham one essential question. "Was Jim under maximum security when he escaped?"

A long silence comes from the phone. "Why do you ask?"

"We saw him in—that place. He said he'd semi-rehabilitated. Kashmir told us it was because of the wood you left in his heart, but I don't know if I should believe him."

Another long pause, then Lanham says softly, "Why does it matter? The tribunal is over, Agent McAllister got a slap on the wrist—"

"Shane knows he may have killed an innocent man." I can't keep the edge of pleading out of my voice. "We need the truth." Not only about Jim's state of mind, but whether someone high in the Control let him go on purpose.

"Tests were done," Lanham says simply. "Results were encouraging."

I swallow, trying not to think about what future Jim could've had. I focus on the bright side: that all Jim had to do to escape was mesmerize one guard and have his progeny create a distraction. No one in the Control is trying to kill us. At least, not this way.

"I have to go now," Lanham says. "But, Griffin, I want you to know . . ."

"Yes?"

He hesitates. "Nothing. It's good to have you back among the living."

"Thank you, sir." I feel a glow inside, warm beyond all reason. "It's good to be back."

When I hang up, I hear distinct sounds of rummaging coming from David's office.

I get up and go to his door. "What's going on?"

Lori is armpit-deep in a three-foot-tall box I recognize as one of our Halloween supply containers. "David called and said they're going to be a few more hours at the ER. It's really busy there, and Jeremy and your mom don't have life-threatening issues. So I figured you and Shane had time."

"Time for what?"

Shane smiles as he holds up a dark wig. "Breakfast."

28

Viva la Vida

On the drive, Shane doesn't speak much at first. He's too busy looking at, well, everything.

We decided to go way out of town for our inaugural human breakfast, across the Pennsylvania border to Hanover. Not that Kashmir's human spies wouldn't cross the Mason-Dixon Line, but it makes us feel more secure. We refuse to cower inside the station on what is literally our very first day out together.

For the secret journey, I donned a black wig, à la 1960s Grace Slick (plus the bitchin' shades), and Shane's wearing a pair of Elvis sideburns and sunglasses, plus a trucker hat. All those WVMP Halloween parties are coming in handy.

As I drive Lori's car down the two-lane state highway out of Sherwood, Shane murmurs words like a kid, naming the marvels as we pass them. "Fields . . . hills . . . trees." Finally he turns to me. "There are mountains over there."

"Yeah, you can see Liberty ski resort from David's house in the winter, since he lives on a hill."

"I know, I've seen the lights at night. Can you see the snow on the slopes in the daytime from there?"

"Yep."

"Wow. We should go."

"To David's house or Ski Liberty?"

He gasps. "We *could* go skiing now."

"We could've before. They have night skiing. And wouldn't it have been better to do it when we couldn't break our legs?"

"No, because if we hit a tree really hard and then walked away, people would be suspicious." He smacks his hands on the dashboard in excitement. "I can go to the doctor! Or the hospital. I can have blood drawn, my reflexes checked, a strep test, anything."

"You are really looking on the bright side of this if you're stoked about a strep test."

He touches his throat. "I have bacteria now. That is awesome."

"In a weird way, yeah." There are so many things vampires don't dare to do for fear of being discovered. We can take more risks—like skiing—as mortals than we could as immortals.

"Of course, what would be ideal is if vampires could live openly without fear of being staked or burned or holy-watered."

He scoffs. "That'll never happen in our lifetimes."

We fall silent. *Our lifetimes.* Which suddenly have limits, though only in length. A vampire's life has limits in everything *but* length.

He reaches for my hand. I give it to him. However long we have left, I hope we'll spend it together.

• • •

"You need cream with your coffee?" the waitress at the diner asks Shane.

"Just black is fine." He raises his head, maybe remembering that he can actually taste cream now. "No. I'll have a triple mochaccino with extra whipped cream and . . ." He turns his dark sunglasses to face mine. ". . . and a splash of coconut."

The waitress gives him a level look. "We got regular and decaf, hon. Take your pick."

"Oh. Regular. With cream." He smiles to himself as she walks away. It is so cute.

Then he turns back to the menu, paralyzed by the myriad choices of pancakes. "When did this happen? It used to be regular, blueberry, and chocolate chip."

"Just remember, Rip Van Winkle, this won't be the one and only stack of pancakes in your lifetime."

"Can we come here every week?"

"Only if you promise to keep working out. You did have diabetes when you were human the first time."

"Shit, what if I still have it?" He flips the menu page. "Maybe an omelet would be better. Wow, there's a million of those, too." He starts to sigh with frustration, but stops himself. "A million omelets. That's pretty cool."

The waitress brings our coffee, but Shane isn't even close to deciding on food yet, so she agrees to come back in a few minutes.

He sends her an apologetic look as she walks away, then his gaze shifts to something behind me. I can't see his eyes behind the sunglasses, but the way his head goes still and the corners of his lips draw back, I know he's gone pensive. Besides, I can hear the baby cooing and giggling.

Clearing my throat, I shift my napkin-wrapped uten-
sil set from my left to my right side, then tap it against
my water glass. Shane refills his coffee, then mine, with
the "bottomless pot" the waitress left.

"We don't have to talk about it now," he says.

"Yeah, we do."

"Let's just have one perfect day, okay?"

"It can't be perfect knowing that The Baby Talk is
out there in the future waiting for us."

The waitress arrives and takes our order. She seems
confused at our sudden change in mood, and speaks
louder and brighter as if to make up for our solemnity.

I order an omelet like Shane, though I really want
crepes. No sense in torturing him—I've got my whole
life to eat carbs.

"When I originally asked you to marry me," Shane
says, "back when I was a vampire and you weren't, I worried that we couldn't have kids. I worried that you would
miss that by marrying me."

"And I told you I didn't want kids."

His chin tilts down. "You seemed like you meant it."

"I did." I force out the painful truth. "I still mean it.
I don't want kids, ever."

"Why not?" he asks, like I've said I don't want pancakes (which to me is a lot crazier than not wanting kids).

"I just don't. I don't want the responsibility and the
stress."

"But there's a benefit, too. You get kids."

"Shane, to me that's not a benefit. I don't *like* kids,
the same way that weird people don't like dogs. Babies
are boring. Toddlers are annoying. Teenagers are cool,
but that's a lot of boring and annoying to endure just

to get to someone I can have a conversation with, when I can just talk to teens at our gigs instead. As people, not as sources of worry about what time they'll be home and what drugs they're taking and who they're sleeping with." I put my hands to my head. "I'm just not interested in the whole deal, top to bottom."

"You might change your mind when you get older."

"What if I don't? What if, ten years from now, I'm thirty-seven and still have no interest? You'll be fifty-two and you'll have missed your chance to be a dad while you can still play on the floor without having to be helped up afterward."

Shane rubs his knee, as if already feeling the aches of age. Maybe he is. "I want to marry you."

"And I want to marry you. But I don't want to disappoint you." My heart feels like it's pinching in half down the middle. A voice inside me insists I give him false hope so I don't lose him right now. "Don't marry me hoping I'll change. Marry me for me. Your wife, not a mother of your potential children."

"I've never seen you as the mother of my potential children."

"Until now. You're imagining it even as we speak, wondering what I'd look like pregnant or holding our son or daughter. Wondering if they'd have my eyes or yours."

His mouth tightens and he looks away, rotating his coffee cup by the handle.

My own voice thickens with emotion. "I need you to imagine all that. Go look at baby stuff in the department store, go look at babies in the park. Go to Mass and watch a baptism, now that you can enter a church without freak-ing out." I put my hands on the table. "Then imagine a life, just the two of us and Dexter. Growing old with no one to take care of us but us, and friends, and hopefully some swank retirement community with shuffleboard and mini-golf. Then think about what you want."

Shane takes a deep breath and lets it out, focusing on the baby behind my side of the booth. Then he takes off his sunglasses and looks at me, studying the angles of my face, the motions of my hands as they twist together.

Finally he says, "I want you."

"It's not that simple."

"Yes. It is." He holds my gaze as he speaks, and even though he's lost those vampire mesmer-eyes, I'm no less mesmerized. "It's that simple because you, Ciara Griffin, alone and unadorned, are everything I need in this world. Mortal or immortal, old or young, I cannot and I will not live without you. If it was ever possible before, which I don't think it was, it's not now." He leans forward and speaks in a near whisper. "We died together. We went to hell and heaven and back. Together. We didn't do that just so we could go our separate ways. Does the thought of never being a father hurt? Sure, but only a little compared to the thought of being without you. That thought . . ." He puts his sunglasses back on. "That thought breaks me."

I stare at him, and though I can't look in his eyes, I feel like I can still see his soul.

Shane moves the salt and pepper shakers into alignment, maybe by habit. "If you don't feel the same way, now that I'm human, I'll understand. Things'll be different."

"Not the things that count," I whisper.

"Sex counts. We'll have to start using birth control. I'm sure I won't be the walking hard-on I used to be." He fidgets with his left sideburn. "It'll only get worse as I get older."

I slide my toes against his calf muscle. "You have experience. Nothing can take that away."

A slight smile escapes his lips. "True." He reaches under the table and grasps my foot. Just as he starts to slip off my shoe, our omelets arrive.

"Oh, wow." Shane's eyelids grow heavy at the scent of eggs and toast. My own mouth waters. It sounds tragic, but at this moment I don't want to have sex. I just want to eat until I explode.

But I wait for him. I want to see his face when he tastes solid food for the first time in almost sixteen years.

His eyes water as he unfolds his paper napkin and places it on his lap, then carefully picks up his fork. He holds it awkwardly, like most people do with chopsticks. His other hand picks up a wedge of toast automatically. Muscle memory from long ago. He carves off a piece of omelet and places it on the toast.

Then he stops.

"What's wrong?" I ask him.

"Nothing. Just give me a second." He closes his eyes, and I realize he's saying grace, though both hands are full and he can't cross himself. I know he's giving thanks for so much more than this omelet.

I look at my own food, and my own hands, unfolded. Who do I thank for what happened? Is there some god or goddess out there who wants to return vampires to a human state, but only under certain circumstances? Will we ever understand it?

I think back to that time in the beyond. There was a presence, but it didn't feel singular, like an old dude with a white beard, or a beautiful woman with open arms and ample bosom, or whatever the goddess-worshippers believe in.

It felt like . . . everything and everyone. It felt like the universe.

Shane whispers, "Amen," and I echo him, slightly louder. What the hell. It makes him smile.

He takes a bite, and the noise he makes is worth all the aging and debilitation that lie before us. A vampire's debilitation is equally inevitable, anyway. It's just slower and affects our minds instead of our bodies.

From now on, Shane and I can eat. We can sustain ourselves on something that can be obtained with mere money and time. No more enslaving ourselves to donors. No more taking human vitality to survive.

We are free.

And this omelet is literally to die for.

29

I Feel Free

I still can't believe Mom's here. Seeing her on the outside, wearing something other than prison garb, is almost weirder than seeing Shane in the sunlight.

"I don't even know where to start," I tell her as we share a pizza in the lounge that afternoon. "But I'm sorry I never told you what had happened to me."

"David explained it all, how you had chicken pox and would've died if you hadn't turned. You couldn't exactly tell me on the phone or in a letter—the prison monitors all our communication. Creeps."

"I know. But I'm sorry you had to find out this way."

She reaches out and takes my right hand. "When that man cut you . . . it was like he was cutting my own heart out." She runs her thumb over mine. "Even though we're not related by blood, you're still a part of me, Ciara."

"I know." I don't bring up the fact that we're not related by marriage, either, since my dad is still married to my birth mom, Luann O'Riley. To me, Marjorie will always be Mom. She did raise me, after all, even though she raised me to be a con artist.

"I wish you'd told me you were getting out of prison in November instead of December. You know I hate surprises."

"Since when?"

"Since ever. Remember that clown you hired for my sixth birthday party? I cried for hours."

She laughs. "Oh, my, I wish I'd had a camera to capture the look on his face when you kicked him in the kneecap."

"He went down pretty fast, didn't he?"

"And stayed down, once that other little girl started beating him with the piñata bat. What was her name?"

"Beth-Ann Moseley. She was my best friend that week."

"Too bad we had to leave that town a little sooner than planned, since the clown was on the town council." She angles her head. "I'm sorry about the surprise. But I'm here now."

"I can't even take you shopping or out to dinner, since I have to play dead." I pull out my phone and check my calendar. "I have a wedding gown fitting tomorrow. I'll have to have Lori reschedule. Or maybe I should just not show up. What would a dead person do?"

"Maybe if you wore another disguise . . ."

I give her a guilty look. They came back from the hospital before Shane and I arrived from our brunch. David was predictably pissed.

"No, Kashmir's people will be looking for me at the bridal boutique. We just have to hide for a couple more days, I hope. We can plan wedding stuff after my funeral is over." I doubt anyone's ever uttered *that* sentence aloud. "You ready to play mournful mommy?"

She waves her hand, like I've asked her to pick up a quart of milk at the store. "You know I'm a good actor. The more emotional the role, the better. I even bought a funeral dress on our way home from the hospital."

"That was efficient."

"I needed all new clothes and toiletries, anyway, to replace the belongings that man stole from me. Luckily it was just one suitcase." She reaches behind her to the coffee table, careful to keep her bandaged ankle elevated on the adjoining chair. She pulls a black dress from a department-store shopping bag. "I held off on the hat and veil. I figured that was just for widows."

"It's nice." I add *the dress my mom just bought for my funeral* to the long list of today's surreal images.

"I also got a couple scarves. I've been missing them so. Obviously we can't have them in prison, not that many people hang themselves in minimum-security facilities." She pulls out a green-and-blue silk scarf.

I scan the long piece of cloth, relieved not to see a security sensor hanging off it. She never needed to steal things, but sometimes she liked the thrill. Maybe she's rehabilitated, just like Jim.

"It's not too garish, is it?" She shakes it to make the colors undulate. "I don't want to look like a Gypsy."

"You mean real Gypsies or Dad's Gypsies?"

"Real ones. Though your dad's kinfolk dress crazy, too." She folds the scarf and lays it back in the bag. "But they don't like to be called Gypsies."

"I know." In April, I met four of my Irish-American Traveller cousins, three of whom were vampires. They carried boulder-size chips on their shoulders about the way they were viewed by "country folk," which is any-

LUST FOR LIFE 277

one who's not a Traveller. I'm a full-blooded Traveller myself, but I'm still country folk to them because my dad stole me from my neglectful teen "bio mom" and ran off with this woman sitting across from me.

Though Dad had escaped a family of enterprising criminals, and though Marjorie was presumably squeaky clean, they soon embarked on a decade-plus tour of deceit as fake faith healers (and, apparently, insurance brokers), gathering more money than our Traveller cousins ever would with their petty short cons.

Lori enters the lounge and passes us with a quick wave on her way to the bathroom. Thankfully it's on the other side of two doors, and I have human ears again, so I can't hear her barfing while I'm trying to eat.

"I should get Lori a congrats-you're-pregnant gift."

"Ooh, you can use this." Mom hands me a coupon from the department-store bag. "There's a sale on sweaters."

"She likes the clothes I buy her. But I don't know what size to get now. How fast do pregnant women swell up?"

Mom laughs. "'Swell up' sounds like she has an inflammation. Freudian slip?"

"What do you mean?"

"You're upset that she's having a baby and you're not."

"Yes. But not because I want one."

"Because you're afraid you'll lose her."

I gape at her. She actually understands.

"Don't look so surprised. I was young once." Mom pulls out another scarf, one with broad red and violet zigzags, a bolder look than I knew her to have. "My close girlfriends all got married right out of high school, and all had babies by the time we were twenty-one. They talked about nothing else all day long. I was the 'weird' one who didn't think potty training counted as high adventure."

Now it's my turn to laugh. "Dad sure gave you adventures."

Stroking the vivid silk scarf, Mom smiles to herself. "Yes, he did."

"If you could do it all over again, would you change anything? Would you run screaming when he said hello, or maybe push him off your grandmother's roof he was supposedly fixing?"

She looks at me like *I* should be pushed off a roof. "Not a thing. It was worth the jail time, the uncertainty, hardly ever seeing my family except at funerals and weddings, and not being able to bring my husband and child home for those."

"That must've been hard."

"Before you pity me for giving up my family, remember that your dad did it, too, but for him it was forever. He was exiled."

Shane and Jeremy enter from upstairs on their way to the studio, discussing the latter taking over Shane's show while we pretend he's dead. They each grab another piece of pizza, though they've already eaten an entire one of their own.

Shane kisses the top of my head. "Ready to go soon? Lori needs to drive us to their place while it's still light. David'll bring Dexter after dark."

"Can't wait." Seriously, I can't wait to get him alone and see what his human body is like. Then I realize we have a speed bump. "Mom, we need to find you a safe place to stay. You can't come to David's house until Dexter gets used to you. He doesn't generally like humans. Dexter, that is, not David."

"Oh, I'm staying with Franklin. He said his house is too big for one person and he needed someone who can cook something other than breakfast."

"Did you learn how to do that on the inside? Because last I remember, your cooking began and ended with Hamburger Helper."

"I'll have you know, I am now skilled in all forms of boxed Helper."

Shane laughs. "That sounds amazing right now. By the way, can I get you anything, Mrs. O'Riley? Drink? Food?"

Mom beams at him. "I'm fine, thank you, and please, call me Marjorie. Or just Mom, since that's what I'll be in a month and two days."

Shane's eyes fill with wonder. "Wow. That is . . . wow." He takes another bite of pizza as he follows Jeremy to the studio.

Mom watches him go. "How old did you say he was now?"

"Forty-two. In four years we'll pass the half-his-age-plus-eight cradle-robbing standard."

"Hm." Mom gives a heavy but ladylike sigh. "If he makes you happy, I suppose that's what counts."

"That is exactly the right thing to say, especially after telling me what a great choice it was to run off with Dad."

She purses her lips like she's trying not to smile. "I wouldn't want to be a hypocrite."

"Mom, you guys were living out of wedlock while

preaching family values to the masses. You were professional hypocrites."

"I do regret that I never made your father divorce Luann. But most of all, I regret lying to you about being your real mother."

"You *are* my real mother." I pick the onions off my pizza, deciding I don't like them anymore. "Did you ever regret not having a baby of your own?"

"Oh, sweet pea." With her paper napkin, Mom dabs the corners of her mouth, then her eyes. "You were always my own."

30

Like a Prayer

It feels weird to go to bed at night.

Shane and I (and Dexter) have slept here at Lori and David's house before, in this downstairs guest room with thick blackout curtains on the window. The only thing that's changed is that now those curtains are hiding what's *inside* instead of what's outside.

As I finish changing into a pair of Lori's pajamas, she knocks on our bedroom door and enters. Shane's in the bathroom, brushing his teeth, and probably taking a good long look in the mirror, though he'd never admit it.

"I have something you might need." She hands me a half-full box of condoms.

"Thanks." I examine the contents of the variety pack. "Funny, all the double-pleasure ones are gone."

"Yeah, those were . . . hmm." She sits on the edge of the bed. "So you think you'll use these after you're married?"

"I'll go back on the Pill until we go for something more permanent."

"Oh." She gives a wistful sigh.

"We're not having kids." At the sight of her disappointment, I add, "We don't even know if we can."

"Won't the Control give you fertility tests? I would think they'd be curious."

"I guess." I riffle through the box. "Between extended pleasure and glow-in-the-dark, which do you recommend for first-time human sex?" I look at the ceiling. "Oh, no, you'll be able to hear us through the vents."

"We sleep on the other side of the house, so you should have privacy."

"Okay, we'll try not to break too much furniture."

She lets out a pealing laugh. "I'm so happy you're back. I mean, I loved you as a vampire, but now we can do all the things we used to do."

"Like hug each other without me wanting to bite you."

"Yikes." She examines my face. "Are you happy to be human again?"

"There were some really cool things about being a vampire"—I pinch my forearm—"but this feels right to me."

"Because you were undead for such a short time?"

"Because something inside me always rejected the magic. I was fading fast, wasn't I?"

Her eyes turn sad. "Yeah. Maybe that was part of why I had trouble accepting it. There was something not quite right about you."

"Well, that's always a given."

"It was still wrong of me to freak out over you changing. I promise it'll never happen again."

I look away to hide the doubt in my eyes.

"Ciara." She puts her hand on mine. "I know you're afraid we'll grow apart after the baby comes, especially if you choose not to have your own. But David and I talked about it, and he said he'll make sure I get at least one girls' night out every week with you. Just the two of us, grown-up stuff."

I smile at the ceiling, where I hear David's footsteps going down the hall. "You know he's amazing, right?"

Lori gives a coy, one-shouldered shrug. "Yeah, he's all right."

"Your kid is going to be ridiculously cute and smart. I'll try to not be a bad influence." I swallow and force out the words. "As a godmother, I mean."

Lori gasps. "You'll do it?"

"If Shane agrees, too. And only if I never have to go to church except that one time."

"Of course!" She throws her arms around me. "I can't stop hugging you. You're so soft and warm now."

"I think the word you're looking for is 'flabby,' but thanks."

Out in the hall, the bathroom door opens. I let go of Lori. "Hey, you know what my only regret is about being human again?"

"What?"

"That I never got to bite you." I snap my teeth. Her cackle fades as she retreats with a good-night wave.

I've just gotten under the covers when Shane enters. He spots the box of condoms on the nightstand and shuts the door slowly behind him.

"I'm all nostalgic now." He climbs into bed beside me. We face each other under the covers, like soap opera characters.

I wonder if he feels insecure now that he won't have supernatural potency and stamina. I worry that, with his decreased senses of touch and smell, my body won't have the same appeal to him. Maybe it's too much pressure for our first night together as humans.

"We can wait," I tell him. "If you're tired, or if—"

He answers me with a deep, hard kiss. I give a low moan and pull him close to me, every inch, not missing yesterday's strength, in my body or his. This is still us. His lips, his tongue, his hands, his thighs—all my favorite parts—are still Shane.

I slide my fingers inside the waistband of his boxers.

Oh. Wow. Yes. All my favorite parts indeed.

His breath catches and he lets out a groan, loud and raw.

"We should probably be quiet," I whisper.

"No." Shane claws at my silk nightshirt. "We're alive." He tears open the shirt, sending buttons flying, then hurls back the covers. "Let's live."

If Shane's insecure, he's covering it well.

Naked, we kiss and grasp and feel every inch of each other. I savor each breath, filling my lungs with his new yet familiar scent. We murmur our usual filthy words of encouragement, stoking our desire to animalistic, pornographic heights. Shane covers my body with his, holding me down and driving me crazy, tugging at my nipples with teeth and tongue, spreading my legs with an exploring hand as I urge him on my with voice and fingers.

Then he stops.

Then I stop.

We stare at each other in the low lamplight.

"We did this before," he says, "the night we got engaged."

"Did what?"

"Planned to fuck mindlessly, to prove to ourselves that we were still young and crazy and full of lust." His hand drifts over my belly. "That a real commitment wouldn't change us."

"But it did. And that night we decided not to go for the porn action right away. We made love first. Even though it was kind of scary."

"So the fact that we went straight to bow-chicka-bow tonight means we're more afraid than ever?"

"Shouldn't we be?" I put my hand over his, wrapping his long, strong fingers around my ribs. "Things are different."

"And we're pretending they're not, at least in bed. We're pretending we're still two animals, tooth and claw."

"We can still be that sometimes."

"But tonight, maybe we shouldn't." He rolls over, pulling me gently to lie against him so we're side by side, facing each other. "I don't know what we should be now, or what we should do."

"First we need to forget the 'shoulds.' It's not like we have some precedent to follow. Let's do what we want."

"I just want to look at you." He fingers the ends of a lock of my hair. "What do you want, Ciara?"

"I want you to do something you haven't done since you came back to life." I touch his throat with my first two fingertips. "Sing for me."

"I don't have my guitar."

"You don't need it."

"I might be off-key."

"I won't notice." I slide my fingers under his chin, then up to his lips. "Sing for me, Shane."

He starts off softly, eyes closed, crooning a song I've

never heard before, a song I could swear he's writing even as it leaves his throat. I have to remind myself to breathe.

His voice is more beautiful than ever. It skates over the middle-range notes, caresses the lows, and lifts the highs with just enough effort to avoid sounding polished.

His words and melody tremble with the awe of being alive, and with the lingering fear of a new kind of death. A human death of blood and weakness, where strength will drain from us one day at a time. A death we won't return from again.

The last verse counters it all, with a hope I've never heard before. In his new-old human form, Shane is a little less lost, a little more certain of salvation. But as bright as he becomes in the sun, he'll never shed the darkness that outlines his soul. If he did, he wouldn't be Shane McAllister.

He stumbles over the final chorus, a lighter variation on the previous ones, as if the new reality is a stranger to be let in only with caution. But he goes back and repeats it, stronger and surer, and by the time it's over, my face is soaked with tears of joy.

"That bad, huh?"

"How is it possible?" I wipe my eyes with the edge of my thumb. "You sound even more incredible now."

"Nah, it's just your weak human ears."

"My weak human ears listened to you for three years." I notice my unintentional rhyme but don't stop to admire it. "You never sounded this good. Were you like this before you turned, and if so, why weren't you a rock star?"

"I didn't sound like this." He rubs the spot where his collarbones meet. "It feels different. Not easier or louder, just . . . I don't know. Like something's there that wasn't."

"Nothing builds character and talent like dying, and now you've done it twice."

"Seems like we should've come back with some sort of superpower to make it all worthwhile."

"No." I shake my head and run my hand down his arm, wondering where the freckles will appear first. "This is enough."

Shane inhales, soft as a cloud, then exhales, his eyes roaming my face like he's seeing me for the first time.

I draw my fingers over his brows, noticing a gray hair on the outermost edge of the right one. A smile pops onto my face.

"What are you doing?" he asks.

"Finding hidden treasure in my own backyard." I follow the new thin line that crosses his forehead, like the Arctic Circle on a globe. Shane's face could be my whole world right now, or at least a hemisphere.

"I still can't believe it," he whispers. "We're alive."

I place my hand over his heart. "You've always been alive to me."

He draws his thumb over my lips, first to trace them, then to part them. Slowly he moves forward, slipping his tongue beside his thumb at the edge of my mouth, then inside.

This time there's no doubt or fear or anything to prove. Our bodies find each other as they are, and it is perfect.

• • •

At 5:50 a.m. my phone rings. I grab it and answer blearily. "Mughrhh?"

"It's Jeremy. Turn on WVMP. Make sure you're both listening." He hangs up.

I reach across Shane to switch on the clock radio on the guest room nightstand. He murmurs my name and pulls me to his chest.

I snuggle close, caressing the smooth planes of his muscles and staring at the window. I know it's still dark out, but my body zings a bit with fear at the thought of the coming sunrise. "We're supposed to hear something."

"Okay." He strokes my hair with just his fingertips. "I woke up in the middle of the night thinking of Jim. The look on his face when I killed him, and when we found him in that place."

"He forgave you. Maybe not in so many words, but he said he didn't blame you."

"I wish there was a way to know for sure if he'd changed."

"Whatever the truth is, you did the right thing based on what you knew at the time. You had every reason to think Jim was a threat."

"I did. But now I don't."

Jeremy's voice comes on the radio. "It's five before the hour here at 94.3 WVMP-FM, the Lifeblood of Rock 'n' Roll. I don't do many dedications here on my indie rock show, on account of the fact that I don't have many listeners." He chuckles. "Anyway. This song is from me, for two of my friends I love very much." He pauses. "And always will."

The first acoustic guitar note makes my lids close

with sorrow. I cry every time I hear this song, thinking of me and Shane, or any couple growing old together and, one day, one of them leaving the other behind.

"Listen to the lyrics," I tell Shane.

Maybe in the last several years since this song came out, in the dozens of times I heard it, it wormed its way into my soul and led me to make that leap from the radio station with no hesitation. Maybe this Death Cab for Cutie song saved our lives.

Shane's arms tighten around me after the first line. He hasn't heard the chorus or even the title, but he can already tell what it's about. Refusing to lose someone to death. Joining them instead.

"I'll follow you into the dark again," I tell him. "A million times."

He swallows, the sound heavy near my ear. "And I'll lead you out again, a million times."

31

Changes

Cruelly, we have to get up early for the Control car to pick us up at seven a.m. Our examinations will take place at a secret facility an hour west of headquarters, since our transformation is supposed to stay hush-hush until we've figured out what the hell happened.

Shane stands at the stove, holding a frying pan and a can of cooking spray. "I forget how to make eggs."

"We have to fast before the blood tests, anyway, remember? I'll get you a cookbook for Christmas, since my breakfast-making skills pretty much began and ended with cereal, not always in a bowl."

"Put down the pan," David says as he enters the kitchen, damp-haired and barefoot but otherwise dressed for work. "The smell of eggs makes Lori barf." He takes the coffee I offer him with a nod of thanks. He goes to sip, then looks at the clock. His mug stops halfway to his mouth. "I just realized I don't need to tell you to go home or hide in the basement before sunrise."

"Sunrise." Shane turns to me. "We'll be able to see it."

"It should come up while we're in the car on the

way." I bite my lip in excitement. "It'll rise over the mountains."

I cross the room and let him envelop me in his arms. He winces, then covers the hiss of pain with a cough.

"You okay?" I ask him.

He lets go of me. "Yeah, my back's a little stiff."

"Sorry about the mattress," David says. "It's pretty old. And since it's usually vampires with tough skeletal systems sleeping there—" He cuts himself off and looks away in discomfort.

"You can comment on our being human, David. We promise not to take offense. Right, Shane?"

"Hmm?" He frowns at the toaster as he lifts it with one hand. Then he sets it down and picks up the base of the blender, which Lori leaves on the counter, since fruit smoothies are one of the few foods she can stomach. "Huh."

David and I watch in silence as Shane circles the kitchen and the adjoining dining room, picking up random objects, then putting them down.

Finally he lowers the corner of the dining room table with a thunk. "I'm weak now. I'll suck as an Enforcement agent."

"Plenty of them are human," David points out. "I was."

"When you were, what, twenty-one? That's half my age."

"You have the experience. Nothing can take that away."

I hide a smile, remembering I said the very same thing about Shane and sex yesterday. It turned out to be true.

David lifts his mug. "And how many Enforcement

agents are ex-vampires? You'll have valuable insights your comrades won't."

"True. I just—it was weird waking up this morning and . . . well, it was weird waking up in the morning, period." Shane gives a nervous chuckle as he glances between us. Then his gaze rests on David. "I don't know how to be middle-aged."

And that is my cue to go take a shower. David's only thirty-five, but he's still got eight years on me. Plus, he's a guy, and a former Enforcement agent. He might be the best anchor for Shane on this crazy new ship.

I spent most of my life learning how not to need others. It's a trick I had to unlearn when I became a vampire. I vow not to relearn it now.

Shane and I spend the morning subjecting ourselves to every medical examination, head to toe and all parts in between, inside and out. We leave behind every kind of bodily fluid.

Well, not every kind. The fertility tests will have to wait, since Shane was supposed to abstain from sex for two days before taking it. As for me, they have to draw blood on a certain day of my cycle—another thing I haven't had for over six months. So it could be weeks before we know if both of us can have kids.

The rest of our results won't be in until late this afternoon, so we meet Colonel Lanham for lunch. Luckily for our new human taste buds, this secret Control facility has an amazing food court, much better than the cafeteria at headquarters.

"I want to start by saying that none of this discussion will go beyond this table," Lanham says as he sets down his tray of spinach quiche (Shane says that "real men don't care whether real men eat quiche," but I have no idea what that's a reference to).

"But it's obvious we're no longer vampires. Will people need a top-secret security clearance just to talk to us?"

"Yeah, won't the rest of the agency want to know how we became human again?" Shane asks.

"Obviously we're playing this as we go along," Colonel Lanham says. "This is unprecedented."

"But I've done something no one's ever done before, right?" When he nods, I continue. "And I bet a huge contingent of the Control would like to harness my power to unmake other vampires."

"That's impossible," Shane says. "To unmake us, you had to (a) be a vampire, (b) die, and (c) come back to life."

"Exactly. And I don't think what I did was a power. It was a unique situation." I explain to Lanham the sequence of the void, the light, and the dark. "I couldn't have made it out of the darkness without Shane."

"And I couldn't have made it without her," Shane adds. "Sir."

"Fascinating." Lanham spears a piece of butternut squash with his fork. "My theory is that at the heart of this transformation is Agent Griffin's anti-magic essence. Your body and soul resisted the idea that you could be destroyed by sunlight. You were able to transfer this notion to Agent McAllister."

"Did my body and soul also resist the idea of the afterlife? Because I didn't feel at home in any of those three places."

"I did." Shane examines the soft wheat roll he's buttering. "I'd been to that darkness before."

"When you died?" Lanham asks.

"Literally, yeah. And figuratively, a few times since then. I think that's how I was able to find our way out."

"So perhaps only a failed suicide like yourself could have accomplished the second part of the resurrection."

Shane keeps buttering, smoothing the condiment evenly over the surface. Finally he says, "Maybe."

"That would be cool." To his questioning look, I respond, "It means that whatever's out there, that thing that's bigger than any religion, doesn't hate suicides. Only someone who knows the darkness the way Shane does can find a path out of it."

"If I may venture a guess," Lanham says, "I think it's about more than your first death, McAllister. It could concern your second life."

Shane creases his brow. "You mean my life as a vampire?"

"Exactly. By every measure, you were a good man when you were undead. You saved lives on more than one occasion."

"And you made people happy with your radio show," I add.

Lanham continues. "In short, Agent McAllister, you redeemed yourself."

"Not that you needed redeeming," I interject.

Shane looks at me, then Lanham, then takes a bite of bread. "Wow," he says as he chews.

We wait for him to add further commentary, but he simply eats his bread, focusing on each bite. Watching him revel in the simple pleasures of a human body, I wonder how much of our journey to death and back was done by me and how much by him.

We'll probably never know, or fully understand why it happened. Maybe it doesn't matter.

All that matters is that we didn't make that journey alone.

"Well! I have good news and bad news."

Shane and I turn from the window, where we're watching absolutely nothing outside, and it is lovely, because it's daylight. Unfortunately, it's also overcast, which meant this morning's sunrise was more of a "cloud-glow."

Dr. Sanders motions for us to sit in the chairs on the other side of his desk. In his white coat he looks just like any other doctor, except for the amber-colored Research Division patch above his pen-lined pocket.

"Thank you for agreeing to meet with me together instead of separately." He switches eyeglasses as he sits and opens our file folders. "As you know, we're under-staffed here at headquarters, so my schedule is a mad-house. But obviously I cleared my calendar for your spectacularly unique case."

I nod, trying to keep my breathing even and slow, despite the fact that these results could hold devastating news: a horrible disease, a lack of some vital element humans need to stay alive. And if I'm perfectly normal and mundane, I'll be kicked out of the Immanence Corps. Dr. Sanders literally holds our fates in his hands.

His trembling hands. If I were a vampire, I could tell by smell whether he was emotionally nervous or simply overcaffeinated. But I'm human now, so I have to use mere con-artist intuition.

"The good news is, you're both in excellent health, for the most part. Cholesterol in particular is fabulous. We'll want to check that again in six months, once you've been eating regularly."

Shane leans forward. "What about diabetes?"

"To be completely certain, we'd want to do a glucose curve, but I see nothing in your chem profile to indicate either hyperglycemia or hypoglycemia, so I think you're good to go."

"I can eat pancakes?" Shane asks, sounding boyish and adorable.

"Go for it." Dr. Sanders flips the page. "Your blood pressure, Agent McAllister, is at pre-hypertension levels, so you should watch your sodium, maybe adopt some stress management strategies. Definitely don't smoke."

"I don't smoke."

"Don't start."

"What about drinking?"

"Fine in moderation, although"—he plants his finger on one section of Shane's file—"with your previous human history of depression and addiction, you might want to be careful with any sort of drugs. Just a moment."

Dr. Sanders fumbles for a bottle of pills on the right side of his desk. He knocks over the bottle. Shane reaches forward to catch it, but by the time he's even moved an inch, the bottle has hit the floor.

"I've got it." Dr. Sanders bends over and picks up the pills.

Shane sits back in his chair and drums his fingers on the arms, as if his slow human reflexes don't bother him at all. As a vampire, he could've grabbed the bottle before it was halfway to the floor.

"Sorry about that." Dr. Sanders shakes out two pills into his quivering palm, then downs them with an energy drink. I wonder when this guy last slept more than three hours in a night.

"Other than those minor issues, Agent McAllister, your health is quite boring. Congratulations." He closes Shane's file and opens mine. "Agent Griffin, soon to be the other Agent McAllister, is that correct?"

"No, I'm keeping my name when we get married." Or possibly becoming McGriffin. Why not?

"Everything checks out with your results. No major issues." He folds his hands atop the file and takes off his glasses. "If I were a civilian doctor, I would tell you to be thrilled."

He doesn't look thrilled. I straighten my posture, bracing myself.

"I've lost it, haven't I? My blood is just . . . blood?"

He frowns again. "Believe me, no one is sorrier than we are here in the Research Division. Your resurrection, or whatever it's being deemed, gave us great hope for the future of vampire medicine. But alas, as you say, your blood is now just blood."

"Can we run more tests? In a week or a month, after I've had time to forget what it was like to be in that place? Maybe once I get more cynicism back, my blood will be anti-magic again."

"We will certainly test you again in a few months. Both of you. What you've done is—"

"Unprecedented," I finish, having heard that word twice from Lanham. I should get it on a T-shirt.

"Extremely unprecedented. Vampires don't unvamp. There's no record of it, at least. I hope you understand if we want to study you closely, for a long time."

I tense, ready to run. "How closely?"

"Don't worry, we're not going to lock you up. That would ruin the experiments. Oh, and it would be wrong." He laughs at his own non-joke with a sleep-deprived giddiness.

We make appointments for follow-up tests next week, then Shane and I leave the office as fast as we can. On the way down the endless corridors of the Research headquarters building, I try to console myself.

"I didn't really want to be in the Immanence Corps anyway. Bunch of weirdos."

"It sounded interesting to me."

"I don't want interesting. I want a desk job in the Anonymity Department, making fake passports and driver's licenses for aging vampires. I'm good at inventing stories. It's where I belong, using all my old con-artist talents."

"Sounds boring."

"Boring, but also a complete lack of getting killed. Since when are you looking for adventure? What happened to the slacker dude I fell in love with?"

"Hey." Shane takes my hand and stops me. "Things change. I'll change. You'll change. But what'll never change is this." He leans over and gives me a warm, soft kiss, laying a soothing balm over my rattling nerves. "Okay?"

I nod and say nothing, knowing my voice would belie my doubt. As we continue down the hall, I remark, "Dr. Sanders said 'extremely unprecedented.'"

"Huh?"

"It's incorrect usage. Either something is unprecedented or it isn't. Nothing is adverb plus 'unprecedented.' Same with the words 'perfect' or 'unique.' There aren't degrees of perfection or uniqueness."

"Not even spectacularly." Shane smiles down at me. "Did you miss that? He said we were 'spectacularly unique.'"

I gasp. "I did miss that."

He squeezes my hand. "That's a good sign."

We walk out the door into the sunlight, two extremely, spectacularly, perfectly unique human beings.

32

Nowhere to Run

Shane and I have no time to enjoy being alive, what with planning our own funeral.

With only a day's notice, we've had to move the memorial service for Jim and us from Crosetti's Monuments to the small clearing next to the radio station. It lacks the fake-graveyard ambience of the headstone maker's lot, but it also lacks police tape and dead bodies.

Jeremy has added an extra security camera to the side of the station where the memorial service will take place, as well as a pair of bright floodlights. Our stockpile of weapons and Control personnel has increased. Now that Kashmir is responsible for the deaths of two agents (four including me and Shane), they're out for his blood. If he's smart, he'll cut his losses and go far away before the Control hunts him down. Adrian hasn't heard from him since we died, so maybe he is gone for good.

Under protest, Monroe prerecorded his "Midnight Blues" show and was taken to a Control safe house for the duration of the night. Noah volunteered to play the prerecorded segments in the studio tonight, interspersing timely commercials to give it a live-show flavor. Hopefully this will fool Kashmir into thinking Monroe is here.

As sunset approaches on Monday, we hurry through last-minute preparations, including loading a dozen holy-water pistols with fresh ammunition. The potency of the water decreases once it leaves the vessel it was blessed in, so they have to be armed shortly before battle. To me it'd make more sense to buy forty thousand pistols, load them up, and have them all blessed afterward, but I'm not in charge of logistics.

Jeremy, Shane, and I sit in the center of the main office, working as a team to fill the pistols. I hold the gun, Jeremy holds the funnel, and Shane pours the water. The process can be done by one person, since it's often performed in the field, but this is more efficient.

Meanwhile, my mother sits at my desk putting the final touches on a heart-shaped collage of photos of Shane and me. Underneath in sparkly red letters the poster reads, TOGETHER FOREVER. The display verges on cheesy, but I appreciate the thought and effort, especially since, if we survive, we can use it again at our wedding.

"That's enough," I tell Shane to signal him to stop pouring. Jeremy pulls out the funnel and I reach for the pistol's reservoir cap, the paint on which is mostly worn off, making it look like a pink pimple on the otherwise coal-black weapon. "You know what I've been dying to do for months?"

Jeremy holds the funnel over a bowl so that no stray drops will fall. "What have you been dying to do, Ms. Poor-Choice-of-Words?"

"This." I smile as I poke my finger inside the pistol's reservoir, wiggling it in the water. "Wheeeee!"

Shane pulls in a gasp, then frowns, clearly unamused.

I think of how much it hurt him when I accidentally splashed him in the eye, and how he had to give up a year of his life to the Control to get healed. I think of my cousin Michael, whose holy-water scar on his face made him unfit for employment as anything but a thief.

I hate this stuff with all my heart. If I could make it stop working, I would.

A sudden shock shoots up my finger. "Ow! What the hell?"

"What happened?" Shane asks.

"Something zapped me. I must've scuffed my foot on the rug and worked up static electricity. Either that or Mom's glue stick is making me hallucinate."

The door at the bottom of the stairs bangs open, distracting me. Adrian shouts up, "Just got a call. Kashmir's coming!"

My mother whimpers, then covers her mouth.

"That's good. I mean, bad." I don't know what to feel, other than sick to my stomach.

"It's worse than bad," Adrian says on his way up the stairs. "My blood brothers and sisters from England are here. Instead of three of Jim's progeny to deal with, we'll have seven."

I'm suddenly glad I have to be inside when they arrive, for façade purposes. Shane and Jeremy and I will be downstairs, watching the security monitors, and Noah will be on the air, while everyone else will be outside, mourning or defending us.

"Kashmir won't leave town until he's killed Monroe for staking Jim in the first place." Adrian looks at Shane.

"Regina's off the hit list now. There's no point in killing her if you're not alive to be hurt by her death."

"Kashmir's insane for coming here," Shane says. "The entire Control is gunning for him after what he did to Rosso and Henley—not to mention me and Ciara. If he were smart, he'd disappear for good."

"You don't get him. He doesn't care about anyone's life, including his own." Adrian turns to Franklin's open office. Franklin doesn't turn to look at him, but Adrian goes in anyway. "I just want you to know, before things get ugly, that I—"

"No." Without looking at Adrian, Franklin holds his glued-together FUCK OFF mug at arm's length.

Adrian retreats back into the main office, looking miserable. "I have to get back downstairs and brief Captain Fox about the other progeny as much as I can."

"Good." Shane starts to rise from his chair to join Adrian, then seems to remember he's been suspended. "The more Elijah knows, the more he can have his Control people ready."

Adrian nods sadly. "As ready as anyone can ever be for Kashmir. I hope he at least waits until Jim's ceremony is over before attacking. He should let him rest in peace."

"I think he already is resting in peace." I picture Jim lying on the grass on the Isle of Wight, gazing up at the bright spot on the arm of the Milky Way, knowing that the path was there for him when he was ready.

I'm hit with a sudden memory that's lain dormant for days. "Lemuria."

Adrian's eyes widen. "What did you say?"

"Jim told us to tell Kashmir that he'd found Lemuria. Do you know what it means?"

He stares at me for several seconds, then shakes his head slowly. "You know, until just now I wasn't sure you actually saw Jim when you died. I thought you were hallucinating or lying."

I'm impressed with his skepticism. I wouldn't believe us, either.

"We both heard him say it," Shane offers, "but I couldn't make out the word. So what does it mean?"

"It was an inside joke between them. Lemuria is a mythical lost continent in the Indian Ocean."

"Like Atlantis?" Jeremy asks.

"Yeah. They always said they'd find it one day and start a vampire colony. There was more to it than that, but they never explained it to me. You know how it is with inside jokes—they take on a life of their own."

I think of all the phrases and songs Shane and I have made up in the last three years, especially since we started living together. We could record an entire album's worth of tunes about Dexter—if there was a market for that sort of thing.

Then I remember an odd thing Jim said to me last spring, just before he broke my wrist and tried to abduct me. Something about the world having been all one continent, and that the gaps were getting bigger, and one day everything would fall into the ocean. He sounded so sad.

David comes up from downstairs. "Everything ready?"

Mom displays the poster to him. "What do you think?"

"It's, um, moving. Well done." He looks at us. "Colonel Lanham called. He's bringing Special Agent Anca Codreanu-Petrea with him."

"He's bringing a date to our funeral?"

Everyone gives me a puzzled glance, then David continues.

"She wants to do a ceremony during the wake. It's a necromancer thing." He explains to my mother, "A necromancer is someone who can talk to the dead."

"Supposedly," I add.

Shane asks David, "What kind of ceremony?"

"To honor the three of you."

Honor, my ass. "Does she think she's going to be able to talk to us from beyond the grave?" And if she somehow can, will she know we're not dead?

"I asked her that." David puts his hands in his pockets, looking abashed. "She took offense. Apparently it's bad manners to contact the dead during their funeral."

"How convenient." I scowl at the dust on the holy-water pistol I'm about to uncap. "We'll keep a close watch on her."

"You still think someone in the Control has it in for you?" David asks. "Even though Jim got out more or less on his own?"

"Someone will always have it in for us." I smile at Shane. "It's the price we pay for being interesting."

Sunset comes, then civil twilight a half hour later, when it's safe for vampires to be outside. As the crowd starts to gather in the clearing near the station, Shane, Jeremy, and I move into the lounge to monitor the goings-on, bringing holy-water pistols and of course Shane's trusty katana sword. Soon we're alone in the building, except for Noah on the air.

Though Shane and I were late add-ons, Lori and my mother managed to put together a pair of beautiful eulogies. Unfortunately the cameras have no sound, so I have to gauge the beauty of their words by the number of tissues used by the onlookers. Just watching my mom's impassioned performance sends a few tears down my face.

I've just finished blowing my nose when Shane says, "What's she doing?" He points to the left side of the screen, where Anca is withdrawing a small object from her purse.

"Maybe it's part of the ceremony." Jeremy picks up a holy-water pistol from the card table. "But just in case . . ."

"That won't do any good against her. She's human." I realize by the pink reservoir cap that it's the same pistol that shocked me. "Be careful with that one."

My mother finishes her eulogy, and Anca steps up to the podium. I wish I could hear what she is saying. Seeing the nighttime video with no sound is creepy.

Anca gestures skyward, then to the ground where our grave markers sit three in a row. As she lifts her hands again, smoke pours between her fingers. It's followed by sparks and flames that don't singe her skin.

"Nice effect," Jeremy murmurs. "But you can buy that stuff at any magic shop online."

The con artist in me has always loved magicians. Like us, they give people what they *want* to see, not what's really there.

I step closer to the monitor. "My dad always taught me that magicians do tricks with misdirection. They make you look at their left hand while their right hand is hiding the secret." I put my finger on Anca and her flailing smoke and sparks. "If you want to see through them, look in the opposite direction from what they're showing you." I draw my finger to the other end of the crowd.

Adrian stands alone near the back of the gathering. He wipes his eyes and lowers his head.

Then he disappears, jerked backward out of the light.

"Whoa." Shane clicks on his field radio. "Elijah, did you see what happened to— Elijah, are you there?" He fiddles with the settings on the radio.

Static comes from the speaker in the ceiling. I hurry to open the door to the studio hallway.

Behind the window, Noah is pulling off his headphones. He rubs his ear, wincing.

A loud bang sounds behind me, beyond the lounge. I realize it's coming from the other hallway.

"That was the outside door." Shane lifts his katana, the blade gleaming in the lamplight. Jeremy aims his holy-water pistol at the closed door.

I grab two stakes from the table, bring one to the studio, and toss it in to Noah. "Lock yourself in. No matter what, stay on the air."

I turn back to the lounge, ready to fight with my puny little human body. In the clearing outside, the crowd stares at Anca, mesmerized. In addition to creating a diversion, her little fireworks show must have interfered with our communications system and maybe even the radio broadcast.

The door to the other hallway opens. Kashmir starts through, then sees me and Shane.

"But you're . . ." He tilts his head. "They told me you were dead."

"Old news." Jeremy steps forward and fires the holy-water pistol straight at Kashmir. Instinctively the vampire throws up an arm to block the stream and—

Nothing happens. No sizzling or burning. The water is only water.

With a roar, Kashmir lashes out at Jeremy, hurling him across the room. Jeremy strikes the wall with a sickening thud, then plops on the floor like a rag doll, his eyes open and empty.

"No!" I run forward, but Kashmir catches me. Behind us, I hear the swish and *shing* of Shane's sword.

"Ciara, run!" he shouts. "You can't fight him."

I twist out of Kashmir's grip and sprint upstairs into the main office. If I could just get outside—

Kashmir tackles me. We roll over and over, across the hardwood floor. I scramble to get away, but his weight is on top of me, and my neck is in his hands.

This can't be it, I think as time stretches out. *I didn't go to hell and back just to be snuffed out again.*

Hell and back.

"Lemuria!" I rasp out with my last breath. "Jim said . . ."

"What?" Kashmir loosens his grip. "What did you say?" He shakes me by the neck. A sharp pain shoots out to both shoulders, but at least pain means life.

"We saw Jim," I choke out, "after we died."

"Where?"

"On the Isle of Wight." I drag in a breath through my bruised windpipe. "Doors were playing. He was bitten."

"Where?" Kashmir's fingers envelop my neck. "Prove you saw him. Where did they bite?"

"His thigh and his wrist and his neck."

"Where else?"

I close my eyes, trying to remember the fourth wound. "His mouth."

"What did he say?"

"He said to tell you he found Lemuria. And that everything was groovy."

Kashmir's amber eyes bore into me. Downstairs the sounds of battle rage on—furniture smashing, a sword zinging, Shane roaring in defiance—but here there's radio silence.

Then Kashmir laughs. His chin tilts up as he bays at the ceiling, long and hard. For a moment his face is pure joy, and again I see the young man he once was. I can almost picture him surfing.

"Thank you," he says, with what sounds like genuine gratitude. "I'm so glad you told me that before you died."

This time when his hands start to squeeze, he's wearing a smile.

Kicking and writhing, I try to pry off his hands, but it's futile, so I lunge for his face instead, hoping to jab him in the eye. He moves his head out of reach, still smiling. Yellow and black patches form in my vision, like spots on a jaguar.

I've been here before, battling for my life, holy water filling my brain until I took away its power by telling myself, *It's only water.*

I've lost those powers, the price I paid for a new life. I'm nothing now. I couldn't even neutralize a drop of—

Wait.

The water in Jeremy's pistol didn't work on Kashmir. The water that I'd touched and wished it had no power. Did I neutralize it with my mind? If Jeremy dies, will it be my fault?

Even so, this is different. I can't wish away an entire vampire. Can I?

Kashmir squeezes harder, his fully deployed fangs a contrast to his beatific smile.

What do I have to lose?

You don't deserve to be a vampire. I wrap my hands around his. *You're not a vampire.*

My mind reaches out, playing those words again and again. The mantra gets louder as my vision turns blacker, and faster as the yellow dots dance.

Finally I feel it with all my being—not a plea, not an insult, just a statement:

You're not a vampire.

I'm zapped by what feels like a million volts. My legs jerk and my back arches.

"What are you—"

Kashmir's eyes widen. His grip weakens, spasms around my neck, then starts to slide off. Air rushes in, an almost foreign feeling.

I close my eyes, hold on tight to his hands, and summon every shred of belief in my disbelief, every bit of faith in my lack of faith.

With nothing but my mind, I *pull*.

The magic shoots into me like a lightning bolt. For one moment I feel everything a vampire feels: the strength, the sadness, the rage, the fear. The glory of a life lengthened by years and shortened by hours.

Then the power streams out of my body, into the air and ground, unable to stay inside me. Where my skin meets the floor, I burn.

My body spasms, every muscle clenching. Kashmir lets go of my neck, but I can't let go of his hands. He falls off me, like a cowboy from a bucking bronco, turning me on my side as I hold on to him.

My vision flares in red and green and yellow. My heart starts to race, twenty times too fast. My chest feels full of wriggling centipedes crawling over each other.

I'm dying. Again. Dammit.

Lying a few inches away, his face to mine, Kashmir ages. His skin sags and his hair whitens. Those amber eyes cloud as they stare into mine. He draws in a wheezing breath.

"What have you done?" he rasps. "What am I now?"

About sixty-seven, I think, as the black curtain falls once more.

33

Magic Man

"Should we zap her again?" Franklin says.

Adrian's voice comes from somewhere to my left. "She's breathing now, and her heartbeat's steady. She doesn't need it."

"I know, but just for kicks? I like to see her squirm."

Without opening my eyes, I use all the strength in my battered body to raise my forearm and give Franklin the finger.

Then I notice the world is mostly silent. Memory comes rushing back, and I open my eyes.

"Shane?"

Franklin sits beside me, on the top stair of the station's main office. "He's fine. The Control agents noticed Adrian was missing and came in to investigate. I followed them." He glances at Adrian, then looks away. "I was curious."

"How do you feel?" A female Control paramedic comes into view. She shines a piercing light into my eyes.

"Everything hurts." I try to raise my head again. "What happened to Kashmir?"

"The Control got him," Adrian tells me. "Shane hacked off Leon's legs, and Elijah staked Billy to save Shane."

I notice Adrian's not rolling around in agony. "They took Kashmir alive?"

"Yep, thanks to you."

"I de-vamped Kashmir somehow. But it almost killed me, didn't it?"

"You went into cardiac arrest," Franklin says flatly, like he's telling me it's partly cloudy outside. "Luckily Adrian knows CPR."

"He saved me?"

"The paramedics saved you," Adrian says. "I just did CPR until they got here with the defibrillator."

"I told him not to bother," Franklin says, "that I've been trying to get rid of you for years, but he wouldn't listen."

Adrian's smile is strained, and when he looks past me and Franklin, it fades completely. I hear Shane downstairs, making grievous noises that bend my heart.

"What's wrong?" I start to get up. "Is my mom okay? Lori? David?"

"They're all fine." Adrian gently pushes me back. "You have to lie down or you could go into shock."

I flail my other hand until I hit Franklin's knee. "Tell me what happened. Is it Shane? Is it—" A sudden memory hits me, of a flying body, an unyielding wall. "Jeremy."

"He's . . ." Franklin rests one hand on my shoulder while the other rubs his forehead hard. "It was quick."

Now I hear Shane's labored, sorrowful breaths coming from downstairs, beyond the open door to the lounge.

Then he starts to sing. His voice is richer than ever, sweeter and rougher than it was as a vampire, even more than it was the other night in bed. He croons "Asleep," the Smiths song about suicide, the one Jeremy wanted sung to him as he was vamped.

Which he'll never be now. He'll never be undead, just dead.

I could've prevented this. I could've turned him, like he begged me so many times, like he begged all of us. And now he's gone.

"Take me down there," I whisper.

Adrian looks at the paramedic, who gives a hesitant sigh. "One minute," she says.

He scoops me up and carries me downstairs. I draw in a sharp breath as his arms scrape the burns on my back.

Adrian kneels in front of Shane, still holding me. Shane is cradling Jeremy's body. They're both covered in so much blood, it's hard to see where one ends and the other begins.

Shane keeps singing, and the lounge is so silent, I can hear the soft piano in my head. The melody's serenity belies the lyrics' unbearable pain, one that Shane and Jeremy understand well, one that I've only just begun to grasp.

Behind me, four other Control paramedics are setting up three stretchers, for Jeremy, Leon, and Billy, who's lying on the blood-soaked floor, unconscious, a stake protruding from his back.

Shane begins the last chorus, which will drift off into a repeated, "Sing to me." I try to watch Jeremy's lifeless face, but it's too hard. Instead I focus on the front of his Dashboard Confessional T-shirt, remembering when he saw them in concert last year, how excited he was to snag front-row seats. Afterward, he walked around starry-eyed for days.

His T-shirt moves.

I hold my breath. That wasn't what I think it was.

The *C* in "Confessional" twitches. But Jeremy can't be moving. He can't be alive. People don't come back to life—not people broken in half who are beyond the help of vampires and defibrillators.

Shane reaches the last line, stretches it out.

I interrupt. "Keep singing."

"What?"

"Just do it," I tell him, never taking my eyes off Jeremy's chest. "Start the song over."

Shane doesn't question, just takes it from the top. I want to reach out and touch him, but I know what I'm capable of now. I could kill his magic with one drop of doubt.

But right now I have no doubt. I remember how Shane pulled me out of the land of the dead, twice. I remember the power of his voice.

Apparently it's no longer just for me.

Jeremy heaves a choking breath, and everyone gasps.

"He's alive!" Adrian sets me down carefully, then reaches for Jeremy's wrist. "His pulse is erratic but strong." He pauses. "And getting stronger."

"Keep singing, Shane. Just like you are."

Shane nods at me and keeps going. His voice shakes a little, probably with the temptation to go louder, bolder. But that's not what this song is like.

Jeremy's eyelashes flutter and he moans softly.

"Don't move," Adrian whispers, his hand on Jeremy's shoulder.

When he finishes the song again, Shane gently lays Jeremy on one of the stretchers. The paramedics go to work, strapping him down and putting a brace on his neck.

Adrian carries me back upstairs to my own stretcher.

Shane follows close behind. I feel a weird thrill, knowing I have nothing to hide from human doctors.

As the EMTs lift me up, Shane bends over and whispers in my ear. "I saw Kashmir before they took him away. Do you know what you did?"

I nod. "I guess I'll be staying in the Immanence Corps."

He glances downstairs toward Jeremy, whose raspy voice is telling the paramedic that yes, he can feel it when his toes are squeezed. Then Shane looks back at me. "I guess I'll be joining you."

Colonel Lanham agrees with that assessment. Not only did Shane save Jeremy, but he also sang Billy back to life after one of the other Enforcement agents pulled out his stake. Adrian recommended a Neil Young song, so Shane went with "After the Gold Rush."

"It says here you used to sing it to your childhood dog?" Colonel Lanham looks up from the incident report, arching his eyebrow.

"When she had cancer, sir." Shane sits in the chair next to me in front of Lanham's desk. His posture is straight, but not stake-up-his-butt Enforcement straight. "It seemed to help her sleep."

I hate when he makes me want to kiss him at highly inappropriate times.

Lanham finishes reading the incident report, or at least pretends to. I find it hard to believe he didn't have the thing memorized before we arrived. When he came to visit me in the hospital Tuesday morning, we discussed how I'd overcome Kashmir by de-vamping him.

Kashmir himself is now in Control custody, one of

their few human prisoners. Since he didn't die per se, none of his progeny felt the agony they normally would at a maker's death. They may never feel it, since he'll eventually die as a human.

As Kashmir's conspirator, Anca Codreanu-Petrea is also awaiting trial. Since Jeremy technically died but was brought back to life, the Control hasn't decided whether to try her for accessory to murder or accessory to attempted murder. Such are the dilemmas of law enforcement bureaucracies.

Lanham closes the report and turns to Shane. "You appear to have what the Immanence Corps has termed the Orphic ability. You can call the dying back to life with your voice."

Shane sinks a little deeper into his chair. "So that's a thing, then. I'm not the only one who can do this?"

"You are the only, but not the first." Lanham tilts his chin down. "The previous Orphic agent had an accident on duty and is currently in a coma."

"When you say 'on duty'"—I give him the side-eye—"you mean trying to save someone?"

"Precisely. The subject was too far gone, and the Orphic agent tried too long and too hard. They were drawn into a near death themselves."

"Shit," Shane says. "I mean, shit . . . sir."

"Every ability has a cost and a trade-off." Lanham looks at me. "As you well know, Griffin."

I fidget with the bandages on my palms, which still have second-degree burns from the magic shock. "I don't suppose whoever else has my power is still alive, huh? It'd be nice to get some training."

Lanham pauses, then says, "Agent Griffin, no one

has ever had your power of neutralization before. You must learn to control it."

"I had to concentrate really hard to de-vamp Kashmir. I doubt I'd accidentally do it by shaking hands."

"You never know what you're capable of until you develop your abilities."

"Let me guess: the Immanence Corps will teach me."

"I think you'll teach them as much as they'll teach you."

"The fact that it literally stopped my heart is a good incentive not to use that power ever again."

"Removing someone's vampire nature is an extreme example. Vampirism affects a person's entire being. It's more than a supernatural ability. But if you were to interfere with, say, a telepath trying to win money at the poker table, or a pyrokinetic agent in the process of starting a fire—each a part-time ability—you would probably feel a smaller shock."

Somehow I am not comforted.

"We would start you off with something small," he proposes, "like one of the IC's telekinetic agents trying to move a feather. Under full medical supervision, of course."

I sigh, wondering if I actually have to believe in people's alleged superpowers to neutralize them, or if my disbelief will be my best weapon. "I suppose a transfer to the Contemporary Awareness Department is out, huh?"

"Out of the question. They need both of you in the Immanence Corps."

"When do we start?" Shane asks. "I'm suspended until mid-January."

"The investigation into Project Blood Leash 2.0 is complete, and the committee will present its findings on January second."

I lean forward a little. "And?"

"I have it on good authority that they expect to ac-commodate all the vampire agents' demands. Things will be back to normal soon thereafter." He opens his calendar. "You are both to report for duty on Tuesday, February first, for a year's full-time service."

"Wait—full time?" Shane looks angry. "What about WVMP?"

"You have over a month to find a suitable disc jockey replacement. Potentially you could maintain your satellite radio duties, since that requires only a few hours per week."

Shane lets out a breath, relieved. "Just for a year. I'll make it work."

I hope he does. Even as a human, he needs music like most people need air. And with his Orphic ability, his music will be like air to the dead and dying.

I'm just glad this power is in Shane's hands and no one else's.

It's a good thing Shane and I, and our friends and family, are no longer being stalked by psychotic vampires. Plan-ning a wedding is stressful enough.

Lori's maid-of-honor dress had to be refitted at the last minute, due to what she calls a "baby bump" and what I call a "burrito bump." Her morning sickness has ended, replaced with an obsessive craving for Taco Bell.

In other bridal party news, a still-recovering Jeremy is now a groomsman instead of an usher. After his run-in with Kashmir, we all decided it would be best if he had a job that involved doing nothing but standing there, looking happy. Which he does more often these days, having finally lost his vampiric aspirations. "Nothing like dying to make you realize death sucks," he told me.

But now, with two minutes until I walk down the aisle, I am doubting that wisdom. I can barely breathe from the nerves.

Our wedding is being held at the Sherwood fire hall. Not the most glamorous location, but with our history of special events involving explosives, we figured it was the safest place to be. It was also cheap.

Noah, who replaced Jeremy as usher, offers my mother his arm. She takes it, then spies me peeking out from the hallway beyond the coatroom. Mom gives me a mischievous wave, then proceeds, looking happier than I've ever seen her.

"You ready?" Monroe asks me. He's wearing a white tux with a black shirt and tie, which looks amazing. For once, he left the hat at home. I'm sure many people will wonder why I'm being walked down the aisle by someone who is not only clearly not my relative but is also the same age as I am. Whatever. He's the closest thing I have to a father, even now.

I take a deep breath, focusing on the scent of the red roses in my bouquet, then step forward toward the closed doors leading to the hall. "I'm ready."

"Yay!" Lori scoots over to take her place in front of me. Regina, my only bridesmaid, glides in front of her. Inside the hall, the prelude music continues. When the song changes, that's our cue for Spencer to open the hall door so we can enter.

Behind us, the outside doors crash open, letting in a cold blast of December night air.

I'm ready for another ambush, and *not* ready to have

my wedding ruined by more rogue vampires. In a flash I lift the right side of my skirt, yank out the small holy-water pistol from my garter belt, then aim for the three men coming through the door.

"Hallelujah, I'm just in time!"

I lower the pistol slowly, staring at the white-haired man in a tux flanked by a pair of U.S. marshals. "Daddy?"

"Surprise, pumpkin!" Ronan O'Riley spreads his arms for a hug. "They gave me twenty-four-hour leave to attend my only daughter's wedding. Isn't that fabulous?"

I shake my head with disbelief, then nod. "Fabulous . . ." Every emotion pinballs inside of me at once. I don't dare move, due to the competing instincts to embrace and slap him. "But you know I hate surprises."

He takes a step back and puts his hands up. "Hey, don't do to me what you did to that birthday clown." The laugh lines around his eyes straighten and droop as he realizes I might actually kick him in the kneecaps. "I thought you'd be happy."

Lori puts her hand on my arm. "We can add a father-daughter dance."

That's what breaks me. I lower my head and blink hard so the tears can fall from my lashes to the floor instead of streaking my face with mascara. Every time I imagined my wedding, this was what I secretly wished for.

"Ciara." My father steps forward. "I'd be honored if you would let me walk you down the aisle."

Behind me, Monroe clears his throat. When I turn to him, he bows his head and steps back, conceding his place at my side.

I blink away the last tear, straighten my posture, then speak to the two guards.

"Take him to the side entrance. He can sit in the back."

Ronan's eyes widen as they lead him away. "But, sweet pea, I'm your father."

"Which is why I'm letting you stay. Enjoy the show." I watch them lead him toward a door on the side of the fire hall. "Regina, tell them we're ready."

She salutes me as she passes. "That. Was totally awesome."

I smile, knowing what the word means coming from a child of the eighties, when it was more than just a default description for anything remotely cool.

Regina cracks open the door and flashes a thumbs-up to Rick, Shane's former donor and front man for Vital Fluid. I hear his acoustic guitar begin the procession music.

I'm still shaking from the encounter with my father, yet somehow calmer about the wedding itself than I was ten minutes ago.

On cue, Spencer opens the doors. I stand off to the left so no one can see me. Regina sweeps forward, provoking gasps of admiration verging on worship from the crowd inside.

Lori gives me a wink and a smile before she sets off. The audience sighs with a series of "Awws" at the sight of her cuteness, enhanced by the little bulge in her belly, so obvious on her tiny frame.

Monroe offers me his arm and I meet his eyes. We're almost the same height, with me in my four-inch heels, but I will forever and always look up to him. For giving me life, then saving that life months ago, even if he can only be a small part of it. I know he's trying, and this right here, walking me down the aisle? Huge.

The music changes, and we step into the doorway. Everyone stands.

For a moment I hesitate, intimidated by the attention. I've spent my life slipping through the shadows, playing behind-the-scenes manager/puppet-master to this hodgepodge set of vampires. Now everyone's watching me.

By the looks on their faces, I'm doing all right.

We walk down the aisle just as we practiced, in time to the music, but not so precisely it looks dancy. My father beams with delight, even though he's not in the spotlight himself. On the right side of the aisle, Shane's family seems endless.

Halfway down I see Shane. He's gazing at me like I'm the world's biggest stack of pancakes. Except with more respect.

My mom peeks out from the front row. To my surprise, she's not crying. Then again, she wouldn't want to ruin her makeup.

When we reach the head of the aisle, Monroe goes to stand beside her, and she hugs him as he passes. He actually accepts the embrace. Miracles abound.

Shane takes his place beside me, looking younger and hotter than ever in his black-on-black-on-black tuxedo. He leans over and whispers, "Is that your dad in the back?"

"He busted in at the last second. I almost put that 'something borrowed' to good use."

He smirks and glances at my thigh, where the holy-water pistol is safely holstered. "Sorry I missed it."

"He wanted to walk me down the aisle, which would've totally taken away my moment. I was like, 'Fuck that.'"

Of course, the music fades just as I am finishing that sentence. Our mothers let out soft gasps, but the rest of the crowd laughs. My face feels redder than the roses in my bouquet.

Which I just realized I've been holding backward the entire time. The plastic holder thingie is facing forward. Crap. Maybe the photographer can edit out my idiocy.

Then again, seeing the backward flowers might be a reminder of all I've been through to get to this point— scratch that, all *we've* been through.

I barely hear the warm words of welcome from the officiant, the same Unitarian minister Lori and David used for their wedding. She says something about marriage being a bold and courageous step, and I have to avoid Shane's eyes to keep from cracking up.

Franklin reads a Keats poem with more feeling than I ever would've expected. I notice he tries—and fails—to avoid meeting Adrian's eyes.

We light a unity candle, something we wouldn't have dared to do as vampires, then the minister turns to us for the vows. Shane and I flipped a coin to see who would go first.

"Will you take this man to be your husband," she asks me, "to live together in the promise of marriage? Will you love him, comfort him, honor and keep him, in sickness and in health; and, forsaking all others, be faithful to him as long as you both shall live?"

I take a deep breath from my core, just like my mom always taught me, so that all the realms can hear.

"I will."

34

You Know You're Right

We indulge our families by spending Christmas with them in Maryland, and then it's honeymoon time.

On the way to our ultimate destination, we take a few days' layover in Seattle, where Shane's idol, Kurt Cobain, spent his final years.

It's a dreary late December afternoon when we touch down at Sea-Tac Airport, twenty degrees colder than normal, and raining, naturally. But he wants to see everything, walk in Kurt's footsteps, drink in the clubs where Nirvana and Hole played.

The next day is windy but sunny, so we take a bus then walk to the neighborhood where Kurt Cobain lived his last few months. Because the area is inhabited by the insanely rich, parts of the road have no sidewalks, and we nearly get mowed down by more than one Mercedes.

"This is it," Shane says as we pass a high hedge wall on our right. "The park is just up ahead."

"Park?"

He gives me an amused look. "Viretta Park. Where all the vigils and memorials are held."

I'm relieved that we have a public place to go instead of just gaping at some stranger's house. Courtney Love sold the place years ago. Can't say I blame her.

We come to a high wooden gate. Shane pauses. "The greenhouse where he died—" He shifts his jaw. "Where he shot himself. It was behind the left edge of the house. Courtney had it torn down."

He takes my hand and we keep walking. After another hundred feet, we come to the grassy park, which is a lot smaller than I imagined—maybe two hundred yards across. It slopes uphill, and a trail leads back through the trees. I'm glad it's cold out, so that we're the only ones here.

Shane leads me to a bench at the center of the park.

"Whoa," I whisper when I see what people have done to it.

More than a park bench, it's a shrine. Covered in graffiti, it expresses the love and grief of a thousand fans, and another thousand, faded and shrouded, beneath those marks. I have the strangest urge to kneel before it.

Instead I sit beside Shane. He's shoved his hands into the pockets of his sweatshirt and sits hunched, his brow knitted in thought or memory, I'm not sure which. His eyes are open, so I assume he's not praying.

"Damn it," he whispers. "I meant to bring music."

I pull out my phone and bring up the MP3 player. "Which song do you want? I can have it downloaded in one minute."

He chuckles. "I love the present more and more each day."

I open the MP3 player's online store. "Which song?"

Shane takes a long breath in and out. "It's weird, but

I kinda want 'Where Did You Sleep Last Night,' even though it's a Lead Belly cover, not one of their originals."

"It was the last song Kurt played live before he died, right?"

"The last one recorded, yeah, at the *Unplugged* concert."

I don't mention that it's at the end of the first CD we ever listened to together, or that I already have it on my phone, or that while he was at boot camp I played it every morning before going to sleep. Shane knows all that. This place isn't about me or about us.

I find the song, place the phone on the bench between us, then hit Play.

The guitar comes crisp and clear from the tiny speaker. As if indulging us, the wind stops and the trees ease their rustle just as Kurt begins to sing.

I stare out at Lake Washington and farther, all the way to the Cascade Mountains. They're the same blue-green as everything in this city: the lake, the Seahawks' uniforms, even the seats on the bus. The color of comfort.

All that blue-green couldn't comfort Kurt Cobain. For some reason that Shane understands but I don't, Kurt slipped into that darkness and couldn't climb out or find a way through. People who loved him dragged him out time after time, the way Regina did for Shane sixteen years ago, but he kept sliding back.

Will Shane fall again, now that he's human? The blood tests showed his pancreas was normal, but what about his brain chemicals?

Without looking down, I place my thumb against my wedding band, which already feels like a part of me. If the darkness comes again for Shane, I'll be there to help him fight it. And if it ever comes for me, he'll be there to guide me through, like a shaman in the shadowy underworld.

When Cobain starts to scream, I close my eyes and let the magic of his pain flow through me and out, just like Kashmir's vampire nature. But this magic leaves no burns, only tears.

Kurt takes that last breath before the final two words, and I hear Shane beside me pull in the same breath.

I open my eyes into the blinding sunlight as the voice pours forth. It fades with an ache so raw and deep, I feel like I'll never breathe again. Then the guitars, drum, and cello come in, sending us out with strength, then applause and a final "Thank You."

Did the people in that audience know how lucky they were? Did they know they were witnessing a farewell? Did Kurt's bandmates know? Did *he* know?

Shane hands me two tissues. I take one and give the other back. He blows his nose, then coughs, as if he wasn't crying, he just has allergies or a bit of a cold. Men.

Then I hand him a black marker so he can write a message on the bench. He takes it with a nod of thanks.

While he's writing, I check out some of the other notes. Most are simple: snatches of Nirvana lyrics or Bible verses, or just "RIP" or "I Love You." Some are from those at peace, others from those with still-sharp grief. One person spelled out KURT with bright-colored Fisher-Price alphabet letters glued to the bench. A bouquet of sunflowers is stuffed between two of the bench slats, and a black garter belt is tied to the end of one of the boards.

I look at the house, its brown roof peeking over the edge of the trees that shroud it. Kurt's voice still rings in my head, even as the wind starts up again and rustles the spruces.

Shane reaches into his pocket. "I wanted to leave something that meant a lot to me. Something I'd miss, that would be like leaving a part of me behind."

He pulls out a string of dark-blue Mardi Gras beads, the one he used as a rosary when he was a vampire, since he couldn't use a strand with a crucifix. Pieces of tape are stuck to the beads at certain intervals to indicate where the Our Fathers are substituted for the Hail Marys.

"Are you sure?"

Shane doesn't answer, just ties the beads around the end of the bench and lets the end length dangle. He taps it to set it swinging, then straightens up.

"Ready to go?"

Shane and I arrive in Hawaii early in the evening on New Year's Eve, with plenty of time to drive to our resort. We greet the brand-new decade at a luau with a few hundred strangers turned friends.

But as the night turns to dawn, we leave them all behind and walk down the beach, far enough that the only light is the one in the eastern sky stretching over the sea. Despite the cool ocean breeze, we take off our shoes to feel the powder-soft sand between our toes.

Our gait is unsteady due to the shifting sand and the multiple mai tais. So, hands linked tight, we wobble like children, waving our arms for balance. Something only humans have to do.

Without a word, Shane tugs me to a stop. The horizon is glowing now, every color from red to green and back again. A pair of small offshore islands flanks the spot where the sun will come up. Perfect.

We sit together on the sand, pressing our sides together, knees to our chest to keep out the breeze. I loop my arm over Shane's knee and rest my head on his shoulder. He wraps his arm around my back, pulling me closer.

There's no music here, and for once, I don't need any. All I want to hear are the waves of the ocean and the breath of my husband.

My husband. That's so unreal. Almost as unreal as the rays of sunlight streaking up ahead of the orb. Any minute now it'll be here.

Shane clears his throat. "I'm going to ruin this with words, okay?"

I squeeze his leg in response.

"Soon I'll be spending lots of time in the dark," he says. "Guiding people out, I guess."

"Are you worried you'll get stuck there yourself, like that other agent?"

"No. That's what I'm trying to say." He lifts my hand to his lips and gives it a soft kiss. "Because of you, there's no darkness I can't escape."

I don't respond, thinking that's an easy thing to say when one is sitting on a Hawaiian beach, waiting for the sun to come up.

"I'll tell you that every day if I have to"—Shane shrugs— "and you can believe me or not. You can believe whatever you want, or nothing at all. That's where your power comes from, and even if it didn't, I'd never take that away from you."

With that, I release my last worry about the two of us. I let it streak across the sky and dive, flaming, into the red-orange sun emerging from the ocean. Then I lift my chin to meet Shane's kiss.

My belief and faith in the rest of the world—in all the worlds—will probably always waver. I'll always question, always examine, always argue. It's what I do.

But Shane accepts and loves all that I am and all that I'll become. Young and strong, old and weak, and every state in between. In the chill of the dark and the warmth of the sun, he'll be there.

Of that, I have no doubt.

Acknowledgments

Wow—how do I thank all the people who've traveled with me on this seven-year journey, from May 2005, when I first had the nutty idea of vampire DJs, to this moment in summer 2012, putting the final touches on the final book?

Thanks first to all the readers. Your passion for music, for vampires, for Ciara and Shane and all the gang has been an inspiration. Special thanks to the 250+ members of the WVMP Street Team—you rock!

Second, to the fine folks at Pocket Books, especially my ever-patient editor, Ed Schlesinger, who should win an Awesomesauce Award (though I don't know what that would be shaped like), and to Jennifer Heddle for her brilliant guidance of the series through the first three books. Also to editor Megan McKeever, Louise Burke, Don Sipley, Renee Huff, Jean Anne Rose, Nancy Tonik, and Rory Panagotopulos.

Third, to my beta readers/critique partners who helped me eviscerate, shape, and eventually rebuild the manuscript until it became the bionic book you see here today: Rob Staeger, Karen Alderman, and Stephanie

Kuehnert, and to Cecilia Ready, who knew the story before anyone else. Also, thanks to the reviewers, bloggers, and book discussion groups who speculated on how the series would end. One of you was right.

Thanks to my agent, Ginger Clark, for understanding how much this series has meant to me.

Lastly, to my family, who are still waiting to get their Jeri back from Deadline Valley. To my husband, for his love and patience, and for learning how to cook ten times better than I can. And to my dog, Meadow, who was always at my side. Long may you run.

More bestselling
URBAN FANTASY
from Pocket Books!